For the whole of his life, Viscount David Drummond has been groomed to inherit the title Earl of Falkirk upon the death of his father. However, instead of enjoying the manly pursuits expected by his father, he finds his every waking moment is consumed with the belief that he should have been born a woman and not a man. For David, it is a desire to compelling to resist.

After being caught in a compromising position while dressed as a girl, David Drummond is cast out of his family home by his father. With just the clothes on his back and a few golden guineas in his pocket, he escapes to London. There, he hopes to seek out a new life when his trust comes to him on his twenty-first birthday.

Through a letter of introduction, Lady Olivia Hamilton, the Countess of Weybridge, is apprised of his secret. For particular reasons of her own, she resolves to help David become Miss Isobel Munroe, the woman he always felt meant to be. Willing to brave the scandal of discovery for a chance to be true to herself, Isobel becomes a reality, and with the help of Olivia and her friends, she begins her new life. She even finds the man of her dreams, Lord Peter Fairfax, a gentleman in need of a wife as special as she. Everything is coming together, or so it seems. But Isobel can't escape her past so easily, for someone is seeking David Drummond — someone who wants him dead.

The unauthorized reproduction or distribution of this copyrighted work is illegal. Criminal copyright infringement, including infringement without monetary gain, is investigated by the FBI and is punishable by up to 5 years in federal prison and a fine of $250,000.

This book is a work of fiction. Names, characters, places, and incidents either are products of the author's imagination or are used fictitiously. Any resemblance to actual events or locales or persons, living or dead, is entirely coincidental.

The Making of a Lady
Copyright © 2021 Charlotte Johnson
ISBN: 978-1-4874-3252-2
Cover art by Martine Jardin

All rights reserved. Except for use in any review, the reproduction or utilization of this work in whole or in part in any form by any electronic, mechanical or other means, now known or hereafter invented, is forbidden without the written permission of the publisher.

Published by eXtasy Books Inc or
Devine Destinies, an imprint of eXtasy Books Inc

Look for us online at:
www.eXtasybooks.comorwww.devinedestinies.com

The Making of a Lady

By

Charlotte Johnson

Dedication

To all who have encouraged me to aspire to be more.

Prologue: Scotland May 1820

Malcolm Drummond, 7th Earl of Falkirk, lay awake in his bed, even though he should have been sound asleep. On retiring that night his mind had been clouded due to the wine and the whiskey he had consumed at dinner, and by rights he should have slept soundly until the morn. But something had disturbed his alcohol-induced slumber, something intangible, unknown, and now sleep evaded him. Groaning, he turned and fumbled for the full hunter fob watch that hung on the stand beside his bed, pressing the button that ordered the tiny bells within to chime the time . . . a quarter past the hour of three in the morning.

"Fuck," he whispered as he rolled over once more.

The earl sighed, his hand bashing his down-filled pillow as he turned over in his bed to seek out a comfortable position. Then a fox barked in the distance and Malcolm laughed out loud.

That must have been it! A blasted fox!

Relaxing a little with that thought, he rolled over once more, this time onto his front, his bloated body pressing down upon his very full bladder. Again, he laughed. Perhaps needing a piss was what had awoken him after all. With a pounding head, he clawed his way out of his bed and lifted the front of his nightshirt. He took himself in hand, and a stream of piss was soon ringing into the chamber-pot that was kept under his bed, a sigh of relief hissing from his lips as he emptied his bladder. Then his eye caught sight of flickering candlelight reflecting from a crystal decanter that stood on a table by the window.

The whiskey called to him. Staggering over to the table, he poured himself one last glass and pulled back his drapes a fraction to peer out into the night whilst he sipped at the fiery liquid. His rooms were at the back of the manor house, overlooking the stable block below, and at first, everything seemed quiet, everything seemed as it should ... That was, until he saw the unmistakeable flicker of a lantern being carried across the stable courtyard.

Finally, there was the truth of it! One of his favourite horses, aptly named Midnight, was due to foal at any time, and the earl grinned drunkenly as he watched his head groom, Hamish Russell, disappear into a stable. Midnight was a superb brood mare and her soon-to-be foal had been sired by no less than Apollo, a magnificent Arabian stallion owned by his friend and neighbour, Lord John MacDonald. Not only would the foal have the pedigree of a champion, it was sure to be worth a pretty penny, too, and its birth was something the earl did not want to miss. That had to be it. Russell was, by nature, a lazy bastard, and the earl knew that the only thing that could possibly have dragged the man from his bed was the imminent delivery of the foal.

In his inebriated state it took some time, but by the light of his candle, the earl dressed himself simply: trousers and shirt, and a pair of stout walking boots that he kept in his room for such an occasion. Then, after throwing his robe over his shoulders once more, he slipped out of his room and made towards the staircase at the back of the house, a staircase that led directly down to the kitchens. As he imagined it would be, the kitchen was deserted, the room still warm from the fire that cook had carefully banked in the stove. Striding purposefully across the flagstones, he made his way to the outside door, only pausing for a moment when he discovered it to be already unlocked and unbolted.

Quietly and with mounting excitement, the earl lurched towards the stable block, the bright luminescence of the full moon making it easy for him to find his way in the darkness. But as he reached the door through which the weak light shone, something made him freeze, his whole body becoming motionless. He had expected to hear the sounds of a horse in labour, perhaps the soft encouraging tones of Russell, the head groom and midwife to Midnight. Instead, coming from behind the door were the unmistakeable sounds of a man and woman enjoying each other's pleasure: the steady slap, slap, slap of flesh on flesh, the deep grunts of man in the heat of passion; the soft moans of his woman urging him on.

"The cheeky bugger," whispered the earl. "Russell must have a lassie in there with him."

Smiling lasciviously to himself, the earl took a step forward and put his eye to the crack in the door. He recognised his groom almost immediately, for he was a giant of a man, his breadth of shoulders alone making it obvious as to who it was. The man was down on his knees amongst the freshly laid straw, his back towards the earl, the kilt he habitually wore hiked up to his waist exposing his massive hairy thighs and naked backside. And, as the earl had suspected, Russell was pounding away at a woman who was on her hands and knees before him, his hands gripping the girl's hips to pull her in each time he thrust forward.

Because of the angle of Russell's body, it was difficult to see who he was with. However, one thing was for certain — the woman was young, and judging by the way she was dressed, was no commoner either. The dress she wore appeared to be of fine cotton, the skirt of which was pulled high over her back to reveal long, graceful legs encased in the finest of white woollen stockings. Her body was slim, almost prepubescent in form, her breasts so small they were invisible beneath the bodice of the dress she wore. As she braced herself on graceful arms, she held her head low, her long red hair hanging loose over her face and concealing her features, and the earthy noises she was making left no doubt that she was enjoying being fucked this way. So obviously near his peak, Russell began to pound even harder into the woman and, fascinated, the earl watched as the woman moved a hand between her legs to pleasure herself there.

Only then did the earl look on in confusion.

For the woman was not rubbing at the top of her cunny as he had suspected she would. Instead, her hand had made a fist, a fist that began moving furiously up and down, its movement in perfect unison to the thrusts of the man behind. Faster and faster they went, and suddenly the young woman squealed as her back arched, her whole body quivering as it was consumed with pleasure. Russell continued to hammer his cock into her. Within seconds, the earl saw every muscle, every sinew in Russell's body contract, his hairy buttocks clenching as he too reached his peak. Unable to tear himself away from the scene, the earl watched on as Russell's body sagged forwards, pushing his partner down onto the straw, his cock still firmly embedded in her body.

It was only then that the girl turned her head to the side, her hair finally coming free from her face, her eyes looking straight towards the door behind which the earl was standing. In horror, the earl staggered backwards as sudden realisation sobered him like a bucket of ice water over the head.

It was no woman. Instead, on his knees and in a dress, was David, his only son.

Chapter One: London June 1820

"Ah, 'tis good to see you in the land of the living once more, sir," said Jenkins.

Lord Peter Fairfax, second son of the Duke of Abingdon, groaned as his valet pulled back the drapes from around his bed, the sudden burst of brilliant sunlight sending shards of pain lancing into his brain. It had been a diverting evening, and as usual, in a fit of remorse, Peter had consumed too much in the way of ardent spirits when he had returned to his lodgings. Now his head pounded like battle drums and his mouth felt like someone had poured sand into it.

"Tell me why I put up with you, Jenkins." Peter flopped back down onto his bed, covering his head with his pillow once more, knowing that if the pain was to subside, he would need darkness, and he would need more sleep.

"Because I am the only one stupid enough to remain in your service, my lord. Besides, who else would employ a one-legged former soldier?"

Jenkins grinned as he tapped the side of his leg, making a sound like a gavel on a wooden table. Late of the Royal Regiment of Horse Guards, Jenkins had been Peter's sergeant when he had served as Major in the peninsular wars. For three long years they had fought together until a bayonet through the thigh had cut short Peter's career, whilst moments later, a French canon ball had neatly severed Jenkins's left leg just below the knee.

Once more Peter groaned, his voice now muffled by the pillow.

"True, so true. So why don't you bugger off and let me sleep, before you find it necessary to seek alternative employment."

"Whilst I would deem it an honour to *bugger off*, my lord, I am afraid I cannot do that. A message has been delivered from your father, the duke. It appears that their graces are in London and you are commanded to wait upon them at three o'clock in the afternoon at Wilton House."

"Christ!"

"Quite," replied Jenkins. "Anyway, I have drawn a bath for you, sir, for as usual you stink of whatever revelry you indulged in last night. I have also laid out your shaving kit so that you can at least make yourself *look* presentable. In addition, a hackney carriage will be here at half past two to collect you, as I suspect you will be in no fit state to ride."

"Tea first. I need tea."

Wincing a little from the pain in his head, Peter sat up in his bed, the blankets falling from his naked muscular frame, revealing the fact that he had, as normal, foregone a night shirt.

"Yes, my lord," said Jenkins. He handed Peter a mug of very strong tea that had been in his hand all along.

Peter took the offered cup and smiled. When they had served in the army, tea had become something of a ritual, and Jenkins always seemed capable of having a pot on the boil, no matter what the weather or circumstances. Now, in the comfort of his own rooms, he sipped at the golden-brown liquid, sighing as the strong tea cleansed his mouth and settled his stomach.

"God, that is good. You are forgiven, Jenkins," said Peter.

"Thank you, my lord," Jenkins replied, unable to keep the sarcasm from his words.

Peter threw on the robe that lay over the end of his bed and padded barefoot into his bathroom, where a copper bath full of steaming water awaited him. For a moment he paused before a small plain mirror that hung from a chain on the wall to inspect his face and rubbed at the stubble of his chin. He knew he was handsome, for he was often told that he was. His features were strong and aristocratic, and he kept his nearly black hair neat and unfashionably short, a style which he had always thought suited him admirably. He was tall, too, a little over six feet in height, years of soldiering having left his body hard, lean, and muscular. It was a physique he was proud of, and one which he maintained with regular riding and irregular visits to Gentleman Jackson's boxing emporium. Then he shrugged off his gown and stepped into the bath, hissing a little as he felt the heat upon his skin.

It was a decadently deep bath, and if he propped his back against the high end, he could almost stretch out his legs. To one side of the bath was a small wooden table on which lay soap, shaving brush, and what he knew would be a freshly stropped razor. But these he ignored for the moment, closing his eyes instead before ducking his head down beneath the surface of the water.

He allowed his mind to wander, to reflect. All in all, he had a good life, a simple, yet privileged existence. His father, the Duke of Abingdon, gave him a generous monthly stipend which allowed him to live comfortably in a suite of rooms in an apartment house that his father also owned. Whilst not overly large, it had more than enough space for him and for Jenkins, who not only acted as his valet but as his butler, housekeeper, cook, and maid all rolled into one. As the second son, he didn't even have to worry about someday inheriting the dukedom along with all of the responsibilities that would entail. No—his elder brother, Thomas, would inherit, and he already had an heir and a spare, his sons Frederic and Edmund. Why, even Peter's twin sister Alice had two sons who could inherit, God forbid anything happening to Thomas and his family.

No... life was good for Peter. He was responsible to no one but himself and was able to do whatever his heart desired. He had no wife or mistress. Not that he ever intended to have either. He was the son of a duke, had enough money, a title, and the respect that came with having served in the wars. That was enough for him.

Besides, it also meant that he was free, discreetly of course, to pursue his own favoured type of sexual fulfilment, even if at times it left a bitter taste in his mouth to do so. As a very young man, still in his teens, Peter had realised that his sexual proclivity would never favour the female form, and as he had grown into adulthood, the feelings he had towards other men had only become stronger and stronger. His first foray into such had been at Eton, when a young and effeminate fag had offered him sexual favours in return for his protection from the inevitable bullies. The experience had left him reeling and wanting more.

There were times when he hated himself for being this way. Society tolerated no aberrations such as he, and had it become public knowledge that he was, in fact, a shirt-lifter, the scandal would have been beyond belief. Yet he could not help himself. He was akin to an opium addict looking for his next pipe, especially when it came to soft and effeminate partners. And just like an addict, he went to extraordinary lengths and expense to keep his needs a closely guarded secret.

There was, as far as he knew, only one other who knew he preferred the company of another man in his bed.

His twin sister, Alice.

With Peter, it seemed she had a second sight, some form of mystical twin connection, as he had with her. Somehow, when he had been one and twenty years of age and newly enlisted in the army, she had divined his preferences and had confronted him about his sexuality. At first he had tried to deny it, but it had soon become clear that he would never be able to hide something so momentous from her. Whilst it been difficult for him, like a torrent of water it had all come pouring out of him as he had sobbed upon his sister's shoulder.

To his absolute surprise, she did not condemn him for the choices he had made. Instead, she embraced them and had even suggested a way out of his predicament.

The Moonlight Club became a sanctuary for Peter. It was a place where, on occasion, like-minded men could meet in complete anonymity, a place where there was no condemnation or censure for desiring to be with another man. He grinned to himself with that thought, for it had been at the Moonlight Club where, in private, he had spent the previous evening. His anonymous partner had been a most delectable and compliant young man whose talented mouth had brought him untold pleasure, a young man who had revelled in being with someone as *masculine* as Peter.

By the time Peter re-entered his bedroom, he was feeling much more human. He had shaved, something he preferred to do himself, and his headache even seemed to have abated somewhat. A freshly pressed suit of clothes had been laid out on his bed, and on the floor was his favourite pair of black hessians which had been dubbed to a mirror-like shine. He dressed quickly in a fresh linen shirt and form-fitting pantaloons. He had just slipped his arms into a plain grey waistcoat and was about to tie his cravat when Jenkins returned, carrying a freshly sponged tailcoat.

"Here, let me." Jenkins stepped forward and relieved Peter of the cravat he was holding. "You will only make a mess of it and then I will have to go and press the silk once more," he grumbled.

Peter stood, stoically enduring his valet's expertise as Jenkins tied a simple but elegant knot, knowing it was one task he could rarely complete on his own. Once satisfied, Jenkins completed the job with a ruby pin before holding up the jacket so that Peter could slip his arms into the sleeves.

With a flick of his hand, Jenkins brushed away an imaginary speck of dust from Peter's shoulder. "There, you'll do. May I enquire as to if you will you be in this evening, sir?"

"Not until late, I would guess. I may be expected to stay for dinner, but if needs be, I shall dine at my club, so there will be no need to wait up for me. In fact, you could take the rest of the day, if you wish."

"Very good, sir," replied Jenkins. With a grin, he picked up a golden pocket watch from its stand before handing it to Peter.

At exactly half past two, Peter slipped into the back of the hackney carriage that had been waiting outside the house for him. Normally he would have ridden his stallion, Ajax, but on this occasion, he found himself glad to have a few moments alone to contemplate what was to come. Admittedly, in recent times, he had been a little neglectful in attending on his parents. He had good reason for that, or so he thought. They lived in Berkshire, a six-hour carriage ride away, and he resided in London.

So why now come to London? he thought. *After all, it is not yet the start of the season, and Papa much prefers the peace and quiet of his country estate. Perhaps this summons is their way of saying they want to see more of me. Or perhaps it is something more serious they want to discuss, an illness in the family, some financial difficulty. No. Surely it would not be that, for the old man is as strong as an ox and rich beyond belief.*

Then he had a sudden dreadful notion.

God forbid if they know where I spent last night!

So lost in thought as he was, Peter hardly noticed the journey, and in what seemed like a matter of moments the carriage was pulling up outside Wilton House, the family's London townhouse in Belgrave Square. Reaching into his waistcoat pocket, he retrieved a silver shilling and passed it to the coach driver before jumping down onto the pavement. Then, with cane in hand, he skipped up the stairs and knocked on the front door. Immediately the door was answered by his father's butler, who stepped aside deferentially to allow Peter to enter.

"Good afternoon, Wilkinson," said Peter. Schooling his face into a neutral expression to mask his growing apprehension, he handed the man his gloves, hat, and cane.

"Good afternoon, my lord," the man replied. "Their graces are waiting for you in the green room and have asked for you to join them immediately on arrival. If you would follow me, sir."

"No need, Wilkinson, I know the way," replied Peter.

The door to the drawing room was tall, solid, and ornate, and as Peter reached it, he found his heart begin to pound a little faster as it always did when summonsed by his father. For a moment he paused to collect his resolve, giving him the chance to draw in a deep breath to steady his trembling hand. Then he reached for the handle and opened the door, knowing it to be unwise to delay any further.

His father was stood by the fireplace looking every inch the senior aristocrat that he was. As usual, he was immaculately dressed in a finely tailored tailcoat. However, he had forgone the old-fashioned wig that he normally wore, and the greying hair which he now sported caught Peter by surprise, as it made his father look every moment of his sixty years of age. Even his face seemed to have aged since the last time Peter had seen him. His father had always been handsome, but now his skin was laced with wrinkles around the eyes, which served only to give him a serious and sombre look.

His mother, on the other hand, was an entirely different matter. One would never suspect that she was five and fifty years old, for she looked so much younger. Her golden blond hair, without even the merest hint of grey, was elegantly styled, and she wore a gown of lilac silk that did little to hide a mature yet curvaceous body. In her day, Mama had been dubbed a *diamond of the first water,* and in her more mature years she was still regularly declared to be one of the most beautiful and elegant ladies in all of England.

And sat next to her on the luxurious sofa was a young lady whom no one could ever mistake for any other but his mother's daughter!

"Alice! What an amazing surprise. Mother, you look as wonderful as always," he added. With a boyish grin, he kissed first his mother and then his sister upon the cheek.

"And hello to you too, Peter," replied Alice.

Her voice was icy, and Peter instinctively paused as he caught what he thought to be a note of warning, a hidden message for him to watch his step. As had always been the way between them, when Peter returned his sister's gaze, his own expression showed his gratitude, a message he knew she would clearly understand in return. It was then that she nodded imperceptibly towards the duke. Peter took the hint, and with a single stride he found himself in front of his father, where he gave a curt yet respectful and deferential nod of his head as he held out his hand.

"Hello Father," he said.

His father took the proffered hand and shook it with what Peter took to be genuine warmth. Then his father smiled. Yes, it was the merest turning up of his lips, but it was still a smile, and Peter found he was once more able to breathe freely, not realising how nervous he had become.

"Peter, it is good to see you, my boy. But in future, I hope we will not have to drag ourselves up to London to do so!" His father's tone of voice was light, almost jovial, but Peter did not fail to recognise the admonishment he had received.

"That will do, Henry," said the duchess.

Peter turned and looked once more at his mother, noting the adoration that shone in her eyes. Whilst his father instilled the discipline, his mother had been the one he had turned to when hurt or upset, a constant source of warmth and love. She had always been there for him, and he knew, if push came to shove, she would act like the fiercest of tigers to protect her children. Had it not been she who had tracked him down after the Battle of Waterloo, refusing to believe the reports that his body had been left upon the field of battle? Somehow, the men she sent to look for him had discovered himself and Jenkins amongst all of the other fallen, and on her orders had removed them both from the filthy squalor of an army hospital. For months afterwards, his mother had acted as chief nurse as they both convalesced, resulting in Jenkins elevating her to almost goddess-like status.

Peter suddenly felt the shame of it spear through his heart, the pain he felt at causing his mother any sort of heartache almost too much to endure.

"No, Mama," he said softly, "Father is right. I have been quite remiss not to come to see you, and for that I am truly sorry."

Lovingly, the duchess smiled. "Never mind, my darling, for now you are here," she said.

Once more the parlour door was thrown open wide, and without waiting to be announced, his elder brother, Thomas, Viscount Fairfax, entered the room. For some unknown reason, Peter shuddered at the sight of him. Whilst Thomas had never been unkind to his siblings, he had always been ready, especially with Peter, to put them in their place. Being four years older than the twins, he was quick to assert his authority as the eldest, as their father's heir, and judging by the supercilious and pompous manner he now subconsciously projected, nothing had changed.

Shit, he said to himself. *Something has to be seriously amiss for all of us to be brought together.*

Peter felt the hairs on the back of his neck stand proud as he recognised the seriousness of the situation. After all, this was the very first time the whole family had been together in the same room since the day he was returned from the war. He had been close to deathbed at the time, and now the atmosphere suggested he was about to be so again.

"Mother, Father, Alice. Peter. It's good to see you here on time, brother" said Thomas. "Father, I am expected by Lord Jenkinson in an hour's time. Do you think we could get right down to the matter in hand?"

The bluntness of this statement compelled Peter to stare. His focus darted from father to mother to sister to brother, each one of them turning their gaze upon him as if he were some prize exhibit in the Tower of London zoo. Heat suffused his face as his heart ratcheted up to a beat higher that it had when going into battle. Something was wrong, something was seriously wrong, and everyone was staring at him as if it were his fault.

"What?" he demanded. "What is it?"

"Peter," his father began. His voice was strong and resolute, and left Peter in no doubt that his father intended to be obeyed. "Do you realise that is has been five years since you were injured at Waterloo. Has it not occurred to you that since leaving the army, your life has lacked purpose and direction?"

"No father, "said Peter defensively.

"Well, I have, Peter. I have therefore called the family together to discuss your forthcoming marriage to Lady Priscilla Weston."

Chapter Two

"So what are you going to do?" asked Alice.

They sat together upon a garden seat, and Alice had taken hold of Peter's hand in an effort to quell his anger. For a moment Peter stared back at his sister morosely. Then he shrugged his shoulders and slumped forward in abject surrender.

The argument had been of epic proportions, a battle to rival anything that Napoleon could have arranged. His father had issued him an ultimatum. He would marry by the end of the season or have his monthly stipend withdrawn. Even his mother had sided with his father and his brother on this matter. She had taken the eminently reasonable stance that she wanted to see him settled, to have a family, to put behind him the years of debauchery and risk that being an army officer had brought. His mama had even sweetened the pot by announcing that his wedding gift would be Winsworth Manor and its estates, along with the guaranteed income of at least five thousand a year that it would bring. Then his brother had put in his two-penny worth. He argued that by marrying and having children, Peter would ensure the ducal succession should anything happen to him and his family. Only Alice had offered an olive branch and had tried to be the voice of reason on his behalf.

"I don't know," whispered Peter. "At least you got them to agree that I could make my own choice of bride."

"Yes," laughed Alice. "Lady Priscilla, despite the size of her dowry and her breasts, would be entirely unsuitable for you in so many ways. That girl is truly vain and spoiled, not to mention that laugh of hers, which always reminds me of a braying donkey. However, you have to admit Father was right when he said that your life lacked purpose. Winsworth might give you that."

"I suppose I could always re-join my regiment."

"No!" declared Alice emphatically. "I will not have that. I nearly lost you once, and I am not going to risk losing you again in some Godforsaken war in some Godforsaken country."

"But . . .but . . .I can't marry, Alice. I can't. Just the thought it sends shivers of horror down my spine, you know it does. How could I possibly marry and not be true to myself?"

"No, indeed. This is quite a quandary, is it not?" said Alice.

"I will have to get a job then, find some form of gainful employment to support myself once I am cut off. Perhaps I could become a Member of Parliament."

"A role for which, with your obvious lack of tact and diplomacy, you are eminently suited," replied Alice sarcastically. "No, you must be wed, for I see no other way out of this. All we need to do is to find you the right kind of girl to marry."

Peter turned his head towards his sister at this comment, and hope flared through his eyes.

"What do you mean?" he asked.

"What I mean is that there are plenty of *ladies* out there who are prepared to sacrifice a love match for the sake of a secure future for themselves. You are quite a catch, brother mine, whether you know it or not. I am certain that we could find you a wife who would be satisfied with a marriage of convenience, in return for becoming mistress of Winsworth Manor. Whilst children would be good to occupy her time, you would not even have to bed her if you didn't want to, for nothing was spoken of having to produce children from the marriage, was it?"

"No, by God, it was not," declared Peter as he jumped to his feet. Then he sat once more, his sudden enthusiasm ebbing away as another thought entered his mind. "No, Alice. I could not do that. It would not be fair on whatever girl who would accept me."

"And there is my true brother. Always thinking of others before himself," said Alice. She smiled fondly at him. "You have a good heart, Peter, but trust me when I say that I am certain we could find you a suitable match, one who would be more than willing to be wife to the second son of the Duke of Abingdon and mistress of Winsworth Manor in exchange for your supposed freedom."

"Do you think so?" asked Peter.

"I know so."

"So . . . so where do I start?" he asked tentatively.

"If it were I, I would go and see Countess Hamilton."

"Who in blazes is she?"

"She, brother dear, is affectionately known as the Matchmaker. If she cannot find someone suitable for you to marry, then no one can."

Chapter Three

Olivia Hamilton, Dowager Countess of Weybridge, was sat in her office, her ledger open in front of her as she neatly penned yet another entry onto the income page. Thanks entirely to her business acumen, the current state of her finances was eminently satisfactory—so much so that she was even contemplating retirement. With what she had squirreled away and had invested in the five percents, she could easily afford to maintain her town house and live in the manner she had become accustomed to for the rest of her natural life, without having to rely on the generosity of her daughters.

When her late husband, the Earl of Weybridge, had died, there had been little left in the estate for her. Not that Olivia minded, as her daughter Amelia had married well, and had often begged Olivia to come and live with her, especially as Amelia was now expecting her first child. In addition to that, there was her particular *friend*, the Duchess of Camberly, who was not only immensely wealthy in her own right, but was married to one of the richest men in England.

However, having been a dependent for most of her life, when the Earl died, she had taken it as a sign to begin again. Whilst by no means destitute, she had resolved to pay her own way, to earn her own money and to become financially independent for the first time in her life. Her solution had been an easy one to find. After all, she had the title of countess, a title that she had used to great effect to discretely facilitate connections throughout the highest echelons of London society. So why not use those connections?

So it was that she became the Matchmaker to the *ton*.

For a *modest* fee, she elicited introductions, negotiated marriage settlements, and took great pride in meeting the needs of her clients. Why, only that morning she had witnessed the signing of the marriage contract between Miss Helena Smythe-Jenkins and Baron Teddy Porchester. Helena was something of an oddball, and after four seasons, her parents had despaired of her ever finding a husband, even though she was in possession of a handsome dowry.

The problem was that, whilst eminently pretty, Helena had been labelled as a bluestocking and could often be found in the gallery of the Royal Society listening to some lecture on astronomy or natural history. However, as Teddy was usually to be found in his own laboratory, Helena had been the perfect choice when he had asked for help in finding a bride. Right from the offset, Olivia had known that they were meant for each other, and the couple now seemed deliriously happy. The fact that the match had added yet another five-hundred guineas to her coffers did little harm, either.

There was a knock on the door, and Olivia saw her abigail and maid-of-all-duties, Mary, enter the room, her ever-present smile preceding her as she curtsied to her mistress.

"Lord Fairfax is here to see you, my lady. Says he has an appointment. Good lookin' one too," she giggled.

"Mary, what have I told you about keeping your comments about my customers to yourself?"

"Oh, sorry my lady," the girl grinned, completely unabashed by her mistress's chastisement.

"You, young lady, are incorrigible. Would you please show him in?"

"Yes'm."

Once she was alone, Olivia closed her ledger, carefully locking the leather-bound book into a hidden strong box that lay behind some panelling in her office. Seating herself back at her desk, she then closed her eyes for a moment and reflected on what she knew about Lord Peter Fairfax.

Like she did with all her customers, Olivia had done her homework and had made discreet enquiries about the man, knowing full well how the gossips of the ton liked to talk. Seemingly, he was one and thirty years of age and had been a Major in the Royal Regiment of Horse Guards. Second son of the Duke of Abingdon, he now kept apartments in London and was attended by a single servant. He had a small social circle of male friends with whom he enjoyed an occasional bawdy evening. Yet he was not seen as a rake and had never been embroiled in any sort of scandal. That in itself had surprised the countess. It was said that he was as handsome as sin, and had he not studiously avoided the London marriage mart, he would by now have been snapped up by one of the eligible ladies of the ton.

So why come to me to find a match? If he is what is reported, surely he would be able to find someone suitable for himself.

Once more there was a knock on her office door, and Mary entered, this time with something of a blush to her cheek.

"Lord Fairfax, my lady," the girl announced formally.

Olivia watched intently as her *customer* entered the room, noting instantly that Mary had not been wrong with her appraisal of the man. He was, indeed, extremely handsome. Tall, broad-shouldered, and with the face of a dark-haired Greek god, he was immaculately dressed in form-fitting buckskin trousers and a perfectly tailored coat. In fact, the only things she could note to mar his appearance was a slight limp where he favoured his right leg, and the red blush in his cheeks that suggested the man was more than a little nervous. She stood and waited until he had bowed respectfully before returning his courtesy with a curtsey of her own.

"Lord Fairfax, welcome to my home," she said. "Please, have a seat." Graciously, she indicated two tall library chairs that had been placed by the fireplace for such an occasion.

"Thank you, Lady Hamilton," he replied. As he took the proffered seat, Olivia noted the shakiness in his voice, so she sat on her own chair opposite him and smiled encouragingly.

"So how may I be of service to you, Lord Fairfax?" she asked, deliberately keeping her voice light.

For several moments she observed the man as he squirmed in his chair, almost as if he could not find a comfortable position to sit. He crossed his leg and then uncrossed it once more. He placed his feet upon the floor only to have a knee jiggle up and down. With knowledge born of experience, Olivia instantly realised that she would have to take control of the situation if he were not to bolt like some thoroughbred stallion spooked by a yapping hound.

"Please, Lord Fairfax. You have my word that whatever we speak of between these four walls will remain entirely confidential. I have built my reputation on such a fact. You may speak freely. In fact, I insist that you speak freely and honestly, for without that, I doubt I will be able to help you."

To Olivia, Lord Fairfax looked morosely miserable as he toyed with some sort of inner demon. But then she saw his resolve stiffen as his back straightened, as his dark brown eyes turned to hers.

He coughed.

"Lady Hamilton. As you may have surmised, I am here today to avail myself of your . . .erm . . .your matchmaking services. I . . .er . . .I am in need of a wife, in need of a wife before the season's end."

With these words, Olivia observed the redness in his cheeks flare even brighter with embarrassment. This was an occurrence that Olivia had come to expect from her customers, who often felt intense discomfort when explaining the reason for their visit. However, some instinct was telling her that the whole process was going to be far more difficult than then norm for Lord Fairfax.

Kid gloves, she thought, *this one needs kid gloves.*

So it was that she replied with the gentleness of a mother holding her new-born babe.

"Well, my lord. I see no reason why I would not be able to help you with this quest. From what I know of you, you will make quite a catch for the right young woman. Perhaps if you were to tell me a little more about the circumstances leading up to this decision."

Her words were spoken softly, in a soothing tone that was designed to make the man feel more at ease, and she knew that they had achieved the desired effect when he looked back at her with a little more confidence in his eyes.

"My parents, the Duke and Duchess of Abingdon, are insisting that I marry, even though I have no wish to do so. To ensure that I comply, they have set certain conditions. I must marry before the end of the coming season. If I do so, I will inherit a sizeable estate with a sizeable income. If I do not, I will be cut off from all financial support."

Olivia smiled. "You are not the first to suffer from this demand, my lord, nor will you be the last, I am certain. So, if it is to be, what sort of girl would you be looking for?"

Olivia stared at Peter intently, watching the play of emotion as it flickered across his face. It was almost as if there were some kind of internal war going on inside his head so, rather that pushing him further, Olivia sat and waited for his to make up his mind about what he wanted to say.

"I have your word, Lady Hamilton, that this conversation will go no further?"

"Yes, of course you have."

Again, he paused, and Olivia took advantage of the delay to stand and to walk over to a sideboard, where on a silver tray there was a decanter of fine brandy. With a clink of glass, she removed the stopper and carefully poured out two measures of the ruby coloured liquid before turning back to

Peter.

"Here, drink this, Lord Fairfax."

She watched as a grateful Peter took the glass from her hand, only to swallow the spirit in a single mouthful. She in turn sat once more and sipped a little of her own drink before placing her glass onto a small side table.

"Lord Fairfax, you do not have to tell me anything you do not wish me to know. But in my experience, the more truthful you are, the easier it will be for me to find the right match for you."

"I know, "Peter sighed. "But 'tis difficult for me to talk about this. The truth of the matter is that I will require a bride in name only. Yes, I will provide for her as a husband should. She will be mistress of a fine house and will want for nothing . . . except . . . except for the warmth of a husband in her bed. You see, I . . . I . . ." he stammered.

"Ah," replied Olivia as the penny began to drop. "Does this mean that you . . ."

Heat flared in the young man's face as he stared down at the floor miserably, and Olivia suddenly felt her heart go out to him.

"Mmm," he said, his voice barely a whisper. "Unfortunately, my sexual preferences do not run to members of the opposite sex, if you get my meaning."

"Ah, I see," said Olivia. "And may I ask where you seek out such liaisons."

"I am a member of the Moonlight Club."

"Ah yes. I am aware of that establishment, my lord. That is well, for I believe the club to be quite discreet."

"So, you see my dilemma, Lady Hamilton. I will not, cannot bed a woman, yet I need a wife if I am to satisfy the demands of my parents."

Olivia slid back into the library chair and picked up her brandy glass once more. With intelligent eyes she viewed the man who was sat before her, looking for any form of subterfuge, knowing how difficult it must have been for him to admit to being such a man. Not that a man with his preferences was unusual. And Olivia already knew of several others with similar inclinations. Why, only the year before, Viscount Jameson had presented himself in a comparable situation and was now embroiled in a very unhappy marriage, one which she herself had reluctantly arranged.

"Very well," said Olivia. "It is obvious that the lady you need will be a little older, perhaps a second sister who has been left on the shelf, someone with little prospect of marriage. I can think of at least three who would match your needs."

"Yes . . . yes . . . that is the sort of girl . . . but . . . but . . ."

"But what, my lord?"

"This is so unfair," he said angrily.

Olivia watched as Peter stood, the agitation he was feeling so clear in the way that he paced over the window, his face hidden so that she could not see the play of emotion. "It is so wrong of me to do this, to inflict myself on such a girl. She is bound to be miserable and more than a little disappointed with the arrangement. And what if she expects a child that I cannot give her?"

It was at that very moment that Olivia knew she would accept this commission to help Peter Fairfax. The man who stood before her was a man of morals, regardless of his sexual proclivity, and her heart went out to the internal struggle that he was so obviously experiencing. Yes, she would most definitely help him.

It was then that, like a bolt of lightning from Zeus himself, a most deliciously wicked idea on how she could help flashed into her fertile mind.

"Damn it!" he shouted. "Perhaps I should take myself off to the Americas instead!"

Olivia could not stop herself.

"No, I would not do anything so rash, my lord, for I think that I might know the perfect *girl* for you," she replied.

"And who might that be?"

Olivia smiled broadly as she looked back at Peter.

"Oh, I think I will keep that to myself for the moment until I have had a chance to speak to her in person. With your permission, I will explain the situation to the lady, without mentioning your name of course. If she is agreeable to the arrangement, I will facilitate a meeting."

"And your fee, my lady? I assume you do not do this out of the goodness of your heart."

Olivia sat back in her chair and laced her fingers together, fighting to keep the excitement and trepidation she felt from showing upon her face. Yes, she could always find a lady to play the part that Peter required. But why should she, when she had someone far more suitable in mind?

"My fee is a flat rate of five hundred guineas, two hundred and fifty in advance and two hundred and fifty payable on completion of the contract. Should I not find you a suitable match, you will of course receive a full refund, my lord."

Chapter Four

David, Viscount Drummond, lay on his bed, and as he counted the cracks in the plasterwork above, he once more he cursed himself for the stupidity that had allowed his father to discover his deepest held secret.

At the time, of course, the lure of being true to himself had been too strong; had been impossible to ignore. For years, his dreams and fantasies had been filled with the desire to act upon what he saw as a natural urge. So, when the opportunity had presented itself, he had found himself unable to resist. This, of course, had led to his downfall, for it had resulted in his father discovering him dressed as the girl he longed to be whilst being fucked in the arse by a great big hairy beast of a man. It had also brought on the beating that he would never forget and the subsequent banishment from the only home he had ever known.

It had been his mother who had facilitated his escape to London. It had been she who had given him a purse with one hundred pounds in gold coin. It had been she who had given him a letter of introduction to an old friend, Countess Hamilton.

Even now, he was uncertain as to what his mother had written in her lengthy letter. Nonetheless, it seemed to do the trick. After he had arrived on her doorstep, the countess had been of immeasurable support. She had found him rooms to rent at a very reasonable rate and had even sent her own physician to treat his bruises. But David knew he would not be able to prevail on the lady's good nature forever, and the sixty pounds he still possessed would not last him very long, especially in London. Of course, he had the trust his grandfather had left him, some twenty thousand pounds at that, but he would not get access to that money until he turned one and twenty years of age. So, somehow, he would have to survive for nearly a year as an outcast from his own family.

Perhaps you can find some form of gainful employment, a clerk perhaps or a schoolteacher. After all, you are well educated. That must be of some value to someone. I will find employment; learn a business, perhaps a business I can invest in when I am in receipt of my trust. Perchance Lady Hamilton could help with that. She is, after all, the only person I know in London!

It was at that very moment that a knock sounded on his bedroom door. David pulled himself from his bed and walked over to the door, thinking it was probably Mrs. Jones, his landlady, holding a meagre supper of bread and cheese for him to eat. However, his mouth dropped open as he opened the door, for standing there was none other than the lady he had just been thinking about, along with a young maid who stood respectfully behind.

"Good evening, David," said the countess.

David stood and stared as the woman breezed uninvited into his room, followed by the grinning maid. Countess Hamilton was indeed a handsome woman. In her fifties, she had the lush, rounded body of a mature woman, a body which she displayed to maximum effect with the beautiful clothes she wore. For a moment, David stood and gawped, his eyes drawn irrevocably to the lovely globes of flesh perched upon her chest, a flash of jealousy spearing his heart. He coughed and then bowed respectfully to try and cover the redness of his cheeks.

"Good evening, my lady."

He spoke softly, not quite knowing what to say next, completely vexed as to why a lady of her standing would want to visit him in the second-rate rooms which he now occupied.

But he need not have worried on that score, for Lady Hamilton was instantly all business.

"If you would follow me, David," she ordered. "I have a carriage waiting downstairs."

Her tone of voice was imperious, and it was obvious that the countess would tolerate no question or discussion. Having little choice in the matter, David smiled and bowed once more as he reached for the jacket that hung on the back of the door. At the same time, he looked on as the maid collected the few possessions he had brought with him from Scotland, placing them all securely in a small carpet bag.

After a twenty-minute journey, a journey conducted mostly in silence, the coach pulled up outside a small townhouse on a quiet street in a much nicer area of London. Respectfully, David allowed the countess to alight first. Then he followed, standing next to her as her maid retrieved yet two more carpet bags from the rear of the coach. A key appeared from the reticule that the countess was carrying, and moments later, all three of them had entered the house.

Whilst the dwelling appeared unoccupied, it was obvious that someone had recently been in residence. The house was fully furnished and was neat and tidy, every surface and window devoid of dust. David followed Lady Hamilton, who seemed to know exactly where she was going, and soon they entered a pretty and well-appointed drawing room. He stood and watched the lady divest herself of her travelling cloak, handing it to her maid, before turning to sit elegantly before the fireplace. With a nod of her head, she indicated a chair to David.

"I suppose you are wondering what this is all about, young man," she said softly.

David looked on as she placed her reticule on her knee to retrieve a letter from it, a letter that he instantly recognised as the one his mother had written.

"Yes, you could say that, my lady."

"First let me tell you about this house. As you may or may not know, I consider myself to be something of a businesswoman. This house is one of several that I own and rent to paying tenants. If you want it, the house can be yours for the next six months, until the present tenants, Doctor and Mrs Cartwright, return from their extended trip to Europe. That should be enough time for you to find your feet in London."

David grinned. "Thank you, Lady Hamilton, thank you," he gushed.

"However," she continued, "I think, perhaps, that your stay here may be shorter than you might expect."

Slowly, and much to David's consternation, Lady Hamilton opened the letter she held in her hand and smoothed it out on her lap before retrieving a pair of half-moon spectacles from her reticule. For a moment she scanned the neatly penned missive before once more capturing David's eyes with a perceptive glare.

"Your mother writes that the reason your father has disowned you was that you were discovered wearing women's clothing and were at the time in a very compromising position with your father's head groom."

Instantly, David felt his face glow hotter than any fire, the very tips of his ears literally burning as he jumped to his feet. His anger flared and he let out an audible groan. How could she? How could his mother write such things, even if they were true? He would be a laughingstock. The whole of London would know by now. He would never again be able to show his face in public. He groaned once more, his feet now moving in a blur as he practically sprinted to the door . . . until a simple command rang out.

"*Sit down, David!*"

The countess's words were harsh and demanding, halting him in his tracks. Like a man in a trance, he felt her words cut through to his heart, and without even realising he was doing so, David found himself turning once more to do as he was told. Then he looked at Lady Hamilton, really looked, and was shocked to see her expression. She sat there looking serenely calm. There was no hatred or malice in her eyes, no perverse enjoyment at his embarrassment. If anything, all he saw was compassion and pity. Heavily, he sat on his chair and resigned himself to his fate.

"Would you like to talk about it, David?" she asked.

"Not in front of her," David whispered. He nodded towards the maid, who was still stood in the doorway to the parlour.

"Oh, you have nothing to fear from Mary, for her loyalty to me is without question. But perhaps, Mary, if you would go and make some tea?" she asked.

"Yes'm," the girl replied as, with a grin, she turned and closed the door behind her, leaving the two of them alone together.

For a few moments, a silence settled over the room, a silence that was only broken by the cracking of a damp log in the fireplace. Again, David found himself looking nervously at the woman before him, and if anything, his face began to glow even more furiously than it had before. Shamefully, he looked at the floor and began to speak from the very core of his heart.

"It is all I ever think about, Lady Hamilton," he said simply.

"What is?"

David looked up, his eyes beseeching, hoping beyond hope that this woman would let him off the hook, would not force him to speak. But as his eyes caught hers once more, he knew that this would never be the case, and something told him that if he was ever going to talk about how he felt, it would be with this extraordinary woman.

"Being a girl, being a woman," he replied softly. "From the moment I awake to the moment I go to sleep, all I can think of is wanting, nay needing to be a woman. Even in my dreams."

"But is this not some deep-seated fantasy? Escapism, some call it. You know, to dress up and pretend to be a girl for a while. I have heard of men like that."

Even Olivia had come across reports of the molly houses of London and of how men therein would dress in womanly garb to satisfy some morbid sense of excitement. Whilst it was more common that was generally believed, dressing this way was behaviour that was fraught with danger. Why, only the year before, a gentleman was sentenced to two days in the public stocks for just such a crime.

"No!" exclaimed David. "It is much more than that, my lady. For me it is no game. If I were to be given the choice right now to remain as I am or to be somehow magically transformed into a woman, I would not hesitate for one second in choosing the latter, even if it meant living in some hovel, selling sprigs of heather in order to survive."

"I see."

"No, I do not think you do, Lady Hamilton. Whilst I know it is futile to do so, I dream of having breasts, of having...well...you know...instead of a...well, you know. I dream of what it would be like to marry, to beget a child, to hold that child to my breast."

"Ah."

"Do you know what is like to hate yourself, to hate your own body, Lady Hamilton? For that is me. I hate being a man! I hate all that being male represents, especially with the expectations of my father to *man up* and to be the *warrior laird* that he expects me to be. From a very early age, I was treated and educated thus, taught to ride and fight with sword, fist and pistol, expected to indulge in all the manly pursuits, sorely disappointing my father when I failed to excel in any of these. Yes, Lady Hamilton, I can truly say that I hate being a man."

Breathlessly, David paused, turning his head so that Lady Hamilton could not see the tears that were forming in his eyes. Never before had he spoken so vociferously about himself. Yet as he did so, it was almost as if a great weight had been lifted from his chest, and David had no idea whether to laugh or cry. As for Lady Hamilton, she did not appear shocked at all. Quite the opposite in fact, her lips forming an encouraging smile, which prompted David to continue with his account.

"What my parents do not know, what no one knows," he continued, "is that because of this there have been times where I have reached real depths of despair. I have twice tried to take my own life, once by holding a loaded pistol to my brain. On that occasion I had discovered an ancient manuscript from the Far East describing something called reincarnation. It is the belief that one's soul would be reborn as another person, once death had occurred. In my madness, I actually hoped that if I took my own life, I would be reborn as a woman."

"Fortunately, you seem to have been unable to go through with your plan however."

"Yes, quite. But in truth, I have recently thought of doing so once more, especially after my father caught me with our head groom."

"Will you tell me what happened?" asked Lady Hamilton. "And please be candid. Think not that I am some shrinking violet who will faint at the mere utterance of the word *sex*."

For a moment, David sat there, his cheeks burning violently from the embarrassment he felt. But as he looked at the lady who sat before him, there was no condemnation in her eyes, only soft compassion and understanding. His mind made up, he sighed deeply as he resigned himself to telling the truth.

"I had amassed quite a collection of feminine clothing, mainly the castoffs from my mother's wardrobe, and would spend hour upon hour locked in my bedchamber secretly changing into the garb of a woman. It is difficult to explain, Lady Hamilton, but it just felt right to do so. I would put on ladies' undergarments to give me some semblance of a feminine form. Then I would slip into a dress before letting my hair down to comb it into something akin a feminine style. Night after night, I would go to sleep dreaming of being a woman, one who might share her bed with a man to make love to her."

"So you are, for want of a better term, a shirt-lifter."

To David, Lady Hamilton's words seemed deliberate and designed to provoke a reaction. Even he could see how she probed the facts, looking for the truth of the matter. Well, now that he had started, that was exactly what she was going to get.

"No, I am not," said David firmly. "I can only explain it by suggesting that my fantasies of indulging in a physical relationship with a man were the fantasies of very naïve young *woman*, the woman I believe myself to be. Is it not normal for a woman to want the love of a man?"

"But you are not a woman, David."

"Confusing, is it not?" groaned David. For a moment, he looked away before once more turning back to his hostess.

"As time passed, I found myself consumed with the very thought of acting upon my . . . how shall we put it . . . my natural sexual urges. Russell, our head groom, was the object of my fantasy, so after discovering the man was in debt, I unashamedly bribed him to be my partner in this enterprise. I arranged to meet him in the small hours of the morning, with me attired as the young woman I imagined in my mind. Unfortunately, my father discovered us together. He beat me within an inch of my life before banishing me from his estates. The rest you know."

It was at that moment that Mary returned carrying a tray with kettle, teapot, and cups which she placed onto a small table before sitting so that she could begin to pour the tea. In silence, David watched on, knowing that he would be unable to continue with her being in the room.

Lady Hamilton was having none of that, and David winced a little as she continued to press.

"So what are your intentions now?" she asked.

"I am not sure. I have a considerable sum of money held in trust for when I am one and twenty, but until then I will have to find some form of gainful occupation I suppose."

"That is not what I meant, David," said Lady Hamilton crossly, "and you know it is not. What I would like to know is what are you going to do about this confusion you have in your mind?"

"Oh, there is no confusion, Lady Hamilton. I know exactly who I am *supposed* to be. But unfortunately, there is nothing I can do about it. I am and always will be David Drummond, and I suppose I will have to live with that," he added miserably.

"But do you?" asked Olivia.

David's mouth fell open in surprise.

"What do you mean?" he demanded.

David suddenly found himself sitting on the edge of his seat, his eyes fixed upon the lady before him. She in turn sat looking completely relaxed about the whole situation.

"What if there was a way for you to be the woman you claim to be? Would you take it?"

"In a heartbeat. But even you must realise how ridiculous that sounds," moaned David.

"Mary," said Olivia, calling over her maid.

With his heart pounding, David watched as the maid stood

and walked over to him, her hands outstretched as if to have him stand. He duly obliged and then felt himself led to the centre of the room. For a moment Mary circled him, looking at him thoughtfully. Pausing at his back, she loosened the ribbon that tied his long red hair into a queue at the nape of his neck. With her fingers she then spread his hair about his shoulders before once more standing before him with a critical eye.

"Well?" asked Olivia.

"Well, my lady! He is not too tall and is very slim. He has little if nothing in the way of beard growth. and his complexion is beautifully pale and smooth. His hands are small, and there is no sign of a manly swelling at his neck. The hair . . .well, that is a real asset. But best of all, he has a really pretty face."

"And?"

"And, yes, I am certain I could make him look very feminine."

"What is this?" demanded David as he once more turned to Lady Hamilton.

"I have it in mind to help you, David," said Olivia. "However, before we proceed further with this matter, before I fully explain my intentions for you, I see the need to conduct a little experiment. Mary is a most accomplished lady's maid, which is why I asked her to be here today. With your permission, of course, I would like her to perform a transformation on you, to make you appear as the lady you purport to be."

Chapter Five

It was a very bemused David who found himself alone with Lady Hamilton's maid, the lady herself having departed to attend dinner at the home of one of her clients. He had been completely stunned by what the countess had suggested; completely excited about it, too. She had offered him the services of her lady's maid in order to facilitate his physical transformation from man to woman, and he was enthralled by the idea. For the first time in his life, he would go *all the way*, would have his hair styled as a woman might, would have cosmetics applied to his face.

Eagerly, he turned to Mary.

"So where do we begin?" he asked.

"With a name, I think. It is unseemly for a maid such as I to be left alone with a gentleman. If you choose a feminine name, I will be able to consider you to be a lady instead and able to remain in your company. Much more socially acceptable," she giggled.

"Isobel," he replied, almost instantly. "I would like you to call me Isobel."

"And such a pretty name, too. From now on I will call you Miss Isobel and you will call me Mary. And I shall also think of you, as so should you, with a feminine gender."

David grinned broadly, for this was a game he had often played as a child. He had picked out his feminine name so many years before, and had always, in his imagination, referred to himself as such.

"So, Mary, what is to come first?" David asked eagerly.

"Well, *Miss Isobel*," said Mary, "as you know, we have until tomorrow noon before Lady Hamilton returns. This evening will be all about preparation. A bath first, so that I can wash your lovely hair and so that I can shave your body."

"Shave my body!" exclaimed David.

"Mmm. Proper ladies do not have hairy bodies, Miss Isobel, so I will shave it for you. Then I shall trim your lovely hair before I set it with papers. That way it can dry properly overnight before I style it for you. And don't look so worried. Should you need to return to being Master David, you will still be able to do so without question. Now come and help me with the hot water I have already on the stove in the kitchen."

It took the two of them twenty minutes to fill the copper hip bath with hot water, David beginning to appreciate how hard a servant was required to work as they did so. When all was ready, Mary helped him undress, insisting that she do so as if he was her mistress. Strangely, David felt no embarrassment at doing this, even though he had never before been naked in front of a woman, and it was not long before he was stepping into the bathtub, hissing a little from the heat.

Mary allowed him to soak for a while as she fussed around the room, arranging a variety of bottles and brushes upon a small table. She came to him then, standing behind him to untie his hair from its queue and running her fingers through his locks to loosen them. When satisfied, she scooped water over his head with a jug, and once his hair was completely wet, she reached for a bottle and began to gently massage the contents into David's scalp. The sensation was like nothing David had experienced before. He sighed and closed his eyes in pleasure as the girl's deft fingers massaged the lotion into his scalp, the soft scent of roses and lavender pervading the air.

"Oh, that feels so good," David whispered. "It smells wonderful too. What is in it?" he asked.

"It is made by a friend of mine, Miss Phoebe. She is an extraordinary African lady who is companion to the Duchess of Camberly, a particular friend of Lady Hamilton. She is also a very talented healer and knows everything about herbs and such. This, as well as a gentle soap and a lovely fragrance, has in it the oil of a plant called aloe vera and will leave your hair feeling smooth and shiny. I believe she grows the aloe plant herself in the hot houses on the Duchess's estate."

David grinned as he listened to her speak, for the more he came to know this girl, the more he realised that she was nothing like the run-of-the-mill servant. No, this girl had a natural enthusiasm for life, and an obvious intelligence, too.

"Why, Mary, do I get the feeling that you are quite an extraordinary young woman?"

"No, just a fortunate one," she said. Mary had him lean his head backwards, and after gathering his hair behind his ears, began to pour clean water from a jug to cleanse his hair of soap. "My father was a well-known clockmaker in London, and Lady Hamilton was a client of his," she continued. "Papa believed that all young ladies should receive an education, and whilst I was but a child, he hired a tutor for me so that I can now read and write as well as any other. However, he died when I was but fourteen years old, leaving me an orphan and virtually penniless. Lady Hamilton, bless her, took me into to her household, or else I would now probably be walking the streets. She must have seen something in me, for she apprenticed me to her own lady's maid. That was near on nine years ago now, and for that I shall be ever grateful to her."

"I see now where your loyalty comes from," said David softly.

"Quite. Now up you get, and don't be bashful," said Mary. David stood, the water sloshing in the bath as Mary reached for the shaving brush, soap and straight edged razor she had placed upon the small table.

For the next forty minutes, Mary carefully shaved David's entire body as he stood and stoically endured her ministrations. She shaved his legs and his arms. She shaved his chest and his back, even though he did not believe it to be necessary. She even shaved beneath his arms, leaving his skin pink and entirely smooth. In fact, the only part of him that was not shaved was his manhood, a manhood that David was struggling to control with every second that passed. Then, once she was finished, Mary took another pot from the table and began to smooth a pleasant-smelling ointment all over his body.

"This is another one of Miss Phoebe's concoctions," she explained. "I have no idea what it contains, but it is really effective in preventing further growth of hair."

When finished, David stepped out of the bath and into the robe that Mary held for him, noting with real pleasure that it was a woman's robe and not a man's. Then he and Mary went into his bedroom, a room that was appointed as a ladies' bedroom and one which was pleasantly warm, thanks to the fire that had been laid. To one side was a comfortable-looking bed that Mary had already turned down to air. There was a large wardrobe against one wall, and along another was a ladies' dressing table complete with a large silvered looking glass. Next to the fire was a ladderback chair, and it was to this that Mary went, retrieving a pretty nightgown that had been warming there.

"Here, put this on, Miss Isobel," she said, smiling broadly once more.

Without speaking, David did as he was instructed. He slipped out of his robe and held up his hands as Mary gathered the material to drop it over his head. As David felt the material float down over his body, he actually moaned out loud. How could he not? The nightdress was floor length and made of the purest cotton, and the feeling of the material against his smooth skin was unadulterated pleasure. What was more, he could see his reflection in the mirror. Despite the fact that he had no breasts to fill out the garment, it was a reflection so perfectly feminine that he instantly felt his blood surge to his groin. Mortified by his lack of control, he sat on the chair before the mirror and placed his hands over his groin, his cheeks glowing with embarrassment.

"Oh Miss Isobel, do not fuss so," chastised Mary, having obviously guessed the reason for David's discomfort. "'Tis only to be expected. Here, let me brush out your hair whilst you compose yourself."

Again, David closed his eyes and surrendered himself to Mary's ministrations. She took a brush and very gently set about taming his wild red hair, smoothing it down behind his ears and brushing it in her hand until it lay down his back in long silky tendrils.

"You have beautiful hair, Miss Isobel," she said softly. "It is so full in body and I love the colour it has. Do you know that it has grown several inches below your shoulders?"

"Yes," replied David. "It was something my father hated, even though long hair in men is quite fashionable. He wanted me to have it cut short."

"Well, I for one am glad you did not, for it allows me something to work with. In fact, I think that I will not put in rags after all. I think it would be better if I left it straight so that we can style it on the morrow. I will, however, have to trim it a little, and that is best done whilst it is still damp, Miss Isobel."

As his hair dried naturally, they had shared a light evening meal together with food that had been stocked in the pantry. Then Mary had spent several painful minutes shaping his eyebrows, plucking out the errant growth to leave them as graceful and narrow arches. It was a little after eleven in the evening when Mary finally announced herself satisfied and had wearily withdrawn to the bedroom she had claimed as her own.

Now completely alone, David once more sat before his looking glass, and his reflection thrilled him. He did not care that his hair was not dressed, that he was not wearing some fine gown. To him he had never looked more feminine, even if all he wore was a pretty lace-trimmed nightgown with a mob cap to cover his hair.

Excitement threatened to overwhelm him as he sat there, turning his head this way and that, trying to imagine what he might look like with his hair pinned up into a fashionable style, with a little kohl around his eyes perhaps. With his anticipation of what was yet to come, blood once more began to suffuse into his groin, his little cock becoming hard and excited, even though he felt a little disgusted with himself for allowing it to be so. He simply could not help himself, for he knew there would be no sleep for him unless he relieved the pressure. Carefully he pulled up the hem of his nightgown, bunching it around his stomach so as to not soil the cotton. Then, he closed his eyes as he took his phallus in hand, his mind once more playing out the scene amongst the hay in the stable.

Slowly David allowed his fist to move up and down his cock as he recalled the moment. It had been his first time with a man, and it had taken weeks of innuendo and gentle coercion—as well as a substantial amount of gold—to persuade Russell to take an active part. He remembered the sheer feminine pleasure of putting on the stockings he had stolen from his mother, of dressing in the old gown he had found in a trunk in the attic. He remembered the heady delight of taking the man's cock into his mouth, his hair loose around his face, like a woman might when making love to her man. He remembered the pain as Russell had pushed himself into his body, taking him from behind as he might any other woman. He remembered the ecstasy of being fucked, of Russell's cock pounding into him.

As his hand beat out a terrible rhythm, David felt the inevitable surge of pleasure. His spare hand shot forwards to protect his nightgown and before he knew it, wave after wave of his essence shot from his cock whilst his body shuddered and convulsed with pleasure. And as he came, he opened his eyes and looked at his reflection in the mirror, his orgasm ripping through him like a cyclone when he saw the young woman that was staring back at him.

Chapter Six

"Good morning sleepyhead," called Mary as she pulled back the drapes from the bedroom window. "Rise and shine, Miss Isobel. We have a lot to do this morning."

Groggily, David pushed himself up onto his elbow, his hair falling over his face as the mob cap had come away from his head sometime during the night.

He yawned. "What time is it?"

"Dawn was about an hour ago, so a little after seven in the morning, I would guess. Now if you would, Miss Isobel, I would like you to break your fast from the tray over there and do your morning ablutions. Not that you have much facial hair, but I would also like you to shave. There is a jug of hot water on the side over there, next to the basin. I will return in about twenty minutes so that we can begin your transformation."

The moment he was alone, excitement began to wash through him like the inevitable tide in the River Thames. He relieved himself into the chamber pot and then drank a cup of tea, the rest of what Mary had provided for breakfast going uneaten as his nerves threatened to overwhelm him. He shaved and brushed his teeth and was sat waiting for Mary when she returned holding a pile of clothing over her arm, clothing which she carefully placed upon his bed so as to not wrinkle the fabrics.

"Good. Now, before we go any further, I would suggest we deal with the little problem of what you have between your legs. Your manhood becoming aroused would not be very lady like, now would it?"

David laughed at her bluntness. How could he not? "No, it wouldn't, at that."

"Here," she said. With a hand, she held up a long strip of cotton muslin. "Try wrapping this tightly around yourself and between your legs. That should suffice to keep everything under control. Then put on your robe. I need to pop back into my room for something I have forgotten."

Once more David did as he was told. He slipped out of the nightgown, carefully folding it onto his bed. Then he took the long strip of muslin, fashioned as a bandage of sorts, and began to wind it around his hips and between his legs. Soon the bandage firmly held his cock between his legs. Yes, it was a little uncomfortable, but needs must be, and on this day of all days, a little discomfort was a small sacrifice to pay.

By the time Mary returned, he was in his robe and once more sat before the mirror, a dressing mirror that Mary proceeded to cover with a sheet she had brought from her room.

"Och! What are you doing that for?" protested David. "I want to be able to see everything you do," he moaned.

"And I want you to wait until I have finished with you. That way you will be able to see the full effect in one go," she said firmly. "The sheet stays."

David was about to protest even more vociferously, but the look in Mary's eyes told him she would stand for no nonsense over this matter. But perhaps she was right. If he were to see himself as a woman . . . to believe, maybe it would be best to see the finished product, not the stages it had taken to get him there.

"Besides," said Mary, "there will be plenty of time later on for you to learn all about how I facilitate this change."

"What?" asked David, as he turned to glare at her. "What do you mean by that?" he demanded.

"Ah! Perhaps I shouldn't have said that," she mused to

herself. "The countess will explain everything to you this afternoon, I am sure. Now turn around and let me start on your hair."

Despite the fact that David could not see what Mary was doing, the next two hours turned out to be a complete delight. For the first hour, Mary worked on his hair, combing it into sections, pinning it, curling little tendrils of hair with an iron she warmed by the fire. David guessed that she was creating some sort of chignon, for he could feel it at the back of his head, secured by a ribbon. But he could also feel loose curls about his face, too.

"Please Mary, may I see?" he begged as she seemed to finish.

"Nope," she said.

Dramatically, David sighed, as Mary set to work with her lotions and potions, starting with the same unguent that she had used on his body to retard any further growth of hair. Once more it took her an hour to achieve the look she was after. David was powdered, had kohl applied around his eyes, had golden powder applied above his eyes. She even added a little colour to his cheeks before applying a tinted lip balm with a rich red hue.

"Is it usual for a lady to have her face painted?" asked David. "I thought the ton frowned upon it."

"That all depends on how the face is painted, Miss Isobel. Ever since Lady Charlotte Winters married the Duke of Camberly, it has become the fashion for ladies to have their faces painted delicately and with moderation. It was she that demonstrated to society that subtle use of cosmetics can enhance the beauty of the woman, not mask it like some of kind of French courtesan. For you, cosmetics will be essential to disguise any masculine traits you might have in your face. The trick is to make it look like you are wearing the absolute minimum. There, you'll do. Now let's get you dressed, shall we?"

Suddenly, David felt his whole body begin to tremble. Up until this point in the proceedings he had been able to remain somewhat calm and composed. But now they were close to finishing, he could feel the mounting excitement that threatened to cause him serious pain between his legs. Slowly he stood, and with a broad grin, he slipped off his gown.

"Stockings first. Here," she said. She held out a pair of white silk stockings which David took from her.

"Where have you obtained all of these things, Mary?" David asked as he sat on the edge of the bed.

"Lady Hamilton said I could have any of her old things. She has trunk after trunk of clothes she never wears, and as the two of you are of a similar size, she said I could use whatever I could find."

Taking care not to snag the material, David pulled on each stocking, fastening the tops around his thighs with a ribbon. It was only then that he allowed himself to luxuriate in the feeling of the silk against his skin, skin that was devoid of hair for the first time in his adult life.

"This next," said Mary.

She held out a simple cotton chemise that had obviously been well worn and washed during its lifetime. David stood as Mary bunched up the material so that she could drop it over his up-stretched arms, being careful not to disturb his hair. Then she settled it down over his body, the short sleeves covering his upper arms, the hem falling to just above the ground so that his toes peeped out from under the material.

"Stays next," said Mary. "Now this I am particularly proud of, Miss Isobel, for I was up most of the night making the modifications required. See, I have sewn bags of rice into the cups that would normally contain a lady's breasts. I have also added some padding at the sides and the rear to give you a little more shape. Now hold up your arms."

David did as he was instructed, and Mary slipped the stays around his body. As he stood still, the abigail began to thread the laces through the eyes at the back, and David soon felt the garment begin to pull against his body. By the time Mary had finished, the stays were tight around his middle, but not unbearably so. Desperate to see, David looked down as best he could, and his mind rejoiced, for he could see the gentle swell of his small *breasts,* could feel how the stays nipped him in at the waist, could feel how his hips and bottom flared outwards in a most becoming way.

"Perfect," giggled Mary. "You have more curves that I do!" she declared.

Next, she handed David a petticoat. This was a garment that tied around the waist and was made of starched cotton. It was soon fastened, and David then felt himself looking hungrily towards the bed, his eyes resting upon a very pretty blue day dress that rested there.

"I hope it fits," said Mary. She picked up the dress from the bed and carefully began to undo the buttons.

Once more, David raised his arms to allow Mary to fit the dress. She carefully lifted it over his head, and with mounting excitement, David felt the material slither down his body, the long sleeves encasing his arms. It was a simple dress in the empire style, made of a pretty blue material with some lovely lace detailing. What was more, it seemed to fit perfectly. As Mary fastened the buttons at the back and tied a contrasting ribbon around his chest, it was all David could do to stop himself from jiggling up and down in excitement.

"One last thing, Miss Isobel. You need shoes. I am hoping that you are of a similar size to the countess, for if not, we may have to have some bought especially for you."

David watched on as Mary knelt before him, lifting the hem of his dress so that she could reach his foot. The shoe she held in her hand slipped on easily, and if anything, was slightly too big for him, although Mary seemed satisfied as she stood up once more.

"Now may I see? Please, Mary," David whispered.

"Just one moment more, Miss Isobel," Mary replied.

She stood before him, her fingers mischievously playing at the curls around his face deliberately prolonging his agony. But then she grinned as she took him by the hand to lead him before the mirror.

For David, the tension he felt was excruciating. His whole body was trembling with anticipation, his heart pounding so violently beneath his stays that he thought it was literally going to burst. Then Mary pulled away the sheet and his heart did just that.

Open mouthed, David stood and stared, not daring to believe that the reflection was truly him. Part of him had expected to see the same image he had seen every day when alone in his bedroom, a masculine facsimile of the person he longed to be. How wrong he had been! Instead, a young woman stood in his place, a beautiful young woman at that. Her glorious red hair was perfectly styled and was held with a blue ribbon that matched the dress she was wearing. Tendrils of hair framed her cheeks in a delightful way whilst, the chignon gave her quite a sophisticated appearance. The young woman's perfect oval face was stunning to look at, too — big, innocent green eyes, framed with kohl and golden powder; high aristocratic cheekbones highlighted with the merest hint of blush; plump lips with the most perfect little cupids bow that David had ever seen. The woman's body was astonishing, too, slim, yet curvaceous in all the right places. The ribbon around her chest served only to enhance the soft swelling of her small faux breasts, whilst the soft material of her dress draped itself perfectly over feminine hips and bottom.

David could not help himself. Without warning, he burst

into tears. Turning, he fled into the arms of Mary, his whole body wracked with emotion.

"I take it you approve," said Mary.

Like a mother comforting her child, Mary had held David against her breasts, allowing him to cry. As the tears subsided, she untangled David's arm from her own, her hand reaching for a small square of muslin with which she could mop away the tears.

"There, no damage done to your make up, Miss Isobel. Now take a proper look."

Once more David turned to the mirror and stared at his reflection in complete awe, his whole body trembling with emotion. For the past twenty years he had grown used to staring at the face of a young man in the mirror. But now, that young man was gone, with not even the merest hint of who he used to be left behind. In his place was the young woman that David had always known lurked beneath the facade, a young woman whose heart was fit to burst with happiness.

"So, what do you think?" asked Mary, almost timidly. "Do you like your appearance?"

David turned and stared at her, unable to hold back his tears. Disbelievingly, he turned back to the mirror yet again, now swivelling this way and that to admire his reflection. Mary even came up behind him, holding a hand mirror so that he could even see his own reflection from behind.

"What I think, Mary," he said softly, "is that *like* is far too weak a word to describe how I am feeling right now. Had I not seen it for myself, I would never have believed it possible for me to look so perfectly feminine. This is incredible. You . . .you are a miracle worker."

"No, I am not. All I have done is put to good use all the features God gave you."

"I do have one problem with how I look, however," said David shyly. As he spoke, he almost smiled when he saw the look of consternation on Mary's face.

"And what might that be, Miss Isobel?"

"I don't think I will ever want to change back," whispered David.

"And why should you? Surely it is up to you to choose who you want to be?"

"Then I choose to be Isobel. As far as I am concerned David Drummond is no more, and from this moment on I shall be *she* and not *he*, I shall be Isobel and not David . . .well at least until this wonderful dream comes to an end."

Olivia arrived outside the house at precisely mid-day. As the hackney came to a halt, she remained seated until, a few moments later, her driver was standing by the door, respectfully holding out his hand to help her down onto the pavement. She did not even have to wait at the door of the house, for the moment her feet touched the pavement, Mary was opening the front door to allow her immediate entrance to the house.

"So how has it gone?" she asked softly as Mary shut the door behind her.

"Well, I think, but I will let you be the judge of that, my lady."

"So, where is he?" asked the countess.

"*Miss Isobel* is in the parlour."

"Isobel. Oh, I like that. Miss Isobel Munroe. It has a nice ring to it, don't you think?" she said as she bustled past Mary.

Without even pausing to remove the spencer she wore, Olivia entered the room and gasped with surprise as she did so. There, her back straight, her hands folded neatly into her lap, was a very pretty young woman sitting nervously on the edge of a chair. Her glorious red hair had been artfully styled into a very feminine chignon that was perfect for someone of her age, and the makeup she wore served only to enhance her beauty. The girl was attired in an appealing blue day dress that Olivia recognised as one of her own, and judging by the curves she had, was all woman beneath. With obvious nervousness, the girl stood and performed a clumsy curtsey, her cheeks blushing furiously as she did so.

"Oh my goodness," gushed Olivia. "Da... er... Isobel, you look simply perfect!"

Olivia marched over to him, grasping David by the hands as he stood before her. Holding him at arm's length, she let her gaze roam up and down, taking in every last detail.

"Thank you, Lady Hamilton," David replied.

Olivia was thrilled, for even his voice was soft and feminine, his Scottish lilt adding to the effect.

"You are incredible, Isobel," gushed Olivia once more. "Here, let me look at you properly. Spin round for me if you would, my dear."

Olivia watched as the young woman did as she had been asked, turning slowly before her, and Olivia's grin grew wider and wider as she did so. Her hair was perfect, and even the dress she wore seemed to fit quite satisfactorily. In fact, it fit her well enough that it displayed feminine curves that no boy could possibly own. Quizzically, she turned back to Mary, one eyebrow cocked questioningly.

"I have sewn some padding into her stays, my lady, to get a little more shape, even though she has a naturally slim waist," Mary explained.

"Oh Mary!" exclaimed Lady Olivia, "You have surpassed yourself...both of you have far exceeded my wildest expectations. Isobel, you look simply perfect. If I did not know better, I would never have guessed you are a boy. Come, my dear, sit. Mary, would you organise some tea for us please? I would guess that Isobel may be in need of it."

Mary curtsied and then disappeared, closing the parlour door behind her, whilst Olivia sat on a chair, waiting for

David to join her. With a critical eye, she watched as he walked across the room to a second chair, noting that his gait was feminine too, the dress he was wearing making him take much smaller steps than he was probably used to. Yes, it would take a little more practice, but his walk could soon be that of a proper young lady. David sat, his back straight, his hands once more in his lap as he looked nervously down to the floor.

"Isobel, how do you feel?" Olivia asked softly. Inwardly she laughed at her use of a feminine name, noting how easy it was for her to think of the person before her as having a female gender.

"There are no words powerful enough to describe how I feel, Lady Hamilton. My rational mind knows that this is some fantasy, a fantasy that has been indulged by you and by Mary. I know it will soon be over, too, and that I will have to go back to being David. But I cannot help but believe that this is who I should be, that this is who God meant me to be. If anything, for the first time in my life I am at peace. Now I am Isobel, even if it is for but a few hours. For that, I thank you from the bottom of my heart for giving me this opportunity. It is a memory I will cherish for the rest of my life."

Olivia sat and stared at him, her own heart pounding with excitement. David's transformation had exceeded her wildest expectations, and there was little doubt in her mind that with a deal of hard work, he would be perfect for what she had in mind. But in saying that, she knew she would have to tread lightly, would have to take Isobel, not David, by the hand and gently guide her into the world of women if she was to achieve her goal.

"If you could," she asked, "would you stay this way? Would you stay as Isobel?"

David's reply was immediate and emphatic.

"Yes, of course I would. You know that. This is who I am

meant to be. But we both know that would be impossible, that the suggestion is simply ridiculous. No one in their right mind would ever accept me as Isobel. I would never be able to leave the house, let alone function in normal society."

"Now that I don't believe," replied Olivia firmly. "You make a beautiful and very convincing young woman, doesn't she, Mary?"

They both turned to see Mary entering the room once more, carrying a polished mahogany tray with teapot, jugs, and teacups. She placed the tray down onto a small tea table and then smiled broadly.

"Yes indeed, my lady," Mary said. "'Tis my opinion that, with a little more work, Miss Isobel could go anywhere looking as she does now and fool anyone into thinking she is a real woman."

"A little more work?" asked Olivia. "What do you mean by that?"

"Well," said Mary, "whilst her physical appearance is quite acceptable, we will need to work on her walk and her mannerisms to make them more ladylike. You know, how she holds herself like a lady, how she moves like a lady. This and much more will have to become second nature if she is to avoid suspicion. Her speaking voice is already quite good but could be even better with a little more practice. I particularly like her Scottish accent, which adds something of a feminine touch already. I would like her to grow her nails, so that I can shape them properly. That will give her hands a bit more of a feminine appearance. Oh, and if she is to go out into society, she will have to learn the etiquette of a lady, will have to learn to dance as a lady too."

"Now, Mary," warned Olivia, "let us not get ahead of ourselves, shall we? What do you think, Isobel? Are you up for a challenge?"

Isobel startled, her mouth dropping open wide. "What I

think is that you must be out of your mind, Lady Hamilton," she spluttered. "Whilst this has been a wonderful experience, it is only a fantasy. I could never be Isobel in real life. That suggestion is totally ridiculous. Why, I could never even venture out of that door."

"Well, I think differently, Isobel. In fact, I can prove it to you, if I must."

"What, what do you mean, Lady Hamilton?"

"Mary, did you bring that spencer I gave you?" she asked.

"Yes, my lady," Mary replied. "Would you like me to fetch it for you?"

"Please."

As Mary left the room, the tea now forgotten, Olivia turned back to Isobel, who was now looking decidedly green. Encouragingly, she smiled.

"Tell me Isobel," she continued. "How would you like to go for a walk? There is a rather nice park a short stroll from here."

"What!" shrieked David. "Dressed like this? Not bloody likely."

"Yes, bloody likely," said Olivia with a grin. "Would you not like to find out how it feels, how it feels to walk out as the lady you appear to be?"

"Yes ... but ..."

It was at that moment that Mary dashed back into the room, a simple navy-blue velvet spencer over her arm. Without even waiting to be asked to do so, she marched over to Isobel and began to help her into the jacket, fastening the buttons around her faux breasts as she did so.

"Perfect," said Olivia as she too stood.

"Now wait a minute," said David. "I can't go out dressed like this."

Olivia's reply was to lead him over to mirror which hung upon the wall of the parlour, placing him before it so he could clearly see his own reflection.

"Tell me, Isobel, what do you see? Be honest."

Olivia watched as David stared at himself, at first lost for words. But she could also see him looking, really looking, as he decided how to reply.

"When I first saw myself upstairs, Lady Hamilton, my initial reaction was to burst into tears of happiness. Nothing has changed, for I now see the woman I have always longed to be."

"And do you see any trace of the man you once were?" asked Olivia.

She watched as his focus once more flickered over his reflection, and Olivia realised he was now looking for any imperfections. Not that he was going to find any. His hair was perfectly styled for a lady of his age and bore no resemblance to any style a man might choose. The cosmetics he wore masked all traces of masculinity, whilst the dress and spencer served to emphasise the feminine body shape that had been created for him.

"N-no . . ." he stammered.

"Then come," said Olivia. She gently took him by the hand.

At first, Olivia thought he was not going to move. However, with a light guiding pressure upon his arm, David took a step towards to door of the parlour. As they reached the entrance to the house, Olivia found herself having to apply even more pressure as David paused, only to rejoice in her little victory as he took his first step into the big wide world.

Together they walked down the street. As the elder of the two, Olivia had tucked David's arm into hers and she could feel just how violently he was shaking. Yet despite this, he kept pace with her, walking by her side with a stride that was decidedly feminine. Within moments they came to the corner of the street, and as they turned into another road, Olivia saw an elderly gentleman walking towards them, cane in his hand

and his top hat at a jaunty angle.

"Oh, God," whispered David.

"Don't worry sweetheart, it will be fine," whispered Olivia. Hoping that David would not bolt, she took an even firmer hold of his arm, just in case.

As the man came nearer, Isobel could almost smell David's fear. His shoulders had slumped, and from the corner of her eye, Olivia could see how he held his head so low that the man would be unable to see her face.

But then, to Olivia's complete surprise, she felt him straighten his back and lift his head just at the moment when the old gentleman walked by. Graciously, the man tipped his hat to them and smiled. It was the benevolent smile of a grandfather, and to Olivia's intense relief, it showed absolutely no indication that he had seen anything amiss with her companion.

"There, what did I tell you?" said Olivia as the man continued on his way.

David hissed and once more began to breathe. "Oh dear God," he panted, relief washing over his face.

Together they continued their walk, soon entering the pretty little park that Olivia had mentioned. It was a beautiful early summer's day. Overhead, white fluffy clouds paraded the sky above a simple path that wound its way through lawns and trees. A gentle breeze rustled across the borders of flowers, the riot of colour a testament to the gardeners attending them.

Olivia could not help but rejoice for David. Somehow, each time they passed someone else taking the air, he found the courage to look up, found the courage to smile, even if he failed to meet anyone in the eye. What was even more remarkable was that not a single person showed the slightest inclination that they had seen anything out of the ordinary. They walked slowly and in silence, until something told Olivia that

David had reached his limits. Without asking, she turned and minutes later, much to the relief upon David's face, they were securely behind the door of the house.

A fresh pot of tea was waiting for them in the parlour, as was Mary who had a decidedly worried expression upon her face.

"Well, Miss Isobel?" demanded Mary. "How did it go?"

David stared at her, a huge grin appearing upon his face. "I'll be damned! That was un . . . be . . . lievable!"

"Did I not tell you so?" said Olivia.

"Never in my wildest dreams did I ever think I would be able to do that," said David. Once more he moved in front of the mirror, and Olivia grinned when she saw the ruddiness of his cheeks and the shine upon his beautiful green eyes. But then his eyes dropped as if a sudden dreadful thought had crossed his mind.

"Oh, bugger!" he hissed.

For some reason, David deflated, his knees sagging so that he sat heavily upon a chair. His head went down, the curls that Mary had created hanging loose around his cheeks and Olivia could see the tears that were welling up in his eyes. Striding across the room, she sat next to him, taking his hand into her own.

"What is it, Isobel? Whatever is the matter?"

"Today has been the most incredible of my life, Lady Hamilton. What with the transformation Mary has performed upon me and then the walk you had me take . . . well, I have done things today that I never thought possible, things I have always dreamed of doing. But I will soon have to go back to being David, will I not?"

"And do you want to go back to being David?"

"No," he replied simply.

"Then do not. Remain as Isobel."

"As if I could!" David said reluctantly. "Going out for a

walk is one thing, but . . ." he stammered.

Olivia rejoiced. David had achieved far more than she could possibly have expected for the first day of his transformation, and with those very words he had given her the opportunity she had thought might not occur for many days to come.

"You doubt that you could be in the company of others, do you not?" she asked, so very gently.

"Yes," David said. This time his voice was morose and miserable, almost as if he was on the verge of crying.

"What if," said Olivia slowly, "I could once more prove you wrong?"

"What? How?"

Olivia thought of her plans, wondering if she dared accelerate the program she had mapped out for David. What she had seen of him so far exceeded all expectations, but if he were to find the confidence to enter society as a lady, Olivia was going to need the help of two very special friends.

"Well," she said, "in two days' time, I am invited to tea by the Duchess of Camberly, and I think it would be a wonderful opportunity for me to introduce you to her. In fact, I have already thought of a plausible story to explain your presence in London."

"What!" shrieked David.

"You are to be the daughter of Captain and Mrs Kirk Munroe, both deceased. Elizabeth Munroe will be my distant cousin from Scotland. Captain Munroe was owner and master of a tea clipper which foundered with all hands when Isobel was but eight years of age. Elizabeth will have recently departed this world, leaving you, Miss Isobel Munroe, as my ward and the sole beneficiary of your late father's estates, worth of course some twenty thousand pounds."

"You are mad, Lady Hamilton. Why on earth would you do this?"

"It is Aunt Olivia now, Isobel, so get used to it," she replied firmly. "And to answer your question, I do this because I want to. I do this because you want me to. I do this because in her letter, your mother asked me to help you in whatever way I see fit, and as I owe her a great debt, I am only too happy to oblige."

Chapter Seven

"God, Mary, I am going to be sick," David moaned. "I must be insane!"

"Maybe you are!" Mary laughed. Reaching up, she pulled a bonnet over David's hair, fastening it beneath his chin with the attached ribbon for the final touch to his outfit. "However, you are still going."

Somehow, and against all reason, Lady Olivia had persuaded David to accompany her to the Duchess of Camberly's home. As a consequence, he and Mary had again been secreted in the bedroom all morning so that Mary could work her magic. David's hair had been pinned up in a pretty daytime style, whilst his makeup was light and subdued. Mary had dressed him in a simple pale green day dress over which she had put a darker green velvet spencer with long sleeves. His reticule and bonnet, of course, matched the spencer and completed the outfit perfectly.

"There," she said smugly, "you'll do."

Once more David moved in front of the large mirror in his bedroom, this time to look at himself with a critical eye. Even to him, there was no denying how pretty and feminine he looked, even if his complexion was deathly white from the nerves that were causing his whole body to tremble.

"Oh God, Mary," he moaned once more. "Remind me. Just how did I get myself into all of this?"

Again, Mary laughed. "I don't think you had much choice in the matter, Miss Isobel. The countess can be quite forceful when the mood takes her. But I don't think you have anything

The Making of a Lady

to worry about. The duchess is one of the nicest people you could possibly hope to meet, and even if she suspects anything, she will keep your secret. Of that I am certain. All you need to do is remember your lessons and you will be fine."

The past two days had been a mixture of delight and dread for David. He had lived and breathed Isobel, albeit in the privacy of his own little home, with Mary insisting that he be in feminine guise at all times. The time had been consumed with preparation: practicing his speaking voice until it was soft and very feminine; practicing his walk so he no longer looked as if he had just got off a horse; practicing his mannerisms and his curtsey, too. Mary had even begun to teach him how to dance as a young woman. Despite the limited time, great strides had been made, so much so that Mary had declared herself more that satisfied with Isobel's progress.

The countess had visited each day to monitor Isobel's improvements. For an hour or so, she and Isobel would sit together and talk, and Olivia was nothing but supportive and encouraging, each day offering suggestions and criticisms designed to help her improve. And of course, the subject of the visit to the Duchess of Camberly's home was never far from her lips.

And that was where the fear had come into play.

As the day to visit the duchess's home arrived, David found himself consumed with doubt, consumed with apprehension and fear. The tension he had been feeling had built throughout the entire morning and now, with but minutes to go before the countess was due to arrive, something told him that he was close to breaking point.

"Mary, I don't think I can go through with this," he whispered as he turned from the mirror.

It was then that sudden panic exploded through David's like a volcano erupting, his whole body now trembling as if it wanted to do nothing but run away. Terror gripped him, and his chest began to heave, his pretty breasts moving frantically up and down as he gulped for air. Without thought, his fingers frantically scrabbled at the ribbons which secured the bonnet, at the buttons which secured the Spencer around his breasts. His mind now consumed with dread, he wanted nothing more than to rip off the dress he was wearing, to pull out the pins that secured his hair, to run far, far away.

"I . . . I cannot . . . cannot do this," he shrieked.

In his panic, David nearly missed the arms that wrapped around him, arms that were surprisingly strong. At first, he struggled, trying to break away. But Mary held firm, hugged him to her chest, and all fight suddenly left him as he sagged into her body. And then the tears began to pour down his face as sobs wracked his body. And Mary held him as if her were a child, her voice soft and soothing as her hand gently rubbed his back.

"I . . .I . . .cannot do this. I can't Mary," he sobbed.

"So, do you not want to be Isobel, after all?" asked Mary.

"Y . . .yes . . .I . . .I . . .do. But I can't, I can't go out dressed like this."

"Why ever not, Miss Isobel? You are perfectly lovely, and not a soul would ever guess that beneath the dress is, well, you know. And going to the Duchess of Camberly's home is the perfect way of testing yourself, for if you can fool her, you will be able to fool anyone. I believe you can do it, and so does the countess. Of that I am certain, for she would not risk taking you out if she did not think you ready."

"Oh God . . .I . . .I . . . I . . .don't . . .know . . .know . . .what to do."

"Can I make a suggestion, Miss Isobel?" said Mary.

"What?"

"You need to stop thinking of yourself as David. Don't deny that you still are doing so. You yourself have said that in your heart you are a woman, so start believing it. Put David

The Making of a Lady

behind you and become Isobel in every respect, for I already have," she declared.

"I am not sure what you mean."

"What I mean is that, from now on, in your mind, there is to be no more *David*. Instead, there is to be only Isobel. Forget the man and become the *lady* you are, and do so with confidence and poise."

"But are you sure I can do that, without fear of discovery? For I am not!"

"Yes, I am certain," replied Mary, "and so is Lady Hamilton."

"Oh bugger," he whispered.

"So how is he faring?" asked Lady Olivia as she entered the hallway of the house, having just alighted from her carriage.

"*She*," said Mary quite forcefully, "is close to breaking point. Why, ten minutes ago, Miss Isobel had an attack of the vapours, a panic attack. She is deathly afraid of what is to come, my lady."

"As is to be expected. But she must start somewhere if my endeavours are to come to fruition."

"Indeed, my lady. Perhaps if you spoke to her, reassured her. She is waiting for you in the parlour."

"Thank you, Mary. I truly appreciate what you have done here."

Quietly, Olivia let herself into the parlour. As was to be expected, she found Isobel standing once more in front of the looking glass, her vacant eyes showing her to be lost in thought. However, she must have heard the door, for Olivia watched as the young woman turned and tried to force a smile upon her face.

"Now let me have a look at you."

She took a few steps towards Isobel and lifted a hand to

gently stroke an errant curl back into place beneath the bonnet. Then she smiled encouragingly.

"Why, Isobel! You look perfectly lovely, my dear. Truly you do. In fact, I would go as far as saying that your physical appearance would stack you favourably against many of the debutants this season."

"Do you think so? Do you truly think so, Lady Hamilton? Please . . . please be honest with me."

"Please, Isobel, call me Aunt Olivia. And I am being honest with you. Each time we meet, I find myself astonished at how pretty and feminine you appear. It is almost as if you were, in all reality, born a girl."

"But both you and I know that there is so much more to being a woman than simple physical appearance, Lady Ham . . .er . . .Aunt Olivia."

"Indeed. But that will come with time if you want it to. For now, your speaking voice is much improved, as is the way you hold yourself and the way you walk."

"So you think me ready for my first public outing, Aunt?"

"Yes, I do," said Olivia emphatically. "But the decision has to be yours, Isobel. Please understand that I will never force you into doing something that you do not wish to do. If you need more time, then you need more time."

"But . . . but . . ." Isobel stuttered.

Olivia sighed. "Look, darling, should you desire to return to being David, I will do everything in my power to facilitate that. As it happens, I have a close friend who has a thriving solicitor's practice, and he is looking for an assistant, a paid position that would be perfect for David. But I do not believe for one moment that this is what you want."

"No, Aunt Olivia, it is not. What I want, with all my heart, is to be Isobel . . . to be the woman I appear . . . that I think I appear to . . . Oh you know," she mumbled. "But I am afraid; I am so dreadfully afraid of the scandal, should anyone find out who I really am."

For a moment Olivia paused, her mind working furiously as she tried to decide how much she was going to tell her young protégé about the future plans that she had. Yes, it was a dangerous game she played, and one which could ruin many reputations. It was also a game that she knew, from personal experience, could be won. However, so much depended upon Isobel's ability to pass as a woman in all respects, and pass within the highest echelons of society. What she needed was confidence in her ability to do so, and the confidence could only come with the reassurance of others.

And no one knew that better than the Duchess of Camberly.

"What say you to this? Come with me to tea at the home of the duchess. Let her meet you and see if your appearance and demeanour is good enough to pass muster."

"But what if she sees me for who I am?" murmured Isobel.

"Trust me when I say that I know the duchess well enough to believe that she would never say anything about the incident, should that happen. But I would wager a great deal of money that it will not. At least if you succeed, you will know that you could be Isobel, should you so choose to be."

"But what will happen to me if I do so choose?"

Again, Olivia paused, but this time for effect. At least this was a question she was more than ready to answer, having expected Isobel to ask it.

"In the letter your mother sent me, she also mentioned your trust fund."

"Yes, that is so. But I cannot access the money until I am one and twenty, a few months hence. Fortunately, it is protected from my father, as the monies came from my mother's side of the family."

"Well, what think you to this," said Olivia. "If all goes well and you choose to remain Isobel, I will take financial responsibility for you until that time. You can live with me as my companion, and I will give you a commensurate salary . . . say, ten guineas a month. Think of that as pin money. If, however, you choose to be Viscount Drummond instead of Isobel, I will loan you sufficient funds for you to live comfortably until your one and twentieth birthday, monies which you can repay from your trust. Then, I daresay if you invest the money wisely, you will have more than enough blunt to see out your life. I can help you with that, too."

"You would do that!" gasped Isobel. "But why are you doing this for me? Surely you risk your own reputation by being associated with someone like me?"

"Yes, perhaps. But I think it worth the risk. And as for why, I have my reasons, reasons which are my own for the time being, but reasons which are entirely honourable. Now what is it going to be? Are you coming with me or not?" she asked gently.

Olivia watched as Isobel turned away from her, her shoulders hunched, her face hidden by the bonnet she wore, and for a moment she thought that it would be David who prevailed and not Isobel. But then she saw the lovely young woman's back straighten with sudden resolve, just as it had when they had gone for a walk. Isobel turned defiantly, her shoulders back, a determined look upon on her face.

"You say I have a choice . . . whether to be David or to be Isobel. Well, I don't think I do! I don't think I have any choice at all but to be honest to myself and to be the woman I know is buried deep inside of me. So yes, I will come with you, but only if you promise that if anything untoward happens, you will get me out of there as quickly as possible."

"You have my word that the carriage will wait by the door, Isobel . . . even if you have no need of it."

The carriage ride through London was conducted in virtual silence. Olivia had placed herself facing the driver with

Isobel sat opposite her, her hands clutched nervously in her lap. Even though she was obviously petrified, Olivia observed with pleasure that Isobel's posture was entirely correct for someone of her apparent gender. The dress she wore was simple yet elegant and clung perfectly to the curves that had been created for her. Her face, whilst tinged with green, was entirely feminine, her golden red curls framing the delicate features that God had granted her, irrespective of her birth gender.

It took twenty minutes for the coach to thread its way through the busy streets of London, finally arriving at the ducal residence. It was an imposing building, much larger that her own town house, yet Olivia found its inviting façade somewhat comforting, especially when she saw the duchess herself appear at the door. The door to the carriage opened and before she could say flibbertigibbet, Olivia found herself in the arms of one of the few people that she truly loved.

"Is all well?" asked the duchess softly as she kissed Olivia on the cheek.

Nervously Olivia looked back into the depths of the carriage. "That, I am afraid, is yet to be seen," she whispered in return.

To Olivia's utter amazement, Isobel, holding the hand of the coachman, carefully stepped down from the hackney, her free hand holding her skirts up a fraction so that she did not trip over the hem. By some means, she had managed to steel herself, and her face was now set with a grim expression that made her lips look quite thin. Her whole body was tremulous, too, the hands that she held before her strangling the reticule she carried as she looked nervously to the floor.

Out of instinct, Olivia reacted in the only way she knew how.

"Isobel, may I present her Grace the Duchess of Camberly, Charlotte Beaufort. Your Grace, may I present my ward, Miss

Isobel Munroe."

Isobel did not speak, but much to Olivia's delight, rather than turning to run, she performed a perfect curtsey.

"Charming, simply charming." Charlotte was smiling, and Olivia watched as the duchess placed a hand under Isobel's chin, lifting it so she had no choice but to look at her. Then, so very gently, Charlotte stroked her face with her fingers. "Welcome, Miss Munroe. Do come inside, both of you. Tea should be waiting in the small drawing room."

The entrance to the house was imposing, to say the least, high ceilings festooned with ornately carved cornices and stucco work which had been designed to impress. A maid was standing there, and Olivia quickly divested herself of her bonnet, indicating that Isobel should do the same. Fortunately, despite her nerves, Isobel had the wit to follow suit, untying the ribbon under her chin before handing her hat to the waiting maid. Imperiously, Charlotte led the way into the house. Soon they were entering a sitting room, and Olivia could hardly suppress a giggle as she saw the look on Isobel's face. After all, the *small drawing room* was in fact quite grand, its feminine furniture and furnishings designed to impress... and perched upon a huge chair placed close to the fire was a very unusual woman.

"Phoebe!" Olivia exclaimed with genuine pleasure.

The beautiful woman was obviously of African descent, yet she was dressed as a lady of quality. Her skin, being the colour of polished mahogany, glowed with vitality, and judging by the size of her belly, it was obvious that she was several months into her confinement. As polite manners dictated, the woman was trying to stand, so Olivia dashed to her side to stop her.

"No, sweetheart, sit," she demanded, as she leant down to kiss the woman on the cheek. "I did not expect to find you here. How long now till your babe is born?"

"I have eight more weeks of this to endure, my lady, and Samson would have me confined to my bed if he had his way." Phoebe grinned as she sank gratefully back onto her chair, the whiteness of her teeth in stark contrast to her skin as she turned her gaze upon Isobel. "Now who is this pretty young lady you have brought with you?"

"This is Miss Isobel Munroe, my ward. Isobel, may I introduce Mistress Phoebe, companion to her Grace, wife to Samson, mother to the rapscallion that is Henry, and soon-to-be mother of her second child."

Her heart was beating so wildly that it was beginning to make Isobel feel faint. But even though she was so close to overwhelming panic, she somehow managed to curtsey, not even knowing if it were appropriate to do so. In return, the exotic woman before her smiled at her broadly. Something quite astonishing then occurred to Isobel. It was a notion that sent her mind a-reeling as she suddenly realised that neither the duchess nor her companion had shown even the slightest indication that they recognised her for what she was. In fact, instead of the horror and disgust that she had anticipated, all she could see was the welcoming faces of two remarkable women.

Isobel sighed deeply with the sudden comprehension of that very fact, a fraction of the tension she felt lifting from her shoulders as a result.

When Olivia sat upon a chaise, Isobel managed to do the same, sitting next to her, demurely placing her hands into her lap as she had been taught to do. At first she sat there hunched, her gaze cast nervously to the floor. That was until she heard Mary's commanding voice within her own memory . . . *back straight, Miss Isobel . . . shoulders back, Miss Isobel . . . hands just so, Miss Isobel.* So she did just that. She forced herself to sit up, to face her fears, and glancing up shyly, she returned the duchess's gaze.

There was no doubt that the duchess was remarkably beautiful. She appeared to be something over thirty years of age and was dressed in a lovely peach-coloured day dress made of a silk that seemed to shimmer with a life of its own. Her lovely auburn tresses had been expertly crafted into a very pretty chignon, a style that left little tendrils of hair framing her face beautifully. Just like Isobel, the duchess wore cosmetics upon her skin. It was remarkable, for she wore it in exactly the same way, too, a subtle application of powder on her face, rouge on her cheeks, kohl on her lashes, and a little ruby stain on her lips, all of which served to emphasise every feminine feature.

Suddenly from behind came a commotion, and Isobel saw a footman holding the door open to allow a young maid to enter the room. Carrying a large ornate silver tray upon which sat an equally elegant silver tea service, she efficiently bustled towards the duchess. Isobel reacted instinctively. In an act of self-preservation, her head went down once more, her face turned so that the girl could not see her clearly. It was embarrassing to do so, Isobel knew that. But she could not help herself from hiding her face as best as she could.

"Thank you, Helen," said the duchess. The maid placed the tray onto a side table then dipped a curtsey.

"Would you like me to pour, Your Grace?" the girl asked.

"No, I think I can manage, but would you ask Stevens to find the duke and inform him that Lady Olivia is here?"

"Yes Ma'am," said the girl. She curtsied and then scurried out of the room.

"Good girl, that," said the duchess as she began to pour the tea. "Now Miss Munroe, pray tell me a little of yourself."

Having no other choice but to do so, Isobel shyly lifted her eyes, only to have her gaze captured in return. To her intense mortification, the duchess was studying her, and to Isobel's complete surprise, her expression was not one of disdain or derision, but of compassion and kindness instead. Once more she breathed deeply, knowing that she had no option but to answer the question.

Isobel had rehearsed and rehearsed, practicing her tone of voice for the very moment she would have to speak. Yet, when she opened her mouth, nothing came out but a squeak. Her cheeks flaring with embarrassment, she politely she coughed and then tried again, speaking a softly as she dared, relying on her rich Scottish accent to see her through.

"My father was owner and captain of a merchant vessel, but he died when I was but eight years of age. However, he left us well provided for, and I lived modestly with my mother, a distant cousin to Lady Hamilton. Regrettably, she passed away last year from influenza, so Aunt Olivia has kindly taken me under her wing, so to speak, as my mother made me her ward."

"And you are twenty years of age?"

"Yes, Your Grace."

As she spoke, the door to the parlour was flung open and a very distinguished-looking gentleman strode into the room, a huge smile upon his face. He was elegantly dressed in a dark blue morning coat and trousers, a richly embroidered waistcoat peeping through the material. Again, Isobel's instinct was to turn her face. However, this time she remained still, gazing in such a manner as to avoid making eye contact with the newcomer without appearing discourteous whilst doing so.

"Olivia," the man gushed. "How good to see you."

Isobel watched Olivia stand, so she did the same, automatically dropping a curtsey as she did so. But to her surprise, instead of following suit, Olivia embraced the man instead, kissing him soundly upon the cheek.

"Hello James," she grinned. "May I present Miss Olivia Munroe. Olivia, this is his Grace, the Duke of Camberly.

Olivia felt her entire being blaze with fear as she watched the man turn his gaze onto her. Again, much to her relief, there was no hint of recognition. Instead, a flare of manly appreciation mixed with the tenderness of a grandfather flashed across the duke's eyes, causing Isobel to blush even more deeply. Then, even more to her surprise, the duke captured her hand and brought it to his lips.

"Welcome Miss Munroe, welcome," he said. The duke grinned against the back of her hand as his lips brushed her glove.

For Isobel, all of this was quite surreal. She had been certain that, by now, she would have been fleeing from the embarrassment of discovery. Instead, everything seemed so perfectly normal. First the duchess and her companion seemed to have accepted her as the young woman she appeared to be, and then no less than the duke himself had done the same. Abruptly, she felt an enormous surge of self-belief flood her mind. After all, this was a duke, for god's sake. This was a duke who had kissed the back of her hand. This was duke who had absolutely no idea that he was flirting with another man, and in that very instant of time, all she could feel was euphoric elation in the sudden realisation that she could possibly make this bizarre plan work! Shyly she smiled, but then she squeaked before somehow finding her voice.

"Thank you, your Grace," she said as she once more curtsied.

"Ah, a lassie from bonnie Scotland. Might have guessed, with all that beautiful red hair, Miss Munroe," the duke said. Gainfully, he had tried to mimic her accent with a terrible facsimile of his own, causing Lady Charlotte to roll her eyes.

"You, my darling, are a terrible old flirt," said the duchess.

"'Tis hard not to be when I am surrounded by such

The Making of a Lady

beautiful ladies. Anyway, just wanted to pop in to say hello. Can't stay, though. Charlotte, my dear, what time are we expected at Lord Granger's tonight?"

The duchess sighed, yet looked on at her husband with tenderness and love in her eyes.

"The carriage has been ordered for eight in the evening, my love. Don't be late!" she added playfully.

"Of course not," said the duke sombrely. "I wouldn't dare."

As the duke left the room once more, Isobel followed the example of the others and once more sat upon the chaise next to Lady Olivia. For the next several minutes and much to Isobel's relief, the conversation was dominated by the duchess and Olivia as they caught up with the comings and goings of their respective families. Grateful not to be included, Isobel used this time to compose herself as she attempted to recall all the lessons of deportment that Mary had taught her.

She sat with her back straight, her hands placed lightly upon her lap. She placed her feet upon the floor with only her ankles crossed, even though she thought that to be somewhat silly, as no one could see her feet due to the length of the dress she wore. She sipped delicately from her teacup, remembering to hold it just so, thankful for the warmth of the liquid as it slipped down her throat but wishing it was brandy instead. Then, as she listened politely to the conversation as it flowed around her, she allowed her gaze to wander, where it finally settled longingly upon a magnificent pianoforte.

With good reason, her mind instantly flashed back to David's childhood. His mother had owned a similar instrument and played it beautifully. As a young boy, David had loved nothing more than to sit and listen, sometimes turning the pages of the music for her as her hands flew across the keys. As he grew older, David quickly became enthralled and desperate to learn how to play. However, his father had had absolutely no intentions of letting him do so. When David had asked his father for permission to engage a music master, the Earl had simply sneered at him and had declared that no son of his would ever be allowed to be such a milksop.

His mother, on the other hand, thought differently. She had taken it on herself to teach her son, in private of course, choosing to time her lessons for when the Earl was away on estate business. Every opportunity was taken, and for David, the time he spent with his mother quickly became the most important part of his life. He studied hard, practicing whenever he could, and to his mother's delight, he quickly proved himself to be exceptionally gifted. Regrettably, when David had been seventeen years of age, his father had come home unexpectedly and had caught him practicing. David had never seen the man so angry. In retribution for going against his word, the Earl had ordered servants to carry the instrument outside, where several of them took ugly axes to the pianoforte, quickly reducing it to splinters of wood. Only then had the Earl beaten David so violently that he had broken two of his ribs.

"I see you admiring the pianoforte, Miss Munroe. Do you play?" asked the duchess.

Isobel started, Charlotte's voice suddenly dragging her out of her own mind. For a moment, she returned the duchess's gaze, not quite knowing how to respond. But then she nodded.

"Yes, but it has been many months since I have had the chance to practice, your Grace."

"Will you play for us now?"

"No . . . no . . . I couldn't," mumbled Isobel, her cheeks once more flaring with embarrassment.

"Oh, but I insist, Miss Munroe. Play for us," the duchess demanded.

With panic in her eyes, Isobel looked at Olivia, her eyes

beseeching her to give her a way out. But all she saw was her mentor nodding with encouragement. Isobel gulped, but what choice did she have? As gracefully as could be managed, she stood and walked over to the piano, her whole body feeling a sudden shudder of excitement as her long, now elegant fingers stroked the polished mahogany. She had thought to be nervous. But instead, from the moment she sat before the keys, a peace she had not felt in months settled over her. It calmed her and stilled her over-active mind, as it had always done for David as a young man. Just for a few seconds, Isobel closed her eyes and allowed her hands to centre, quickly rehearsing in her mind the piece she intended to perform.

Then she began to play Beethoven's piano sonata, no 13, Opus 27.

The piece she had chosen was a favourite and was a composition she would know by heart until the day she died. It was not a technically difficult piece, but all the more soulful for it, and soon the emotional notes of the *Moonlight Sonata* were drifting through the room. It did not matter if occasionally she played a wrong note, for she knew that perfection would come with practice. What mattered was that she was playing again, putting her heart and soul into the music. What mattered was that she had been transported back to a time when, as a growing lad, she had been the happiest of all.

"Oh my," whispered the duchess as the strains of the final note echoed through the room. "That, my dear, was simply wonderful."

"Oh Isobel. I had no idea you could play so beautifully," added Lady Olivia.

Isobel sat still, now feeling the intense heat in her cheeks once more. But then she looked up and could not help but smile at the praise.

"My mother taught me to play," she replied. Reluctantly, she closed the lid of the pianoforte and stood. "But I am a little out of practice."

"Well, you can come and play for me whenever you like," Charlotte declared. "In fact, I have a wonderful idea. I am hosting a small dinner party and musicale two weeks hence. I would love for you both to come, and then perhaps you might play for us again."

"No . . . no . . . I couldna . . ."

"We would love to," interrupted Olivia as she turned and smiled broadly.

"So, Phoebe, what did you think of Miss Isobel?" Charlotte asked.

Phoebe had been quiet during the afternoon, obviously preferring to observe rather than converse. But now that Olivia and Isobel had departed for home, Charlotte needed to know what her companion thought. When Olivia had visited to apprise her of the situation, Charlotte had not been shocked by the truth of it. How could she be? Instead, Charlotte had listened with compassion and had then resolved to do everything in her considerable power to help the girl. That of course, would involve Phoebe, provided she also agreed to help.

Phoebe laughed and grinned mischievously at her. "She is prettier and far more convincing than you were at her age."

"Yes, I know, dammit," replied Charlotte, a chortle of amusement in her voice.

"So, what do you think Lady Olivia is up to?" asked Phoebe.

"What I know is this. David Drummond has been disowned by his father after being caught in a compromising position whilst dressed as a girl. Seemingly, his mother and my mother are acquainted, which is why David appeared on Olivia's doorstep. All else I know is that Olivia's *ward* has designs to live as I do, as a woman, that is, and that she has decided to help the child to do so."

"And do you intend to help as well, knowing the risks that you take?"

"How could I not?"

"Indeed," said Phoebe. "How could you not, Missy Charlotte?"

"So, will you make your medicine for her?"

"That, I will have to think upon. As you know, it is a very powerful preparation and will cause permanent physical change. I think it would only be right for me to tell her of what my medicine would do to her body before she starts to take it. That means I would have to reveal that I am aware of her secret."

"Yes... quite. But, again, I think it is the right thing to do," murmured Charlotte.

"As do I, my lady, as do I."

"Only, whatever you do, you must not reveal anything else!"

"Of course not, your Grace," Phoebe replied, knowing exactly what her mistress was trying to say.

The moment that Isobel found herself with Olivia in their carriage, she gave out a very unladylike shriek of triumph and then dragged her mentor into a huge hug.

"Oh... my... God!" she exclaimed. As Olivia untangled herself, Isobel sat back onto her seat to face the countess once more, her hands covering her flaming cheeks. "That was unbelievable!"

"You could say that, Isobel. Well done, well done indeed."

Isobel giggled in the most ladylike of fashions. "Did you see the look on the duke's face? He had not a clue that he was kissing the hand of a boy!"

"And why should he? You were perfect in there, darling. And as for that piano playing . . . you never told me you could play like that. It was simply sublime. The duchess was entranced."

That statement hit Isobel like a sledgehammer and took all the air from her sails. Somehow, Olivia had agreed for them to attend dinner with the duke and duchess and had actually volunteered for her to play . . . to sit in front of an audience in the guise of a woman and to play the piano!

"But how could you?" she whispered.

"How could I what?"

"Volunteer for me to play the pianoforte, and in front of an audience no less."

Suddenly the countess looked a little guilty. Then she laughed.

"Truthfully, I had already received the invitation to attend dinner. I was waiting to see how you were received by the duchess before I accepted. I had no idea she would ask you to play."

"Oh God!" moaned Isobel once more. "What am I going to do?"

The countess grinned. "What you are going to do is this. If you are in agreement, Isobel and Mary are to move out of the house in Cricklewood and are to take up residence in my town house with me. And I do mean Isobel, not David. After all, I cannot risk my reputation by having an unrelated young man living in my house. Mary has already told me that she is more than willing to serve as your ladies' maid. Between now and the musicale, both she and I will continue your training in how to be a lady. You can also have access to my music room, where you will find a pianoforte to practice upon along with a selection of sheet music. I don't play myself, but my daughter Amelia plays, so I keep the instrument for her visits."

"I did not know you have children."

"Mm, I have been married twice. My first husband died in a riding accident. My second husband was the Earl of Weybridge and already had a son from a previous marriage. By him I had my daughter, Amelia. My stepson, Henry, is now the Earl of Weybridge, and Amelia is married to the Earl of Manchester, so is a countess in her own right now."

"And have you grandchildren?"

"Not yet, but all being well, soon. Amelia is expecting her first in a few months' time. Anyway, what think you of my plan?"

"What I think is that I must be meant for Bedlam. But I accept . . . I think. However, I must insist on a codicil attached."

"Oh, and what might that be?"

"That I retain the right to say no to attending the duchess's musicale," said Isobel firmly.

Olivia grinned. "Naturally," she said.

The rest of the trip back to the countess's residence passed in quiet conversation. Olivia sat and mused for most of the journey, her fertile mind jumping from one place to another as she laid plans for the person sat opposite her. Under the circumstances, Isobel had performed admirably, considering she had only two days to prepare. Yes, there had been moments where it had been obvious that something was amiss about her. Just the way that she turned her head away each time someone entered the room might suggest that she had some secret she wished to hide. Even so, she had the wherewithal to greet the duke properly, and she had even found the confidence to play the pianoforte. Yet Isobel still had so much to learn, and only a short amount of time in which to do so.

Olivia winced a little with that thought. Unbeknownst to Isobel, Charlotte had suggested that she be the one to sponsor

Isobel for the forthcoming season. After all, they both knew that having a duchess do so would lend much credence to Isobel's story and make her entry to society far less difficult.

To Olivia, it seemed like the perfect solution, even if it meant revealing to Isobel that Charlotte knew of their secret. She just hoped that Isobel would not fly off at the handle when she found out. And then, of course, there was the insignificant matter of introducing her to Lord Fairfax to contend with!

Looking up to the heavens, Olivia offered up a silent prayer for help.

Chapter Eight

"Morning, sleepy head," said Mary.

Isobel moaned and dragged her eyes open to see Mary bustling across the room to pull back the curtains, thus allowing the bright morning sunshine to flood her chambers.

"What time is it?"

"A little after seven in the morning, Miss Isobel. Time to be up and at 'em. You know it takes time for me to make you look beautiful."

Isobel flopped back down onto the pillow. She had slept badly, the night-rail and mob cap she wore making her feel uncomfortable, the thoughts of what the future had in store even more so. And the dreams she had had ... such dreams ...

"Just five more minutes Mary, please," she pleaded as she pulled the pillow over her head.

"Now, none of that. Lady Hamilton will be expecting you for breakfast at nine sharp, so up you get," she said. Grinning childishly, Mary pulled away the covers with a flourish that any Spanish bull fighter would have been proud of, only to have Isobel throw a pillow at her.

Ninety minutes later, Isobel was once more stood before her looking glass. She was dressed in a simple eggshell blue day dress, another of Olivia's hand-me-downs. Whilst the dress was a trifle on the large side for Isobel, the *enhanced* stays that she wore over her linen petticoats provided perfectly adequate feminine curves. Mary had, of course, braided her vibrant red hair and had pinned it up into a very pretty style. Then she had then applied the usual cosmetics to her face, and in Isobel's opinion the result was again quite remarkable.

For Isobel, her reaction at seeing her own image had become quite fascinating. That she would never tire at seeing herself dressed as a convincing young woman was undisputed in her mind. But more importantly, she was becoming more and more comfortable with the person she had turned out to be, the image of David in her mind fading with every passing day. Smiling happily, Isobel tore herself from her mirror and skipped towards the door, only to stop and look at herself in the mirror yet again, just to be certain.

Since the meeting with the Duchess of Camberly, some three days earlier, it had become routine for Isobel and Olivia to breakfast together, so that they could discuss the program for the day. With Olivia she practiced behaving as a lady of the ton, hardly daring to believe how difficult it was to do so. There were so many rules. A well-bred lady was expected to tread a very fine line between being polite and not being over familiar. Heaven forbid if the lady was overly friendly or flirtatious. She was expected to move with grace and poise, every gesture and movement having connotations that gave Isobel a headache when thinking about them. Why, the simple act of pouring a cup of tea had a set of rules that would have confounded any member of parliament.

Strangely, the hardest part for Isobel was to forget all the words and phrases she might have used as a man. Whilst her modulated and feminine voice seemed to come naturally to her, the choice of language did not, and Olivia was constantly chastising her for when the occasional blaspheme or raucous laugh slipped from her lips.

Now, as a new day dawned, Isobel found herself eager for her next lessons, so she joined Olivia, who was already sat at the breakfast table, broadsheet in hand. On the side table was a large silver salver, and when Isobel lifted the lid, the rich aroma of eggs and sausage assaulted her nose. Hungrily she began to pile to food upon a plate.

"Steady there, missy," admonished Olivia. "Not too much. Young ladies, in particular, are expected to maintain their willowy figures, unlike the more mature of us who are allowed to carry a few extra pounds of flesh."

Isobel giggled, for when she looked at the countess, it was quite evident that despite her voluptuous curves, she carried little extra weight.

"I wish I had your curves, Aunt Olivia. How I would like breas . . . well you know what I mean . . . like yours."

"Would you, if you could?" asked Olivia, seizing upon the opportunity.

"In a heartbeat, you know I would."

"You know what would happen if you did?" said Olivia. She sipped at her tea, and to Isobel it appeared that she used her teacup to hide a mischievous smile.

"No, what?"

"Well, a pretty young woman like you with large breasts and a dowry of twenty thousand would be sure to attract the attentions of every undesirable rake in the ton."

"Oh!" said Isobel. Heavily, she sat next to the countess, her cheeks turning red.

"Would you like that, Isobel? You know, to garner the attraction of a man?"

For a long moment, Isobel sat, not quite knowing how to answer that question. From the corner of her eye, she looked at the woman who was looking back at her, her expression far more serious that the conversation had suggested. Isobel decided to be honest and allowed a wry smile to cross her face.

"In her deepest fantasies, Isobel would have it all—a loving and passionate husband, a home of her own to be mistress of, children to love and nurture. But we both know how unrealistic that is. The very most I can hope for is to wait until I come into my inheritance and then to retire to some town or village to live out a simple life as Miss Isobel Munroe. Just being able to do so would be beyond my wildest dreams."

"But what if there was a way? What if there was a man out there who would accept you for who you are, who would allow you to be the woman you are now?"

"Now 'tis you who is being unrealistic, Aunt."

"Mmm, perhaps," said Olivia thoughtfully.

Silence settled over the pair of them as they steadily consumed their breakfast. Then Isobel looked at Olivia as Olivia looked at Isobel, and instantly Isobel recognised that look upon her mentor's face, the look that suggested nothing but trouble.

"So, what think you of Lady Charlotte?" Olivia asked.

"I liked her a great deal. She was not at all what I expected."

"Quite! She is a remarkable and very perceptive woman, and she is without doubt my closest friend."

Suddenly, Isobel looked sharply at her mentor.

"Where is this conversation leading, my lady?" she demanded.

"Well," said Olivia, drawing out the word for emphasis, "I received a note from the duchess this morning. She has requested that she be allowed to let it be known at her dinner party that she will be your sponsor for the forthcoming season."

Isobel dropped her fork in shock, the silver rattling on her almost empty plate.

"She wants to do what?" she shrieked.

"The Duchess of Camberly wants to sponsor Miss Isobel Munroe for the forthcoming season," repeated Olivia.

"What! No! She would not! I could not accept . . . but . . . but . . . no, but what . . . why?" Isobel stammered.

Olivia, whilst wanting to grin, kept her expression sombre and serious. "Charlotte does not have children of her own. She met the duke a few seasons ago, when the duke's daughter, Lady Anne, persuaded her to be her chaperone for her debutante season. I think that now Lady Anne is settled and married, the duchess is looking for another protégé, and has chosen you."

"God no . . . I couldn't. What if she were to find out about me!"

"Then we would face that when it came," said Olivia. Under the table, she crossed her fingers as she told her little white lie, not yet wanting to reveal that Charlotte already knew. That tiny morsel of information would come later in the day. "OH, don't look so worried, Isobel. I explained that you will soon be a *woman* of independent means and that you were in no particular hurry to marry. The duchess is not suggesting that she sponsor you as a debutante and squire you to every ball and house party for the entire season. What she suggests is that you and I accompany her to an occasional and very select number of functions so that you can be introduced to society in a much more subtle manner."

"Like the musicale?"

"Yes, quite. Just think, Isobel! Even you must agree that having a duchess's approbation will lend much more credibility to your presence as a woman. Ultimately the decision, however, is yours, as it has always been."

Stunned, Isobel sat in silence. Whilst her mouth no longer seemed to function, her mind worked furiously. It truly was a magnificent opportunity, and had she been a woman in all respects, she would not have hesitated to accept. But how could she? After all, she was only a man in a gown, and surely this game of fantasy that she was playing would soon come to an end, bringing scandal and shame to all associated with her. But on the other hand, had she not fooled the duchess into thinking that she was indeed a real woman? For sure, the duchess would not have made such an offer if she had known differently, no matter how close she and the countess were.

Suddenly Isobel wanted to scream.

But it was at that very moment that a knock was heard on the breakfast room door and Mary let herself in, performing a little curtsey as she did so.

"Yes, Mary?" asked Olivia

"Beggin' your pardon my lady, but the Duchess of Camberly is here. She is with Miss Phoebe and some footmen."

"Very good Mary, thank you."

It was then that Isobel did scream. "I . . . I . . . I might have known . . . you planned this all along, didn't you!"

"I'm sorry, darling. Did I omit to tell you that the duchess also wrote of her intention to pay a quick call this morning? I believe she has a few things she would like to gift you."

"Buggery," hissed Isobel.

"Now darling, that is not very ladylike, now is it? Come on, let's not keep the duchess waiting."

Reluctantly, her mind still seething from the way she had been *played*, Isobel followed the countess into the entrance hall, where Lady Charlotte was stood with Phoebe. Behind them, four very large footmen had carried in two equally large trunks, placing them on the floor next to the staircase. Isobel curtsied almost automatically whilst Olivia went over to her friend and kissed her on the cheek in the most affectionate and familiar of ways.

"Good morning, Miss Munroe," said Lady Charlotte. She turned to Isobel and surprised her with the warmth of her expression. "I thought I might bring you a few of my castoffs.

Hope you don't mind. My husband seems to think I have far too many clothes, and as you and I are of a very similar size and build, I thought some of them might suit you. Do with them what you will, for I do not want them returned."

Stunned, Isobel stood with her mouth open, not quite knowing what to say. So far, she had avoided a trip to the modiste and had subsisted on what the countess could lend her. But many of her clothes were for an older lady and were not something she could wear for an outing. Again, not knowing quite what to do, Isobel curtsied once more. "Thank you, your Grace," she said softly.

Olivia smiled broadly. "Please, come through into the sitting room for a moment. We have a lot to discuss."

It took but a few moments for the four of them to be seated in the parlour, Isobel sitting next to Olivia, Miss Phoebe next to her mistress. It was only then that Isobel noticed the wooden box that Phoebe had carried in, a box that reminded her of the family medicine chest back home.

"Right, to business," said the duchess. She turned her gaze on Isobel, her expression benign and compassionate. "As I hope Olivia has explained to you, Isobel, I would like to be your sponsor during the forthcoming season."

"Yes . . . but . . ." Isobel replied

"No, hear me out, Isobel," said Charlotte tenderly. "Before you say anything more, you need to know that I am aware of who you *truly* are."

Instantly, Isobel was gripped in all consuming panic. Before the duchess could finish speaking, she was on her feet, running to the door, running to the stairs as tears of shame started to flow down her face. The duchess knew! Olivia had broken her promise! The duchess knew, and so probably did the whole of London by now. The duchess fucking knew!

As quickly as she could, Isobel ran into her room, her only thought about how she could escape. In the back of her wardrobe sat the one suit of masculine clothes that she had arrived in London with. She would change into them, never look back. As David, he would run away, perhaps even take passage to the Americas.

Frantically, Isobel rushed to rid herself of any and all of her feminine trappings, tears streaming down her face as she did so. As quickly as she could, with one hand she began to unpin her hair, the other grappling with the buttons of her gown. It was then that the door to her room opened and a stern voice called out.

"Isobel, stop this nonsense," it commanded.

Isobel turned, and to her complete and utter surprise, it was not the countess who stood in the doorway, but the duchess herself. To Isobel's unqualified amazement, she did not look angry or horrified. Instead, she looked worried, almost ashamed, as she stepped tentatively into the room.

"Oh, darling, I am sorry," the duchess whispered as she pulled Isobel into her arms.

Isobel's knees sagged, forcing her to sit upon the bed, her head held low, her loose and wild red hair now hanging over her face, hiding her tears from the world. Her whole body cried, huge uncontrollable sobs of shame and pain consuming her. Still, she felt the bed sag next to her and felt the arms around her that pulled her into the warm feminine body to hold her and comfort her like a mother might do.

"I'm sorry Isobel. I did not know how else to tell you," said the duchess softly. "And before you say anything, it was not Olivia who betrayed your secret—well, not exactly, that is."

"What?" hiccupped Isobel.

"It was Phoebe who saw you for what you are. I, on the other hand, was completely fooled by you, so perfect was your appearance when we first met."

"What! But how?" demanded Isobel.

"Phoebe has a rather unique skill set, principle amongst

which is that she is a very talented healer. Her story is her own to tell, but I would trust her with my very life and far more than any of the quacks who call themselves doctors. I am still vague as to what she noticed, but when she came to me and told me she thought you to be a boy, I challenged Olivia on the matter and forced her to confess all."

"Oh."

"And you must know that it was only *after* I discovered your true identity that I decided that I should be to one to help Miss Isobel Munroe establish her credentials as young woman."

To Isobel's utter amazement, the duchess's voice was so soft, so sincere, that there could be no doubt as to her honesty. Now Isobel looked at the beautiful woman, her eyes wide with astonishment.

"But . . . but why . . . why would you do this?"

Isobel watched as the duchess sighed deeply, her intelligent eyes betraying the fact that she was trying to decide what she was going to reveal.

"My story is long and some of it not in the least bit pleasant. Suffice it to say that many years ago, when I was in Jamaica, a very special person helped me when I was at the lowest point in my life. I vowed to that person that one day I would do the same for someone in need. I have chosen you!"

"But why? Surely you risk your reputation if anyone finds out."

"Pish! Being a duchess means I don't have to worry about such things. But as to why . . . you tell me . . . you tell me why it is that you want to be a woman."

Once more Isobel sniffed. "'Tis hard to put into words, but ever since I can remember, all I have ever dreamed of is being a woman. It is almost as if God made a mistake when I was born, giving me the body of a man instead of that of a woman," said Isobel. "It is all I want. It is all I have ever wanted."

"And it is for that very reason I would like to help you. I believe you, Isobel, I believe every word you say, just as I believe in your God-given right to choose to be so."

"Thank you, your Grace."

"Now, no more of that. I think we know each other enough for you to call me Charlotte, at least in private that is. So, Isobel, will you permit me to help you?"

Isobel lifted her watery eyes to Charlotte and looked at her, really looked. Her beautiful face was soft and compassionate, and yet again, Isobel had the strongest of feelings that she could trust the duchess.

"Yes, Lady Charlotte. And thank you, thank you from the bottom of my heart," she whispered.

Charlotte smiled broadly. "Good, that is settled then. I will call for your maid to help you repair the damage. Then I would like you to come downstairs and join us in the parlour. We have a lot to discuss"

"Yes, your Gr . . . erm . . . Lady Charlotte."

It took Mary some twenty minutes to repair the damage done. Isobel's hair was re-braided and her eyes cleaned so that a little fresh kohl could be applied. Then after Isobel had donned a different day dress, the other having been damaged beyond repair, she had walked slowly back down the stairs to where the other ladies waited for her. In the most surreal of ways, it was almost as if she had never left, had never had the fit of vapours that had caused her to run. The conversation was light, with no one wishing to admit anything untoward had happen.

"Olivia tells me that you have been practicing hard on the pianoforte, Isobel. Do you think you will be ready to perform?" asked Charlotte.

Isobel tried to force a smile onto her face. "Yes, Lady Charlotte, I think so. But I am not certain as to whether I will be able sit before everyone's scrutiny."

"Nonsense, I am certain you will be fine," said Charlotte.

"Her playing is certainly quite beautiful," said Olivia. "I could sit and listen to her for hours."

"And do you have a suitable dress to wear?"

For a moment, Isobel looked up and heat flushed through her cheeks. "I was going to borrow one from Lady Olivia."

"Oh no, that will not do. Come with me," said Charlotte.

Isobel followed Charlotte out into the entrance hallway as the duchess marched over to one of the trunks that had been delivered, pulling open the clasps and throwing open the lid.

Isobel gasped when she saw what it contained. There, all neatly folded, seemed to be dress after dress, all of which appeared to be of superior quality.

Like a gardener, the duchess dug into them, pulling at the top layers until she found the gown she sought.

"I had this one made last season. But it never quite felt right on me, so I have never worn it. Yes, I think this will be perfect for you." The duchess held it up for all to see.

Even with her limited knowledge of women's fashions, Isobel recognised the dress for what it was. The gown she held was made from the finest silk, which had been dyed a soft shade of emerald. Together with short sleeves, a modest neckline, a matching sash for the waist, and full skirts, it was dress that Isobel instinctively knew would look wonderful on her. It was also a dress that she sensed must have cost a fortune to make.

"Oh! Lady Charlotte! It is too much."

"Nonsense. I only hope it fits."

"Not to worry," said Olivia. "Mary is a capable seamstress. I am certain she will be able to make any alterations necessary."

It was then that Miss Phoebe appeared next to her mistress, her pregnancy preceding her as she somewhat waddled out of the drawing room. She was carrying the medicine box by a brass handle and had a serious look upon her face. Strangely, Isobel sensed the deference and respect that both she and Charlotte had for the woman, for both instantly became quiet, the duchess nodding her head in approval.

"If all be well with you, your Grace, 'tis my turn now," she declared. "Miss Isobel, would you be so kind as to accompany me out into the garden, for I wish to speak to you privately."

Nervously, Isobel nodded her consent. After all, there was much she wanted to ask, especially as it was Miss Phoebe who had recognised Isobel as the man she had once been. Silently, she followed.

The garden was small in comparison to many London town houses but was beautifully kept, with flower borders and specimen roses in abundance. It was a favourite place for Isobel, as it was a safe and secluded spot for fresh air during the day. A stone path wound its way through the blossoms and ended at a garden bench that seemed to be bathed in sunshine for most of the afternoon. Phoebe was clearly familiar with the garden, for it was to that bench she led them, gingerly lowering herself down as she arrived.

Isobel spoke first, hardly able to contain herself, every fibre of her being needing to know what had given the game away, what it had been about her that had shown her to be a man and not the woman she purported to be.

"Miss Phoebe. The duchess told me it was you who saw me for who I really am . . . when we first met. Can I ask? What made you think I am a boy and not a girl?"

For Isobel, the thought that someone had so easily seen past her disguise was quite disturbing. After all, she had so much to lose should it become public knowledge that she was a boy dressed as a woman. Yet she wanted this so badly, and desperately needed to know what was required of her to avoid such an occurrence in the future.

"It was not one thing, nor was it your physical appearance, Miss Isobel. It was more to do with the way you walked, the way you held your head and placed your hands. Your lack of confidence on the day we met also spoke volumes. But might I add, I already see huge improvement in all of these areas."

"That is because Mary schools me incessantly and scolds me when I get it wrong."

"Ah yes, Mary . . . she is a good girl. Treat her fairly and kindly and she will offer you her undying loyalty."

"I know. She has already proved herself to be so."

"Now, Miss Isobel, let me tell you a little of myself and of why I wished to speak with you alone. I was born and raised as a slave in Jamaica after my mother was taken by slavers whilst still carrying me. She was a remarkable woman, Miss Isobel. A princess within her tribe, she was trained as a healer from a very early age and was recognised as an adept. In Jamaica, our master appointed her as doctor and midwife to his slave workforce, and when I showed an interest, she started schooling me in the arts when I was but six years old. As a girl, I was fortunate that my master recognised some ability in me. He was so unlike any of the other slave owners. He treated me kindly and even had me taught to read and write, so that when Lady Charlotte came along, I was in the position to become her companion and maid. Anyway, it was my mother who told me of the men in our tribe who are exactly like you."

With utter surprise, Isobel stared at Phoebe, doubting she had understood the woman's final sentence. "What?" she said. "What do you mean?"

"In my tribe in Africa, there are men who, like you, prefer to present themselves in womanly guise. Unlike western society, these men are revered, many of them becoming holy men and spiritual leaders. In order to help feminize their bodies to such an extent that they appeared as tribeswomen, they would enlist the help of the healers. As part of my training, my mother taught me how to prepare the medicine they took to do so."

Slowly Phoebe leant down to pick up the wooden box beside her, placing it upon her lap so that she could open the lid. Inside Isobel could see a number of crystal bottles, each with a sealed stopper and each full with a muddy brown liquid.

"This medicine, Miss Isobel, is extremely powerful and is not to be taken without giving the consequences a great deal of thought."

"What? What does it do?" whispered Isobel in awe.

"It will effect some permanent changes in the body, although to what extent depends mainly on the individual. Some experience rapid change whilst for others it may take years. Hair growth associated with men can be reduced to practically nothing. There will be loss of muscle, and some of the fat in the body will relocate to more feminine places such as hips and bottom. Facial features may soften because of that and become more feminine. Some experience growth of breasts, and some experience a partial loss of sexual function in their manhood, for want of a better word."

Suddenly, Isobel found herself lost for words. What Miss Phoebe offered, if it could be believed, was beyond hope, beyond all of the boyish fantasies that a young David had dared to dream about. A potion that would give all the attributes of a woman! No, it had to be impossible, did it not? Yet a tiny part of her rational mind wanted to believe that it would, her heart now beating wildly with the thought of it.

"Surely," she whispered, finally finding her voice once more, "this cannot be true."

"I believe it to be, Miss Isobel," said Phoebe.

Again, Isobel stared at Phoebe, and all that she could see in her dark brown, expressive eyes was honesty and a conviction that could only suggest that the woman truly believed in the effect of this potion.

"Oh my goodness! What on earth is in it?"

"The full recipe, Miss Isobel, is a closely guarded secret, although I will say that it is a combination of natural plant and animal products, some of which come from my African roots. It does, however, have quite an unpleasant taste, as you will find out if you decide to start taking it."

"You ... you ... you are offering it to me?" Isobel exclaimed.

"Yes, but it must be your decision to take it."

"And how much would I need to take?" Isobel asked, now finding it difficult to contain her excitement.

"One teaspoon in the morning and one in the evening, so there is enough in these bottles to last for about six weeks. After that, I will provide you with more, should you wish to continue with the treatment. You need only ask Mary, as she will get word to me. Oh, and one other thing, Miss Isobel. Many who start taking this medicine initially experience similar symptoms as do women in the early stages of pregnancy until their body becomes used to it. So, if you take it, expect to suffer from sickness in the mornings."

Later that evening, Isobel sat at her dressing table clad only in her night-rail as Mary carefully brushed out her long red hair. On the table before her, the lid open, sat the box. It had called to her all evening, had tempted her, yet her mind remained undecided.

After a simple evening meal, she and Mary had unpacked the two large trunks that the duchess had delivered that morning. Isobel had been thrilled and overwhelmed by Charlotte's generosity, for the large trunks had practically contained an entire trousseau, most of which appeared to have never been worn before. There were day dresses and spencers. There were evening dresses with matching gloves and head adornments and even a fur-lined mantle to wear over them on a chilly evening. There were petticoats and chemises and both long and short stays, silk stockings, and shoes. Surprisingly, when Isobel tried on one pair of evening slippers, their fit was almost perfect. In one chest they even found an assortment of accoutrements: a parasol, two shawls, a selection of reticules, and even some delicate white elbow-length gloves.

Then at the bottom of one of the trunks, Isobel discovered a small leather jewellery roll. She recognised it immediately, as David's mother had owned a similar one. In it, amongst other smaller pieces, was a stunning opal necklace with matching earbobs, complete with a handwritten note from the duchess herself, refusing to allow Isobel to return the jewellery and ordering her to wear the opals to the forthcoming dinner party.

But now, as she prepared for bed, it was not the clothes which consumed Isobel's mind. Instead, it was the wooden apothecary's box which called to her with the force of a giant loadstone. All day she had wrestled with the thought of it, wondering if she could actually believe it would have the effects that Phoebe had claimed. Yet, on the other hand, all she had ever dreamed of was having breasts, of having a womanly figure, and if even if there was the remotest chance of it happening, Isobel had determined to try. Well, almost.

"What would you do Mary?" Isobel asked softly.

Before the duchess had left, Miss Phoebe had sought out Mary to give her instructions as to what to do with the box. Mary was therefore privy to its contents and their effects. Standing behind her, brush in hand, Mary looked seriously at Isobel's reflection in the mirror.

"I think it does not matter what I think. You are going to take it anyway, are you not?"

"I would like your opinion anyway. It is important to me,

Mary."

Mary smiled broadly with the compliment. "Well, Miss Isobel, have you not repeatedly stated that you would do anything to enable you to live openly as a woman? It sounds to me that this medicine of Phoebe's will take you one step closer to achieving that. So if I were in your shoes, I would take the medicine, and damn the side effects."

Her fingers trembling, Isobel took the first of the bottles from the box and carefully broke the wax seal that secured the stopper. Gingerly, she brought the bottle to her nose and sniffed, instantly recoiling from a putrid odour.

"Oh my. You could use that for smelling salts." She coughed, a rueful smile passing her lips.

In a purpose-built slot to one side of the box, Isobel found a small silver spoon. Holding it in one hand she started to tip the bottle, yet her hand was trembling so much that she threatened to spill the muddy brown liquid all over the carpet.

"Here, let me," said Mary softy.

She took the bottle and spoon from Isobel and carefully poured out a measure. Then, holding it to her as if she were a babe, she slowly pushed the spoon into Isobel's mouth.

"Ugh... that is truly disgusting." Isobel winced as the medicine hit her throat, yet still she swallowed every last drop of it.

Chapter Nine

"Have you any thoughts on what you might play at the musicale, Isobel?" asked Olivia.

It had been two days since Charlotte's visit, and for Isobel the time seemed to have flown by. In preparation, Mary had accelerated her training, insisting that she practice over and again every single inflection of the head, every pose, and every step. Olivia had been involved too, tutoring Isobel in the etiquette of a woman, demanding that they share their meals each day so that they could discuss her progress.

"I have three pieces in mind, but you don't seem to have the sheet music for them," Isobel replied. "In fact, I was wondering if I might send Mary to purchase what I need later this morning."

"Oh no, that will not do," replied Olivia, a smile playing across her face.

Isobel sat as Olivia rang the bell, knowing that it would be Mary who would answer. Within moments, the maid appeared in the doorway with a curtsey and a smile.

"Mary, would you be so kind to ask Cartwright to order us a carriage for eleven this morning? Miss Isobel needs some sheet music, so I am taking her to Skillern and Challenor's in Oxford Street, so she can select what she needs. Then can you run upstairs and select something appropriate for Miss Isobel to wear please?"

"Do you wish me to accompany you, my lady?" Mary asked.

"Yes, I think that would be wise," Olivia replied.

Throughout, a stunned Isobel sat motionless, her heart suddenly pounding as her breath caught in her throat. Whilst she knew this moment would come, she was not at all certain that she was ready for her first foray into the big wide world. Yes, Olivia had convinced her to attend the musicale but that was days away, weeks. But going out onto the streets! What if someone recognised her for who she was? What if she was publicly humiliated upon the street by some vagabond or street urchin who could see past her disguise? What if . . .

"Isobel?" demanded Olivia.

"No. I can't," she said as she half stood, pushing her chair back from the table. "I can't do that! I can't!" she moaned.

"Yes you can, and yes you will." The countess's words were firm and forthright, and anyone would know from the tone of her voice that she meant every syllable.

"No, I can't. I'm not ready. I'm not."

"I disagree, Isobel, as does Mary. Ultimately though, it is up to you, as always. I will not force you to do so. But you cannot remain housebound for the rest of your life. You will sometime have to face venturing out into public. Now is as good a time as any. Besides, I am certain that you would rather select the sheet music for yourself. All we will do is go into the music shop, nothing else. You have my word on that."

"No! I cannot, Aunt, I simply cannot!"

"At least do this for me. Go and change, as if you were to go to the music shop. Put on a pretty dress and spencer, a bonnet too, and see how you feel. Make your decision whether to go or not when you come back downstairs. If your answer is still no, I will send Mary and one of the footmen with a list of what you would like."

Isobel sighed, for a part of her longed to be able escape the confines of the house and gardens. She also knew that Olivia was correct in her assumption that Mary also thought her ready to do so, for her maid had said as much that morning as she dressed for breakfast. But the fact still remained that the thought of venturing abroad scared her witless.

Mary was waiting for her when Isobel entered her room, a dress already laid out upon the bed.

"How exciting. It will be your first outing, Miss Isobel," she said. Without asking for permission, Mary moved behind Isobel to begin unbuttoning the simple muslin day dress she was wearing, giving her little choice but to disrobe. "I thought the cream dress with the brown velvet spencer would be perfect, as there is a matching bonnet to go with it. Oh, and you will need those walking shoes that the duchess included, and a reticule, too."

Bewildered, Isobel stood still as Mary undressed and then dressed her once more. In fact, the abigail did this in such a fashion that Isobel felt almost like a petulant child being told off by her governess. In a matter of minutes, she had put on the dress and the velvet spencer, to then have Mary tie the matching ribbon of the bonnet around her chin before artfully teasing her hair into the prettiest of styles beneath.

"There. What do you think?" asked Mary. She steered Isobel in front of her mirror and then fussed around her a little.

The truth of the matter was that Isobel did not know what to think. Her appearance was everything she could ever have hoped for. The bonnet she wore, the hairstyle that Mary had created, and the cosmetics upon her face all resulted in a very pleasing and very feminine appearance. The clothes she was wearing were those of a fashionable young lady and were perfect for the occasion. In short, even she had to admit that the young woman she saw was more than a little pleasing to the eye.

But inside was a totally different matter. Her heart was pounding, her mouth was dry, and her whole body was trembling like a calf's foot jelly on a plate held by a drunken sailor.

Fear was the overriding emotion she felt, but it was fear that was tempered with a smidgeon of excitement, too. All her life, Isobel had dreamed of this moment, of the day she could step out into the big wide world as a young lady. She had spent many a day wondering what it would be like to be a lady of fashion wandering through the shops of Edinburgh or London, to buy this lace or that ribbon or even visit a modiste to order a ball gown or two.

"Oh God," she whispered to herself.

It was then that Mary did something quite extraordinary, for a maid that was. From behind, her arms snaked around Isobel's middle, to pull her back against the softness of her bosom. Then she felt Mary's chin rest upon her shoulder so that their faces were side by side in the mirror.

"You can do this, Miss Isobel," she said firmly. "I know you can, for I would not let Lady Hamilton take you out if I did not think you could do so without fear of discovery. But more than that, I think you should do this. How else are you to find the courage to venture further afield in the future? What other choice do you have?"

Isobel put her hands over her maids and hugged her in return. "I could always return to being David?" she whispered.

"As if you could. We both know that is only going happen when the sun fails to rise in the morning."

Isobel sighed deeply. "I know, I know. There is no need to remind me."

"Look, when you get to the music shop, all you have to do is to stand there and look pretty. Let Lady Hamilton do the talking, or myself if necessary. You will be fine, I promise."

Olivia sat opposite Isobel, who in turn was sat next to Mary as the hackney made its way towards Oxford Street. Although she did not show it, Olivia was almost as nervous as Isobel.

After all, much depended on Isobel's ability to remain in *character*. If she were to fool all and sundry into believing her to be a lady, she would have to move and talk and behave like one in all respects. One little slip and the game might be over, and if it became known that Isobel was a man in ladies' clothing, the scandal would be even greater than that of Lord Nelson and Lady Hamilton, before Nelson was killed at Trafalgar.

But in her heart, Olivia knew that David deserved to be happy, and the only way that he could achieve that would be to live his life as Isobel. Towards that goal, great strides had been taken. Isobel's physical appearance was far superior to anything Olivia could have imagined, and in truth, she was really quite beautiful. But that would only take her so far. If she were to live as Isobel she would have to walk and move like a young woman, converse as a young woman and act in a manner that was so far removed from the man she used to be.

Whether she could do so was yet to be seen.

Little conversation passed during the journey into London, and even Mary's usual enthusiasm failed to break the tension within the Hackney. But that was only to be expected, considering how nervous all three of them most certainly were and how desperately they all wanted Isobel to succeed. Far too soon, judging by the look on Isobel's face, the carriage pulled to a stop, and as Olivia glanced out of the window, she could see that they were directly opposite the very shop they intended to visit, Skillern and Challenor, music sellers since 1806. A little squeak of terror slipped from Isobel's lips as the carriage creaked and tilted a little. Then the coachman opened the door, and politely held out his hand. Olivia alighted and was followed by Mary.

Of Isobel there was no sign.

"Come along Isobel!" demanded Olivia. She turned back

to the coachman, handing him a silver shilling that she took from her reticule. "Would you please wait for us here, coachman? We should not be more than half an hour. Isobel, come along!" she repeated as the man tugged at the peak of his cap in deference.

Olivia did not realise that she was actually holding her breath as she searched the darkness of the coach for Isobel, part of her willing her ward to find the courage she needed to step down.

Mary, on the other hand, was having none of that. As Olivia watched, she poked her head back inside the coach, her hand reaching out for Isobel. For an instant, Olivia thought that Isobel would refuse to move. But Mary pulled firmly upon her hand, and to Olivia's relief, Isobel clambered clumsily to her feet.

Giving Isobel no time to think, moments later all three of them entered a paradise of music. Everywhere one looked there were instruments of all shapes and sizes. Violins and violas lined the walls on specially crafted shelves. Cases of flutes and oboes could be seen in display cabinets, whilst larger instruments stood to one side. But most impressive of all was the line of polished pianos and pianofortes, all of which gleamed in the sunlight that streamed in through the large front window. As Mary closed the shop door behind them, a well-dressed, middle-aged man approached and bowed politely before allowing himself a smile of genuine pleasure.

"Lady Hamilton, what an unexpected pleasure," he said as he bowed once more. "How may I be of assistance?"

"Good morning to you, Mr Skillern. May I introduce my ward, Miss Munroe. She is in need of some sheet music, as the Duchess of Camberly has requested she play the piano at her musicale on Saturday next."

"What a great honour, Miss Munroe. Have you in mind

what you will play?" asked Mr Skillern.

Olivia was about to reply on behalf of Isobel when, to her absolute surprise and delight, she heard a soft, feminine, but very shaky Scottish voice begin to speak.

"Do you have Mozart's *Sonata in C major?*" she asked.

Olivia turned to look at Isobel, who in turn was looking at Mr Skillern. She was standing tall, with her shoulders back, her hands held in a feminine posture that Olivia knew had been practiced for many an hour. Yes, her face was pink in the cheek, but there was also a strange look of defiance, too, and Olivia felt her heart go out to her wonderful protégé.

"Yes, of course," replied Mr Skillern.

"And I would also like piano arrangements for J.S. Bach's *Jesu Joy of Man's Desiring* and *Spring* from the Four Seasons by Vivaldi if you have them."

"The Vivaldi, yes, but I only have Maestro Sussemeyer's arrangement of *Jesu Joy* in stock. Perhaps you might like to try it before purchasing the sheet, Miss Munroe, for even I find it a very challenging piece."

Olivia could hardly believe what she saw. Isobel smiled, she actually smiled, her whole face lighting up as she did so. With a rustle of her skirts, she was soon sat in front of the piano, where Mr Skillern had placed the sheet music. As before, Isobel closed her eyes for a moment, her fingers reaching for the keys. And then the strains of beautiful music began to fill the shop.

It was at this moment that the shop door once more opened to admit two ladies, one middle aged and somewhat elaborately dressed, the other much younger. Olivia recognised both instantly as Lady Justine Farthingale, Viscountess of Salisbury and her daughter Lady Felicia Farthingale, neither of whom Olivia cared for one little bit. The viscountess was typical of her type, privileged and with little interest in anyone she deemed below her in station. Accordingly, her daughter was nothing more than a spoiled madam who believed herself destined to marry a duke. The viscountess was an inveterate social climber, too, and one who, in particular, wanted to get into the good graces and social circles of no less than the Duke and Duchess of Camberly.

Mr Skillern, it seemed, was enraptured by Isobel, so much so that he missed the grand entrance of the viscountess and her daughter, all of his attention focused on the beautiful music that Isobel was creating. All doubt that she could play the piece had obviously evaporated, for he was stood at Isobel's shoulder with his eyes closed as he savoured the music. This obviously did not please Lady Farthingale, who quite deliberately rapped the man on the shoulder with her fan in an effort to garner his attention.

"Mr Skille . . . ."

"Shush," he replied without turning.

"Well, I never," exclaimed the woman, her voice deliberately pitched so that it would carry over the music.

"Oh, please be quiet for a moment, madam," snapped Mr Skillern.

Olivia grinned as she saw the head of Lady Farthingale about to explode with rage. Therefore, Olivia placed herself in front of the woman and smiled.

"Lady Farthingale, I would deem it a great favour if you would allow a moment for my ward to finish playing."

Olivia spoke in voice that barely disguised the disdain she felt. With huge satisfaction, she watched as Lady Farthingale rounded on her with all the indignation she could muster, only to have the wind taken out of her sails when she saw who had spoken to her. They had bumped heads before, and Olivia had often taken great pleasure in using her own superior title and her *friendship* with Charlotte to put the woman in her place.

"*Mother*," whined Lady Felicia. "Who is that girl?" she

demanded.

It was at that very moment that Isobel, still unaware of the unfolding drama, played the very last note, the sound softly dying away as she sat back onto her stool.

"Oh, bravo Miss Munroe, bravo!" declared Mr Skillern. "That was simply wonderful. You play so beautifully and so skilfully," he added. He graciously held out his hand to help Isobel stand, a hand which Olivia was pleased to see her take.

"Isobel, would you come over here please," called Olivia.

Thankfully, Isobel did as she was asked and came to stand next to Olivia, only this time her head was held low, her eyes cast down a little so as to not make contact with the other ladies in front of her.

"Isobel, may I present Lady Justine Farthingale, Viscountess of Salisbury, and her daughter, Lady Felicia Farthingale. Ladies, may I present my ward, Miss Isobel Munroe. Isobel is requested to play for the Duke and Duchess of Camberly at their musicale, Saturday next, and is here to select her music."

As she spoke, she sensed Isobel dipping a respectful curtsy, garnering a withering look from the Viscountess and the barest of acknowledgement from her daughter. The reply she received in return was nothing short of vitriolic.

"What a coincidence, for Felicia will also be playing in her string quartet. You say this is your ward?" sneered Lady Farthingale as she glanced at Isobel. "She received an invitation through your friendship with the duchess, no doubt."

"No, Lady Farthingale. She received an invitation so that their Graces may once again enjoy her sublime playing. In fact, her Grace so much favours Isobel that she has even offered to sponsor her for a season. Now if you would excuse us, our carriage is waiting outside. Mr Skillern, how much do I owe you for the sheet music?" she asked as she reached for her reticule.

The man smiled broadly with genuine appreciation. "No, please, Lady Hamilton, let it be a gift from me. It has been a very long time since I have heard such talent, Miss Munroe."

Olivia watched as Isobel yet again blushed. But Isobel was smiling broadly as she dipped yet another curtsey, this time to the man who stood before her.

"You have my thanks, Mr Skillern, for it is praise indeed when it comes from such a renowned musician as yourself."

Chapter Ten

Since visiting the music shop, Isobel's progress had been swift, and each day Olivia recognised that she seemed to grow in assurance and poise. In particular, her self-confidence had grown exponentially, especially after she had received the compliments of Mr Skillern. On a number of occasions over the past few days, the two of them had even ventured out into public—a visit to the British Museum, a walk along the Lady's Mile in Hyde Park, a short shopping expedition in Bond Street, where Olivia had Isobel purchase some ribbon. Each and every time, Olivia had been amazed at how easy it had been for her protégé to pass undetected. In fact, the only sour note in the whole process had been bouts of morning sickness, brought on by Phoebe's medicine.

But now, the moment was rapidly approaching where Olivia would have to confess the final reason why she was so adamant to help Isobel.

Lord Peter Fairfax

Oh, she knew that ultimately, Isobel had no need to accept him. She had, after all, her inheritance to fall back upon. If that be the case, Olivia was aware of at least three different young ladies from good backgrounds who would jump at the chance of becoming Lady Fairfax, even if that did enter them into a loveless marriage. But in saying that, she also hoped that Peter and Isobel might see the beauty of her plan. A *marriage* between them would certainly lend credence to Isobel's claim to be a *lady*. Besides, did not both of them deserve the happiness that a union between them might bring? In her heart, something told her they would be perfect for each other, even if they risked public humiliation should Isobel's true gender become common knowledge.

She sighed and checked the mantle clock, noting the time of two in the afternoon. As per her letter, Lord Fairfax would be arriving in precisely one hour to hear of a potential match, and now she had to find Isobel and break the news to her.

Isobel was at the pianoforte when Olivia entered the small music room. She looked up and smiled broadly as the countess walked over to her, a smile which faded away to nothing as she took in Olivia's expression.

"Good heavens, Aunt. Whatever is the matter? You look like you have lost a sovereign and found a farthing."

"Isobel, would you come into the parlour? There is something of import that I need to discuss with you." Olivia watched as fear flickered over Isobel's face and silently cursed herself for worrying her so. "Don't fret, Isobel. It is nothing to do with you. Well, it is. But is nothing to worry about, not yet, that is," she mumbled, trying hard to keep the embarrassment from her face as she swiftly turned to leave the room.

On entering the parlour, Olivia indicated that Isobel should sit, choosing to perch next to her so that she could take her protégé's hand in her own.

"What is it, Aunt Olivia? You are scaring me a little."

Olivia looked up, knowing the redness in her cheeks and the dark circles under her eyes from the sleepless night she had endured still showed upon her face.

"I have a confession to make Isobel, and it is something you are probably not going to like. All I ask is that you listen and let me explain before you get angry with me."

Isobel nodded, so Olivia launched into the explanation she had rehearsed in her mind so many times.

"My second husband, the Earl of Weybridge, was a horrid beast of a man who, when in his cups, thought it his God given right to hurt anyone who got in his way, including me. My back still bears the scars to prove it. Unfortunately, his son is cut from the same cloth, so when my husband mercifully died, my *delightful* stepson refused to help me financially and practically cast me out onto the street. Not that I would have been destitute, for my daughter Amelia and the Duchess of Camberly both offered me a home. Instead, for the first time in my life, I determined to help myself. I sold what jewellery I had, and with the money, I set myself up here. Then I began to use my title, my contacts, and my influence to broker and arrange matches for those within the ton."

"I do not think I am going to like where this conversation is taking us, Lady Hamilton," complained Isobel.

"Recently, a gentleman of the ton approached me to find him a bride. He is being forced to marry by his family, by the way. At the time he admitted to me that whomsoever I chose for him would be his bride in name only, as his sexual preferences lay very much on the other side of the sheets, if you get my meaning. His plan was to marry a suitable girl, ship her off to the countryside, and then continue with life in London. It was at this time that a somewhat unique solution presented itself to me."

"Me, you mean," hissed Isobel angrily.

"Yes, you, my darling. *David* had just turned up in London with that letter from your mother explaining the circumstances of your departure, and I had a wild thought that, if you were able to present yourself successfully to the ton as a woman, you might make the perfect match for my client."

As the countess had expected her to, Isobel exploded with anger.

"How could you!" Isobel yelled. Her face a picture of rage, she rounded upon Olivia, snatching her hand away as she did so. "This has all been a game to you, has it not, a means to an end, a way of making money from me."

"No, it has not," replied Olivia, so firmly that her words stopped Isobel in her tracks. "*Everything* you have done has been by your choice alone. Was it not your decision to have Mary perform her transformation on you? Was it not your decision to come with me to meet the duchess, to go to the music shop? Everything you have done as Isobel has been by your choice and will remain so. You have my word on that. My client knows *nothing* about you, absolutely *nothing*. He doesn't even know you exist. Whilst I would like it to be so, the decision to meet him would be yours and yours alone, and my word is gospel on that. But think on it, Isobel. You have in the past told me that, if you could, you would be a wedded woman, with a home of your own."

"Oh God!" moaned Isobel.

"Has that changed, Isobel? Have you changed your mind about that?" Olivia demanded.

"No. But . . ." Isobel stammered.

"The man in question is the second son of a Duke. I will not tell you his name, in case you decide not to meet him." She laughed then as an obvious thought flicked across Isobel's eyes. "No, not the Duke of Camberly, another Duke. My client therefore is a Baron in his own right. He is one and thirty years of age, and as a young man, spent several years serving as an Officer in His Majesty's army. However, he sold his commission after he was wounded at Waterloo, nearly losing his life in the process. Other than an occasional limp, a relic of the wound he received in his leg, he is hale and hearty now. A fine prospect for any woman, he will inherit an estate and five thousand a year on his marriage. It does not harm that he is tall, athletic, and devilishly handsome, either."

It was at this point that Olivia saw a flicker of interest in Isobel's eyes and could guess at the imaginings of her mind. The man she had described would be the ideal for any young woman, especially for one like Isobel. If only she could see that.

"And you say, aunt, that he has no knowledge of me?" she asked. Her voice was small and almost childlike in its breathless quality.

"None at all. He is coming here this afternoon to discuss..."

"He's coming here this afternoon?" screeched Isobel.

"Yes, this afternoon. He is coming to meet me, thinking to discuss the prospects I have in mind for him. I had thought to introduce you as my ward and to see how you feel about him. But as I have stated before, it must be your decision and yours alone."

"Oh God, I do not know what to do."

"Nothing will change for you, Isobel. If you do meet with him, I will introduce you as my ward, so that he believes you to be a lady, the lovely young lady you are rapidly becoming. After all, he will need to see that you can function in society as a woman if... well, you know. Then, should you wish it and only when you give me permission to do so, I will reveal the truth of your true gender."

"You have given this a great deal of thought, have you not?" said Isobel.

"Mm, and have lost a great deal of sleep in doing so from fear of broaching this subject with you. Note the dark circles under my eyes, Isobel. So, what say you? Will you meet him?"

For the longest few seconds in eternity, Isobel sat without speaking. Olivia watched Isobel's eyes become glazed as she stared off into the virtual distance, her mind obviously working at a frantic pace. It was then that a half-smile flickered across her lips.

"At what time will he arrive?"

"At three this very afternoon," replied Olivia.

Isobel glanced over at the mantle clock, and Olivia laughed out loud as her ward gave out an un-lady like screech. She laughed even louder as Isobel stood to dash out of the room.

"I need to change... I need to change. Mary!" the girl shouted as she ran for the stairs.

The hackney cab that carried Peter arrived outside the countess's modest town house at precisely two minutes before three o'clock. Wanting to make an impression, he had dressed stylishly yet conservatively in a dark green morning coat and buckskin breeches, the only flamboyance being the gold fob watch he wore across a muted waistcoat. He had shaved carefully, and Jenkins had both trimmed his hair and tied his cravat so that his appearance was as immaculate as he could make it.

Yet still his heart was heavy.

Ever since the countess had sent him a missive requesting that they meet, he had felt a strong sense of foreboding. After all, there could be only one reason for her to do so: the presentation of the choice of a lady to be his bride. And of course, that was the very last thing in the world he wanted to do. Still, he had promised his father... had determined not to disappoint his mother, so he hoped that the countess might have found someone at least mildly suitable to be his *de facto* bride.

"God," he moaned to himself as he paused at the oaken front door to the house.

He knocked, and the door was answered by a footman, who ushered him inside and towards the parlour where he had previously met with Lady Hamilton. He was announced, and as he entered the room Lady Hamilton stood to greet him. To his surprise, however, there was another young woman with her, and she too stood, her eyes cast down as if she were quite shy. Peter appraised her quickly. She was a little on the tall side for a lady and had a lovely willowy figure draped in a pretty light green day dress. A mass of red-auburn hair had been artfully arranged upon her head and framed a perfectly pretty face.

It was as he stopped courteously before the countess that something quite extraordinary happened.

As propriety dictated, the girl had risen from her seat to curtsey, her head still held low. Then she had looked up, had looked him firmly in the eye. In truth he had not a clue to whom she was, but the look of horror that instantly covered her face gave every indication that she had definitely recognised him. It was at this point in the proceedings that the girl gave out a loud and very un-ladylike shriek before dropping the embroidery hoop she was clutching. She then dashed from the room, slamming the door behind her as she left.

Stunned, Peter looked at the countess, his mouth open with the surprise of it all. If anything, she looked even more startled at the girl's reaction than he.

Olivia found Isobel in the music room, her whole body shaking, a green tinge around her face indicating that she might soon be physically sick. The tears had not yet started, but from the look of her, they were mightily close to the surface.

"Isobel, what on earth?" Olivia kept her voice soft and gentle, knowing it was the only way to speak to her as she too perched next to her protégé upon the broad piano stool.

"I know, I know him, Lady Olivia, I know him!" she garbled.

"What? How?"

Isobel looked up, and Olivia watched as the girl caught her bottom lip between her teeth, her hands clutching her dress to twist it as if she were a washer woman wringing out the dirty water on wash day.

"Oh God!" Isobel moaned. "I did not tell you, for I did not see the need."

The Making of a Lady

"Tell me what Isobel?"

"I . . . that is, David, arrived in London two days before he presented himself to you with his letter from his mother. You see, even he had heard of the Moonlight Club, and during the journey from Scotland, he determined to spend an evening there."

"And that was where you met Lord Fairfax?" asked Olivia incredulously.

"Yes. Only he was called Archie when I met him."

"And David and he . . . they . . ." asked Olivia.

"Yes, they spent the evening together."

The countess laughed. How could she not? It was a rich, deep, throaty chuckle that pronounced how pleased she was with this revelation.

"And?"

"Oh, Aunt Olivia. It was wonderful," Isobel gushed. "He was everything that I — that is, David — would want in a man. He was strong, gentle, but dominant in a take charge sort of way. He brought me — that is David — to such heights of pleasure, Aunt Olivia. Three times! My body still aches from thinking of it. God, what must you think of me?"

"What I think, Isobel, is that without doubt, this is the best thing that could possibly have happened."

"Oh my God," moaned Isobel. She once more covered her glowing face with her hands. "What am I going to do?"

"That is very much up to you Isobel, as always. What I will say is that Lord Fairfax appeared to have absolutely no idea of who you are in reality."

"He didn't?" squeaked Isobel.

"No, he didn't. Instead, it was quite obvious he thought you to be nothing but hysterical young woman prone to fits of vapours. Anyway, let me offer you a hypothetical question, Isobel. Should Lord Fairfax be interested in pursuing this matter with you, once he has been made aware of the pertinent facts, that is, would you be interested in reciprocating that interest?"

Isobel's cheeks grew even redder as she spoke in a very small and uncertain voice. "Yes, I think I would. But that would mean telling him who I am, would it not?"

"I think that would only be fair, as he too would be risking his reputation, should anyone discover who you are. It would have to be a mutual decision between both of you. You can, however, trust him with your secret, of that I am certain. How about this? I will take you into the parlour and introduce you properly as Isobel and only Isobel. Judge for yourself as to how he perceives you. If he takes you for the lady you appear to be, it will make it much easier for him to accept the proposal I have in mind. Then, if *you* deem it to be, *you* can tell him of your real identity."

Olivia watched as a wry smile slowly drifted across Isobel's face. There was still indecision, she could tell, but part of her was clearly thrilled at the idea.

"So how do I look, Aunt?" she asked coyly.

Peter was starting to lose patience with the whole situation. First the girl and then Lady Hamilton had vanished from the room, leaving him alone, when all he wanted to do was to get this whole sordid affair over and done with. He found himself pacing around the room, his hands firmly behind his back as anger began to flare within him. It was as he reached the fireplace for the fourth time that the door to the room opened, allowing Lady Hamilton and her companion to enter.

"Finally," he muttered under his breath as he turned to them both.

"Lord Hamilton, may I present my ward, Miss Isobel Munroe. Isobel, this is Lord Peter Fairfax, second son to the Duke of Abingdon," began Olivia formally.

The Making of a Lady

Peter watched as the young lady curtsied gracefully, bowing to her in return. There was no doubt that the girl was pretty, especially with that glorious red hair he so admired. But in saying that, like many young women of the ton, it was clear this girl was also prone to fits of the vapours, judging by the way she had reacted to his mere presence. Ruefully he shook his head.

"Lady Hamilton . . ." he said

"Please, sit," said the countess. Interrupting him, she sat upon the settee, Miss Munroe sitting down next to her.

Peter, however, indignantly remained upon his feet. "Not to sound rude, Lady Hamilton, but I would rather discuss our business alone," he said as he nodded towards Isobel.

"Yes, quite. But as it happens, Miss Munroe, Isobel, is the first candidate I would like to present to you."

"Ah. Now I understand," he replied as realisation dawned upon him.

Peter now looked more intently at the girl sat next to the countess. She was young, perhaps no more than twenty years of age, and had the greenest eyes that Peter had ever seen. The cosmetics she wore on her face had been subtly applied, and rather than making her look garish, served to enhance her natural beauty. Peter particularly liked the pale complexion against her golden red hair. It was also clear that she had been raised a lady, simply from the graceful way she walked and sat. There was an intelligence in her eyes, too, eyes that were now studying him intently. Yet, after her outburst, Peter had real reservations as to her suitability for the role.

Still, might as well go on with the game.

"Tell me about yourself, Miss Munroe," he asked softly.

"Well," she replied. Her husky voice was pleasing to the ear, her gentle Scottish accent revealing much of her ancestry. "I will be one and twenty in a few months' time, and as you can probably tell, I hail from Scotland, Edinburgh to be exact. My father was a gentleman and master of his own vessel, who died at sea when I was but eight years of age. I then lived with my mother, a distant cousin to Lady Hamilton, until she died of influenza. Hence the reason I am now here."

Peter fixed his gaze upon her. Just that short statement had told him much about the girl. She had been left an orphan by the death of her mother so would be looking for the security of marriage. No doubt she had little or no dowry either, and on paper, she appeared to be the perfect choice for him.

"You are aware of the conditions I place upon marriage, Miss Munroe?" he said. Inwardly, he cringed as his words came out somewhat more imperiously than he had intended.

"Yes, my lord, I am aware that it would be a marriage in name alone. But I have to ask. What is it you would offer *me* in return? After all, I am to have a season this year, and I could, perhaps, hold out for a better offer, perhaps even a love match."

When Isobel uttered these words, Peter heard Lady Olivia splutter as she obviously found herself fighting the urge to laugh. That angered Peter. To him it was obvious that the little minx had completely turned the tables on him and that Lady Hamilton could not help but smile as she watched the play of emotion on his face.

"On marriage, I am to receive Winsworth Manor and estate. The house has twelve guest bedrooms and is sat in three thousand acres of tenanted farmland that generates an income of five thousand a year. The woman I marry would be mistress of the house."

"Yet mistress in name only," said Isobel softly.

"Yes, quite," replied Peter. Anger was close to the surface, and Peter was now starting to feel more than a little uncomfortable that a mere chit of a woman would question him thus.

"And what of children, my lord? Do you not desire children, a boy to pass on your title to?"

"I require no children, Miss Munroe. My title is honorary

and will revert to the duchy when I pass on. Eventually, it will go to the second son of my brother when he becomes duke."

"But what would I say to your parents if I fail to get with child, my lord? Surely they will expect grandchildren."

Now Peter was really starting to get angry. How dare this chit question him so? Surely the countess had counselled the girl to the terms of the marriage, without, of course revealing the whole truth behind those terms.

"I care not, Miss Munroe," he snapped. "You can tell them I am impotent, for all I care."

Silence reigned for a second as Peter uttered those words. Then Olivia grinned once more as Isobel looked Peter squarely in the eye, almost as if she already knew exactly what was yet to come.

"Oh, we both know you are far from impotent, *Archie*, don't we," said Isobel.

"Yes . . . what . . . what did you say?" gasped Peter.

Peter gaped at the young woman in abject surprise, his mouth flapping like a fish out of water.

"You do not recognise me, do you Archie?" said Isobel softly.

"What? What is this? Lady Hamilton, what is this game you play?" Peter stared at her wildly, not knowing if he should run or not.

"'Tis no game, Archie, I promise you. When last you and I met, you knew me as Fergus."

As Isobel looked up, she saw Peter begin to buckle from the shock, his solid, muscular frame sagging at the knees until he sat down heavily upon the nearest chair. Without asking permission from her aunt, she stood and walked over to the silver drinks tray. There she poured a generous amount of brandy into a glass and handed it to him, watching as he drank deeply, his face a deathly white in colour.

"What is this, Lady Hamilton? Please, please explain," he demanded as he turned back to Olivia.

In reply, Olivia stood and started towards the door.

"I think, Lord Fairfax, that I should give you and Isobel a little privacy so that you may talk. Isobel, I will be in the music room if you need me."

As the door closed behind the countess, Isobel turned to look at Peter, the atmosphere between them so tense it was almost as if battle were about to commence. Isobel once more went over to the drinks tray, this time to pour herself a brandy before tilting back the fiery liquid in the most un-ladylike fashion. Then she sat before him and sighed deeply in an attempt to still her beating heart.

"Only one other knows my story in entirety, and that is Lady Olivia. I need your word, Peter, that whatever is spoken of here, remains between us. Your word, Peter."

"Yes, of course."

Once more she sighed. "My real name is David, Viscount Drummond, and I am the only child of the Earl and Countess of Falkirk."

"My God!" exclaimed Peter.

"What I am about to say next is difficult to explain. You see, for my whole life, I have believed myself to have been born into the wrong body, that I should have been born a woman instead of a man. 'Tis all I dream of, Peter, and it is so much more than simple fantasy. It is almost as if my life depends on becoming a woman. Well, a few weeks back, my father caught me wearing a dress, and to say he was somewhat displeased is putting it mildly."

Isobel paused then, deliberately omitting the fact that when she had been caught, she had been on her hands and knees with a great hairy Scotsman tupping her from behind.

"He beat me so violently that my mother feared for my life.

It was she who gave me the few pounds she could scrape together along with a letter explaining the circumstances of my departure to give to Lady Hamilton. She and Lady Hamilton have a history which I am not privy to, but one which ensured she would help, despite what had happened. On arrival in London, I should have gone straight to her. But instead, I went to the Moonlight Club. I suppose it was an act of defiance against my father that prompted me to do so. I am glad that I did, for it was there that I met this devilishly handsome young man who proceeded to take me to previously unknown heights of pleasure."

"'Twas a night I will never forget either," said Peter tenderly.

"When I finally made it to Lady Hamilton's, she did not know what to make of me, what to do with me. But then you turned up with your request for her to find you a match. I think she put two and two together and made sixty-four."

"So she is forcing you to dress this way?" demanded Peter.

"Oh no! Absolutely not! She offered to help me look like this, to be the woman I desired to be, and I gladly accepted that offer. I want nothing more than to be Isobel and to live my life as such, despite the obvious physical limitations. My plan was simple. David comes into a substantial trust when he is one and twenty. Until that time, my aim was to establish myself as Isobel and then to lead a quiet life as such in the county somewhere. Lady Hamilton offered to help, irrespective of her plans for you and me."

"So you are not being coerced?" asked Peter.

"Far from it."

"But . . . but . . ."

"I know. Complicated, is it not? Anyway, Lady Hamilton had always planned for Isobel and Peter to meet, thinking we would be perfectly matched for each other. Believe me, I did not know we would do so until this afternoon when she revealed all to me. Even then, she allowed me the choice as to whether I would meet you. What she didn't know, however, is that Archie and Fergus had met before."

Peter stood, and Isobel watched as he marched over to the brandy decanter once more, then poured himself another generous drink. He motioned to Isobel, but when she shook her head, he re-joined her on the settee instead.

"This is quite surreal, is it not," he said, as this time he sipped at his drink. "If I understand correctly, Lady Hamilton thought that you and I might make the perfect match, with you in the guise of a woman."

"It is not a guise, Peter. Isobel is who I am, irrespective of anything else. Yes, I will always have a cock," she said crudely, "but I will also always have the heart and mind of a woman."

"But think of the scandal should anyone find out about you."

"No less than the scandal if someone should find out about you, Peter. Besides, no one has yet suspected anything," she lied. "The countess and I have been seen in several different public situations, and I have been successfully introduced to the Duke and Duchess of Camberly. The duchess has even offered to sponsor me for this forthcoming season."

Isobel paused at this point, for there was no need to tell him that Charlotte and her companion also knew about her true identity. Instead, she let him think that, like others she had met, they had accepted her for the woman she appeared to be.

"So, what do you think David?" continued Isobel. "Were we to *marry*, in public I could be your adoring wife, whilst in the privacy of a bedchamber I could be the person you made love to three times that night we met."

She watched as David grinned at the memory, only to have his smile replaced by an expression of dejected concern as he shook his head.

The Making of a Lady

"In truth, I see not how we could take the risk, no matter how much it appeals to me to do so."

For a moment, Isobel thought she had lost the argument, that Peter would never agree to being seen publicly with someone like her. But something deep in her heart was telling her that this was exactly what she wanted, that she would take any risk on earth to make it so with this beautiful man. Then she had a flash of inspiration.

"Are you invited to the Duchess of Camberly's musicale on Saturday hence?"

"I believe my mother and father will be attending, but I have not been invited."

"I will be accompanying Lady Hamilton, so what if I asked for you to be included? I am certain that Lady Hamilton could sway the duchess into offering you an invitation. Then you and I could *meet* for the *first time* in a social setting, and you could judge for yourself as to whether I could perform this role without suspicion or scandal. I would be the only one taking a risk, for if I am discovered you could easily claim no knowledge of me."

From the look on his face, Isobel knew that Peter was seriously contemplating her suggestion. Then a smile appeared on Peter's lips, lighting his face.

Isobel's heart almost stopped as she saw how handsome it made him look. "I think that is settled then," she said. "We will *meet* at the musicale."

"Not quite" said Peter. "There is one more thing."

Before Isobel could react, she was pulled into Peter's arms, his lips settling onto hers as he kissed her deeply. Isobel's toes curled in her slippers, her arms, with a will of their own, snaking around his neck as she returned the kiss with every ounce of passion she possessed. This was everything that she remembered, the passion, the excitement, so much so that when he pulled away, she felt herself breathless with desire.

Peter grinned. "For that I will not apologise. After all, even I needed proof that it really is you, *Fergus*," he whispered as his lips once more met hers.

Chapter Eleven

It was a little after four in the afternoon when Mary and Isobel retired to her rooms to begin preparations for dinner at the Duke and Duchess of Camberly's that night. Mary had deemed it so and had ordered Isobel upstairs to give her time to perform her magic upon Isobel's appearance.

Even though apprehension coursed through her, Isobel had been looking forward to this. After all, this was to be the first time that *Isobel* would dress for a formal event, and the prospects of it gave her incredible goosebumps. So for the next few hours, she determined to ignore the trepidation she felt and instead submerge herself into the world of femininity. The notion of it thrilled her to the core.

The process started with a hip bath filled with scented bath water in which Mary allowed Isobel to luxuriate for a few minutes. Then Mary washed her hair with some of Miss Phoebe's special hair soap and encouraged Isobel to stand so that she could once more take razor to skin, even though there appeared to be little or no re-growth of hair. As she stood in her bath, her naked body on display to her maid as Mary took razor to skin, Isobel turned to look at her maid.

"Do you think Miss Phoebe's potion is having any effect yet?" she asked.

For a few moments Mary stared at her, unashamedly assessing Isobel's body.

"Methinks it is too early to see any real effect, Miss Isobel," said Mary. "If anything at all, your face has softened a little and I see a little more swell in your hips and bottom."

"I wish my breasts would hurry up and grow."

"I know, I know, Miss Isobel. However, talking of breasts," said Mary, "I have modified your stays somewhat by adding some cotton padding over the rice. It will make your breasts look a little bigger but also ensure that should accidental contact occur, no one would feel anything out of the ordinary. In truth, I am quite pleased with the finished result. Come now, out of the bath."

By the time Isobel had dried herself and donned her robe, Mary had everything else prepared in the bedroom. Now used to Mary's ministrations, Isobel sat before her dressing table and surrendered herself to the delights of having her maid brush through her hair. It was as she did so that Isobel broached yet another item which had been plaguing her mind.

"Mary, may I ask you a question? And I do want you to be truthful with your reply."

"Of course, Miss Isobel," replied Mary as she fetched the styling tongs from the fireplace where they had been warming.

For Isobel, the hardest part of making her transition into womanhood remained her own self-belief, and a huge part of her still expected the moment in which her secret would be revealed. Having been raised in an aristocratic family, she also had absolutely no doubt it was the servants who were most likely to divine the truth. It was the servants who were also most likely to reveal that truth to others, either as gossip or even for profit by selling a juicy scandal to one of the less reputable broadsheets. Now, she needed to know.

"Tell me, what do the other servants of the house make of me?" asked Isobel.

Mary laughed, a genuine smile appearing on her face. "Oh Miss Isobel, you have no need to worry about them. Cook adores you, especially as you regularly pop into the kitchen to compliment her on her dishes."

"How could I not. That lemon pie she made last night was to die for."

"Of the two footmen, well! Davis, I am sure, is half in love with you, judging by his mooncalf eyes every time you pass by. Cartwright, on the other hand, always seems to find time to linger near the music room every time you practice. Of the maids, you only have Brenda to worry about, and that is only because she is in love with Frank Davis herself and sees you as her rival. No, let me reassure you that there has not been a single moment of doubt in any of their minds as to your true identity."

Isobel sighed in relief, not realising that she had actually been holding her breath.

"Thank you, Mary. You do not know what it means for me to hear you say so."

"Oh, trust me when I say I do."

"And trust me, Mary, when I say that I will never be able to repay your kindness and your discretion."

"Oh pish, Miss Isobel. Now this is what I suggest we do with your hair."

It took another two hours for Isobel to *dress*. The hairstyle Mary created seemed perfect to Isobel. Most of her hair had been braided and then gathered into an elaborate chignon held by pins adorned with tiny green silk flowers the colour of her dress. To the side, however, hung delicate ringlets of flaming red hair, which proved the perfect frame for her face. Again Mary had painted her face delicately, the makeup serving to mask any and all traces of masculinity that remained. She had even buffed Isobel's growing nails to a shine and shaped them a little to give her fingers a far more feminine look.

Then Mary had helped Isobel to dress. They had begun with the muslin bangages between her legs, as neither wanted the possibilty of an embarrassing buldge. Petticoats and stays came next, and Isobel delighted in the slightly more curvaceous appearance they gave her, thanks to the extra padding. Then came the beautiful emerald green dress, cut low enough to give the hint of decolletage, and tied at the waist with a very pretty satin sash that served only to emphasise her trim waist. The dress had needed a little altering, but with Mary's expertise it now fit Isobel as if it had been made for her. The final touches were matching slippers and the beautiful opal knecklace and earbobs that the Duchess had gifted her.

"Oh my," said Mary as she circled around Isobel, smoothing away this imaginary crease and that imaginary piece of fluff. "Even though I say so myself, Miss Isobel, you look spectacular. Had I never met you, I would never have thought it possible that a young man could look so perfectly feminine. To my eye, you are every inch a lady."

"Thanks to you, Mary," replied Isobel in the soft melodic voice she had adopted as her own.

"Why, even your speaking voice is quite spectacular, Miss Isobel. I still don't understand how you speak so."

"Perhaps it's my musical ear," said Isobel. "I seem to be able to hold a suitable pitch for my voice, especially when I am concentrating. Just don't ask me to sing. I tried it yesterday, and I sounded like a demented pig."

"Then you and I would be a match, Miss Isobel, for I cannot sing a note either. Last time I tried, even the cats ran away. Now here you are, put these on," said Mary. She handed Isobel a pair of long white gloves made of the finest buckskin leather.

"Oh, must I? I hate wearing these. They make my arms all sweaty."

"It is expected, Miss Isobel, so yes."

Isobel rolled her eyes but then made to pull on the gloves,

up and over her elbows. For her, it was another example of some of the negative aspects of the transition she had made. In truth, David had never really considered the restrictions that would be placed upon him on the occasion of becoming a lady of society. As a young man, he had been free to go wherever he wanted, whenever he wanted. Now a simple trip to a music shop involved elaborate planning, a chaperone, and at least one footman for protection.

Yes, these restrictions were a nuisance, but when she glanced upon herself once more in the mirror, she knew that it was worth every moment of the limitations placed upon her. Of course, should she remove her clothes to stand naked, she would look like some extraordinary mixture: woman from the neck up, man from the neck down. However, in her finery, she looked every inch the woman she knew herself to be, and even she had to admit that the long gloves added an element of elegance. Surely it was worth enduring a million of these restrictions so that she could remain so forever more.

"Come now, Miss," said Mary, "Lady Olivia will be waiting for you."

Olivia was sitting in the parlour, trying hard to quell her own nerves. That Isobel was ready to face the challenges of the evening she had no doubt, and in truth she had taken to every lesson like a duckling to water. Yet Olivia knew that there was still the possibility that someone might recognise her as David, Viscount Drummond, and the very thought of the scandal that would ensue had her on tenterhooks every moment of the day.

Olivia turned as she heard someone enter the room, and moments later, her mouth dropped open in abject surprise. Right from the start of this adventure, she had known that David would make a pretty woman. However, the young lady who had entered the room could never be described as merely pretty.

No, she was beautiful.

Dressed in a gown that flowed over feminine curves that any woman would be proud of, she walked with the grace and posture of a duchess. Her gorgeous red hair had been artfully dressed in a style that suited her to perfection, and her face had been ingeniously sculpted with powders and paints so that not even a hint of the boy was left behind. But without doubt the piece de resistance was the delicate opal necklace and ear bobs that served to emphasise the graceful lines of her neck and the subtle swell of her faux breasts.

"Oh Isobel," she gushed. "You look incredible, truly stunning."

A broad smile lit the young woman's face, and for a second, Olivia felt her breath catch in her chest, for the smile had transformed her face into one which might bring princes to their knees.

"Thank you, Aunt Olivia. And might I say how beautiful you look, too."

Olivia allowed herself a moment to preen, for in her come-out season she had been acknowledged as a *diamond*. Even now, many still considered her beautiful. Accordingly, she had dressed carefully, her gown of dark red velvet being more in keeping with her age, as were the feathers she wore in her hair. But something told her that even though Isobel was actually a boy, the woman she had become would outshine every lady that evening, even her.

If only she could maintain the disguise.

"So, darling, you have the looks down to perfection, but how are you feeling about this evening?"

"Oh, Aunt Olivia, it is almost as if I am living in a fantasy. You know, like being transformed into a princess, knowing that on the stroke of midnight, all will be revealed. I am nervous . . . so very, very nervous. But at the same time, I am so very excited, too. Irrespective of Lord Fairfax, this evening is everything I have dreamed of being able to do. I can only pray that I can pull it off!"

"Of that, Isobel, I have no doubt," lied Olivia. "Very well, Isobel. Let us go over what to expect this evening once more. As you know, when the guests arrive it is usual for them to congregate for drinks before dinner. Please do not drink more than one sherry, even if your nerves are threatening to get the better of you."

"Yes, Aunt."

"We will be taken around the room, probably by Charlotte, and introduced to the other guests. I am told there are to be forty for dinner tonight."

"Forty," squeaked Isobel. "I had thought it to be the duke and a few friends."

Olivia laughed, a throaty chuckle escaping her lips. "Forty *is* the duke and a few friends. I went to one dinner where there were close to two hundred in number. Anyway, as arranged, I am expecting Viscount Drummond to be in attendance, and I hope he might find it within him to escort you into dinner. "

"Mmm, yes," murmured Isobel. Her cheeks once more blushed a very rosy colour with the thought of that.

"Just make sure you don't consume too much wine," warned Olivia. "The duke's footmen tend to have a heavy hand when it comes to refilling a wine glass, and one can easily over imbibe without even knowing it. After dinner, the ladies will retire to the music room, leaving the gentlemen to their cigars and brandy. This will give time for the musicale part of the evening to be organised. I daresay you will not be the only one playing or singing tonight, so take your cue from the duchess as to when your turn will be. I have even heard that Madame Helena Hargreaves may be in attendance tonight."

"Who! The celebrated soprano? The one who starred in Mozart's *Marriage of Figaro* last season? Her fame reached even Edinburgh."

"Yes, the very one, although I am not absolutely certain she will be there."

"Oh, there is one thing I do not know, Aunt. What do I do with these blasted gloves?" Just for emphasis, she tugged one of them tight up around her slim bicep.

"A nuisance, are they not? At table it is permissible to slip them off. Most ladies lay them on their laps. You will, of course, have to put them back on, until you play that is. Now, do you have your music?"

For a moment Isobel looked a little sheepish, but then she smiled once more.

"I have no need of it, for I have committed each piece to memory," she said softly.

"You have?"

"Yes. I seem to be able to do so without much effort. My mother used to call it my special talent."

It was a little before eight in the evening when their carriage arrived outside of Camberly House. Unfortunately, it had taken longer than Isobel had thought it would, thus allowing her more time to grow in anxiety as they joined a queue of other guests arriving at the same time. Eventually they were greeted at the door of the carriage by a liveried footman who helped the ladies to alight before the butler took them through into a formal reception room, announcing them both as they entered. Immediately, Charlotte had appeared by their side.

"Lady Olivia, how wonderful you look."

"As do you, my darling," replied Olivia.

And to Isobel, Lady Charlotte did indeed look every inch the duchess. Her dress was of the finest deep blue velvet, and

The Making of a Lady

tiny crystals cleverly sewn to it sparkled in the candlelight. Her dark hair had been artfully dressed, and, as did Isobel, she wore a subtle application of cosmetics upon her face. But it was the jewellery she wore that took Isobel's breath. Around her neck she wore the most stunning and elaborate necklace of huge sapphires and diamonds, the stones of which matched the fabric of her dress and the crystals thereon.

"And you, Miss Munroe. Don't you look simply perfect! I knew that dress would suit you."

Isobel curtsied, taking a moment to compose herself, only then realising how hard her heart was beating.

"Thank you, your Grace," she said softly, making sure to modulate her voice. "But . . . but do you truly think so?"

Charlotte lowered her voice to barely a whisper. "I would not say it if I did not think it, Isobel. You look beautiful, and every inch the lady." To Isobel's surprise, she softly brushed Isobel's cheek with her gloved hand in the most motherly of fashions. "Tell me, how are you faring with Phoebe's tonic?"

Isobel grinned. "Oh, not too badly. I seem to be over the initial symptoms. I just wish the tonic would work a little faster, if you know what I mean."

"Oh darling, have a little patience," said Charlotte. "Phoebe might be a genius, but she is no miracle worker. Now, come, I have something to show you before I throw you to the wolves."

To Isobel's surprise, Charlotte linked her arm into hers and led her away from Olivia. Instead of moving into the reception, the duchess took her down a hallway and into a second room, closing the door behind them to ensure a modicum of privacy.

"There, what do you think?" asked Charlotte.

Astounded, Isobel gasped out loud. The music room was stunning, its high vaulted ceiling a profusion of sconces, plaster mouldings and painted panels. Mirrors adorned the wall, and in front of each sat ornate candleholders, the light coming from them giving welcoming warmth to the room.

However, it was not the room that had taken Isobel's breath away.

The moment that Isobel had walked into the room, her eyes had been drawn to a magnificent grand piano, its lid already propped open so that it was ready to play. It was the piano of Isobel's dreams. A stunning solid rosewood case announced it as a very expensive instrument, as did the ornate brass inlay that festooned its sides. The keyboard lid was also raised, and Isobel had the sudden urge to run her fingers across the polished mahogany and ivory keys.

"Is . . . is that . . . is that a . . ."

"That, Isobel," said Charlotte proudly, "is a John Broadwood grand piano. It is rumoured that there is one exactly like it in the Royal Pavilion in Brighton. I bought it especially for this evening."

"You did not!" exclaimed Isobel. "But it must have cost a small fortune."

"The perks of being fabulously wealthy in my own right, Isobel," said Charlotte. "So, do you think you will be able to do it justice this evening?"

Gracefully Isobel walked over to piano, her fingers coming to rest upon the ivory keys, searching for middle C. A single note rang out, its sound far richer in tone than anything Isobel had ever heard before. Turning, she looked at Charlotte with a radiant smile that did nothing but answer the duchess's question.

"Now, Isobel, tell me of you. How are you faring?"

Shyly, Isobel glanced at Charlotte, her hands now clutched before her, even though she had expected such an inquisition at some stage during the evening.

"I fare well, Lady Charlotte, I think. As you may imagine,

I find the whole of this event quite daunting, yet I am truly excited to be here. Being able to attend a function like this as Isobel has been a lifelong dream for me. I only hope I do not let you or Lady Olivia down."

"Nor shall you. Had I even a moment's doubt about that, I would not have asked you here this evening. Truly, what I see before me is quite remarkable, Isobel, for you make the most adorable young lady."

"Th . . . thank you, Lady Charlotte," said Isobel in a whisper. She could not help but smile broadly, for the duchess's comments had been made with sincerity, and Isobel's heart could do nothing but swell with happiness.

"Good. Now shall we return to my guests? I think it time to introduce you around."

Isobel followed the duchess into the reception, where Charlotte began to gently lead her around the room, introducing her to Lord and Lady this and Viscount that. In the main, it seemed to be husbands and wives, Viscount and Viscountess Farthingale amongst them. However, to one side of the room was a party of younger people, and it was to them that Charlotte led her next, her very presence commanding their attention as they approached.

"Isobel, let me introduce Lady Juliette Kirklees, Lady Georgia Richardson, Lady Felicia Farthingale, and Miss Francis Devon. We also have Viscount Stephens, Viscount Tremain, Mr Francis, and Mr Quentin. Ladies and gentlemen, this is Miss Isobel Munroe, our pianist for this evening. Isobel, these four ladies will be performing as a string quartet tonight. They will play first, followed by you."

For Isobel, the response of the group spoke volumes about what she would have to face if ever she entered polite society in a full and active way. In particular, Isobel felt her hackles rise as Lady Felicia Farthingale, whom she had briefly met in the music shop, wrinkled her nose as if she could smell something quite foul. In fact, judging by the look on Lady Felicia's face, the girl had every intention of treating her like dirt upon her shoe.

But if being introduced to four ladies of roughly her own age wasn't bad enough, all four gentlemen had turned their eyes upon her, more than one of them with a predatory look upon his face. Inwardly Isobel giggled, for she should have been mortified by their response. Instead, her heart gave a little dance of victory. By rights, she should have been running, running far, far away. However, every fibre of her being was rejoicing, for each and every one of these *gentlemen* was looking at her as yet another notch upon their bedposts . . .

. . . and was something that Lady Felicia had also noticed, if the expression on her face was anything to go by.

"Your Grace," said Lady Felicia. The girl spoke in a tone of voice that reminded Isobel of molasses being poured onto porridge, and she had little doubt Lady Felicia had done so in an attempt to garner attention from the duchess. "I heard a rumour that Madame Helena may be singing tonight. Is it true? Are we to be graced by the diva's presence?"

"Yes, she will be here later this evening, all being well," replied Charlotte.

To Isobel's delight, Lady Charlotte once more linked her arm into hers. Then she turned a little to subtly give Lady Felicia a cold shoulder. "Now, ladies and gentlemen, if you would excuse us."

As they walked away, Isobel clearly heard the ladies whispering to one another, and even though she could not make out all of what was said, she clearly heard the word "upstart" spoken by Lady Felicia. The duchess heard it too, for she leant towards Isobel's ear.

"Heed them not, Isobel. Ever since it has become known that I will be sponsoring you this season, Lady Felicia has shown herself to have a jealous streak as wide as the Thames.

She most probably sees you as nothing but a rival for this year's marriage mart, and one who is most definitely prettier that she. Now come, let me introduce you to the Duke and Duchess of Abingdon."

Towards one end to the grand room, Isobel could see another group of people standing and chatting. One was no less than the Duke of Camberly himself, who seemed to be in quite a jovial mood. Next to him stood yet another couple who, judging from their dress and demeanour, could only be the Duke and Duchess of Abingdon. Lady Olivia also stood with them, and she smiled encouragingly as they approached.

And stood next to her was no less a person than Lord Peter Fairfax.

Abruptly and without reason, Isobel froze, pulling back on the duchess as she did so, her heart practically leaping into her mouth. He looked magnificent in a dark tailcoat that hugged his broad shoulders to perfection, his hair cut short as was his style. Yet, in spite of this, the expression on his face was sombre and severe, suggesting that he would rather be anywhere else at that very moment.

"Oh God," she whispered under her breath.

The duchess, for her part, smiled confidently, and firmly pulled upon Isobel's arm, leaning into her to whisper her words of encouragement.

"It will be all right, darling. Trust me, you have nothing to fear. Come on, let me introduce you."

Somehow, Isobel found the courage to allow the duchess to lead her over to the group and watched on as Charlotte instantly caught their attention.

"Henry, Katherine, may I present Miss Isobel Munroe, the young lady I have been telling you about. Isobel, may I present the Duke and Duchess of Abingdon and their second son, Lord Peter Fairfax. And of course, you already know my husband."

Isobel curtsied deeply, her cheeks flaming red as she did so. She cursed herself for that, hoping that those around her would believe the cause to be the heat of the room and not the fact that she felt like casting the contents of her stomach all over Peter's highly polished Hessians.

"So is this the young lady you will be sponsoring, Charlotte?" said Katherine.

"Yes, indeed. She is the ward of my dear friend, Lady Olivia Hamilton, and whilst she is in her second season, this will be her first in London. I find this young lady quite enchanting, and as a consequence, I am, for once, really looking forward to the season."

"And where are you from, Miss Munroe?"

"From Edinburgh, your grace," said Isobel. Her voice was so soft that it was nearly inaudible, even to her. She coughed then and spoke with a little more conviction. "I had my first season there."

"And your parents?"

"They are both deceased," said Isobel. "My father was a gentleman, and owner and master of a schooner that went down in the south China seas when I was but eight years old. Mother succumbed to influenza last year. Mother and Lady Olivia were distant cousins, which is why she has agreed to take me under her wing."

"You are a most fortunate young lady Miss Munroe," said Katherine. "With Countess Hamilton on one side and the duchess on the other, you are certain to be at least engaged by the end of the season."

Again, Isobel felt herself blush, even more furiously this time, her mind once more cursing the pale skin that came with her red hair. Part of this came from the words that Lady Charlotte had spoken. But mostly it was a result of the statement that the Duchess of Abingdon had made. For, as the duchess had spoken her words, her gaze had not been on Isobel, but on Peter instead.

And how had Peter reacted?

Nervously, Isobel allowed her eyes to flicker towards him, not quite knowing what to expect from him. Interestingly, Peter returned her gaze. However, his expression could hardly be described as friendly. Instead, much to her intense disappointment, all Isobel could see in his eyes was a detached disinterest that suggest nothing but indifference.

When the invitation to the musicale had arrived, Peter very nearly declined. Part of him, a very large part at that, had decided that to go ahead with this venture would be fraught with danger. Unfortunately, his mother had caught wind of the invitation and had insisted that he be present, especially as both Lady Juliett Kirklees and Lady Felicia Farthingale would be in attendance. Neither of them were great beauties, but both came from respectable families along with substantial dowries, so he knew that his mother's resolve was just another way of putting him in front of a potential bride. So here he was, attending the musicale, his mind made up that he would not go ahead with this ridiculous undertaking.

Then David had entered the room, and to say that Peter was merely stunned would have been the understatement of the century. He had half hoped that David's appearance would be that of a mere facsimile of a woman. In his mind's eye, he had even imagined what would be the reaction of others at the gathering. She/he would walk into the room, whereupon someone would declare *egads, that is a man in women's clothing,* and that would be the end of it. A few minutes of uproar would occur, and then he could put the whole sordid business behind him, *never* having spoken a single word in public to the person in question.

But never had Peter been so wrong, or so glad that he had

been so.

David's appearance had been nothing short of astonishing. His lithe, elegant body was dressed in a beautiful emerald-green gown that did little to hide curves that any woman would be proud of, and his hair had been arranged in a fashionably feminine style. Whilst some might have frowned upon it had she been a young woman, he again wore cosmetics upon his face, subtly transforming it into one which could only be described as beautiful.

To nobody's surprise but his, the duchess herself had taken David by the arm to escort him around the room. Earlier, she had made it known to all that she would be sponsoring Isobel for the coming season, so it was quite natural for her to do so. However, this very fact had given Peter pause for thought. Did the duchess know? Surely she could not, for despite her obvious friendship with Lady Olivia, even a duchess would not risk her reputation by being associated with the likes of David. But as they wandered around the room, all seemed as it should be, the duchess treating her protégée as if she were a true diamond of the first water. That fact alone gave Peter cause to hope that the duchess had not a clue about David's true gender.

As the two of them circulated, occasionally stopping so that the duchess could introduce her companion to someone else, Peter discovered himself unable to take his gaze from David, even if he were forced to look out of the corner of his eye to do so. That he had fooled the duchess was clear, for he was truly remarkable in his disguise. He walked like a lady and held himself as a lady would. He greeted each person that he was introduced to with a perfect curtsey and could even been seen answering questions in what could only be a feminine voice. In short, the lady that David had become was simply charming, and it came as no surprise to Peter that the duchess had accepted her as such.

The Making of a Lady

Then, for Peter, something utterly bizarre happened, something which shocked him to the core. Keenly, he had observed the duchess introduce David to the ladies of the string quartet and to the gentlemen accompanying them. He was acquainted with all of them, especially Samuel Tremain and Justin Quentin, as they had all attended Eton at the same time. He knew them as gentlemen, and they had reacted to David as gentlemen would.

However, the same could not be said for Viscount Gregory Stephens.

The man was rumoured to be a profligate rake and in serious need of a favourable and profitable match. When David had been introduced to him, the expression on Stephens' face had told many stories, as had his actions. What could only be described as lust and avarice flickered across the man's eyes, and he had leered at David in such a way that a shiver of loathing had Peter nearly undone. But when Stevens had grabbed David's hand with the intention of bringing it to his lips, an inexplicably intense surge of rage and jealousy stopped Peter dead in his tracks. An insane need to protect David's honour then very nearly had Peter marching across the room to plant one on the man's nose.

That very thought frightened Peter to the core, as did his mother's reaction when David was presented to her.

When the duchess had brought David over to be formally introduced to his parents, his father had barely noticed, for he was deep in conversation with the Duke of Camberly. His mother, on the other hand, had taken a great interest in the girl David had become. Thankfully, it was more than evident that she had absolutely no idea that the person she was talking to was in fact a man, just as it was also obvious that his mother perhaps saw the young lady as a possible match for Peter. He, of course, knew everything, except perhaps how to react to David's presence. So he resorted to an age-old tactic that he had often employed in the army. As he had often done before, he schooled his face to make himself look vacant and disinterested, his mind not failing to register David's disappointment as he did so.

It took dinner being announced to bring Peter out of his reverie as the duchess clapped her hands to garner everyone's attention.

"Ladies and gentlemen," she began, "I hope that you will indulge my little idiosyncrasies when you go in for dinner. It occurred to me that, at every dinner I have attended recently, I have found myself placed next to the same two or three people. Whilst I dearly enjoy the company of my fellow dukes and duchesses, I thought it high time that we mix things up a little. As a consequence, there will be no order of precedence at table tonight. Instead, you will find your name on a place card indicating where you will sit, and I pray that you will take advantage of talking to someone different during tonight's meal."

There was a general hubbub of conversation and more than a few smiles as people stood and moved to enter the grand dining room. It was then that Peter saw Stevens move towards David, abandoning the musical foursome as he did so, much to the disgust of more than one of the ladies he was supposed to accompany.

"Miss Munroe," he said, as he came to stand before her, "may I have the honour of escorting you into dinner?"

The man's voice was obsequious and fawning, with him obviously believing that a mere *Miss* would be flattered to garner the attention of a Viscount. To Peter, it was more than evident that Stevens saw Miss Isobel Munroe as an easy target. Without thought, he instinctively reacted.

"Sorry, *old boy*," said Peter. "Miss Munroe has already accepted my arm."

He watched as David smiled, his whole face coming alive

as he did so. Peter offered his arm, and something inside him shivered with pleasure as he felt David slip his gloved hand into the crook of his elbow. Stevens, however, did not look at all pleased, especially when the *young lady* leant into Peter to whisper a thank you.

The dining room was awash with light. No less than three superb crystal chandeliers, each with twenty or more candles, cast their light into the room, accompanied by numerous candelabras and candlesticks upon the table. The table was magnificent. Each setting gleamed and glistened, candlelight reflecting from the solid silver and polished crystal. In a spirit of mirth and gaiety, guests circulated the room looking for their names, which had been carefully written upon a folded card. To Peter's relief and also to his disappointment, he did not find himself seated next to David. Instead, he found himself firmly between Juliette Kirklees and Lady Felicia Farthingale.

No doubt at his mother's insistence, he thought to himself wryly.

Fortunately, David seemed to have escaped the torture that Peter knew he would be forced to endure. Instead of being seated with the likes of Stephens and Quentin, David had been placed between the Duke of Camberly and Baron Gregson, a kindly man in his late sixties, whose wife now sat on the opposite side of the table and who was watching her husband like a hawk.

If it hadn't been for his companions, dinner would have been quite pleasant for Peter. Regrettably, both Miss Kirklees and Lady Felicia flirted mercilessly, droning on and on about where they had bought their gowns and which balls they were going to attend during the season, both of them making it blatantly clear that they would entertain courtship should Peter choose to pursue it. Whilst he answered politely, he showed no actual interest. Instead, when he could manage without appearing rude, he focused his attention upon David, who from time to time would raise his now un-gloved and very feminine hand so that he could giggle politely at some anecdote that the Duke had told him. Even Peter had to laugh when the Duke spoke to the whole table, recounting fondly the story of how the three-year-old son of his wife's companion, Phoebe, had burst into his office one day wearing nothing but a smile.

During the five courses of dinner, Peter observed David with as much slyness as he could muster, intrigued to learn how those around him would react to his presence. To his complete astonishment throughout, David conducted himself with the grace and dignity of a lady, not for a moment making even the slightest mistake that might give the game away. Even the duke thought him to be quite enchanting, if his ready smile and the twinkle in his eye was anything to go by.

When dinner was concluded, the ladies retired to leave the men to their spirits and cigars, and as he sipped at his brandy, Peter gave himself a moment to reflect. That David had fooled everyone into believing him to be a lady of quality was beyond question. In fact, it had been quite remarkable how feminine he appeared throughout the meal. Surprisingly, it was that vey thought that had his mind wandering back to the first time he had met David.

The Moonlight Club had been quiet that night, as he liked it to be. There had been few in attendance, and David had been standing nervously alone in the salon when Peter had approached him, seeing him for the effeminate man he was. The attraction they had shared had been immediate and intense. At the end of the evening, they had both slipped away to their own individual rooms, only for David to sidle through Peter's bedroom door unnoticed some twenty minutes later, as they had arranged. What had followed had been the most sublime night of his life, for David had proved himself to be everything Peter wanted in a bed partner. Soft and compliant, he had taken everything that Peter could offer and had then taken more, bringing Peter to the heights of pleasure that he previously not thought possible.

It was a final round of ribald laughter that dragged Peter from his thoughts. He watched the Duke of Camberly, now in his familiar position at the head of the table, stand. The other gentlemen stood too, so he followed suit to walk with them down the hallway and into the music room.

The room had been set up into something of an informal concert room. Scattered throughout the room were comfortable chairs, all arranged so that they pointed towards a magnificent grand piano, leaving no doubt to the audience as to why they were there. Sat to one side were four excited-looking young women, each holding a stringed instrument, two with violins, one with a viola, and one with a cello. Next to them, but apart, sat David, who was looking decidedly green.

On the other side of the room stood the duchess, who was deep in conversation with a well-dressed yet portly woman of about fifty years of age. The lady was unknown to Peter, but to him it was quite apparent that she was in something of an agitated state, for it was taking every ounce of diplomacy that the duchess possessed to placate the woman.

Eventually, once everyone was seated, the duchess held up her hand once more and silence descended within the room.

"Ladies and gentlemen," she began. "We will be having three performances tonight, the first our string quartet, the second a piano recital, and finally, I hope, a performance from Madam Helena Hargraves. First will be Lady Kirklees, Lady Richardson, Lady Farthingale, and Miss Devon who will play J.S Bach's *The Art of Fugue*."

To Peter's untutored ear, the four ladies played with more enthusiasm than ability and scraped their way through the piece in question. On occasion Peter found himself wincing a little when this violin or that viola screeched, and by the end of it he decided that the applause was more for them finishing than it was for their playing. Whatever, all four girls seemed inordinately proud of themselves as they curtsied to the room to the enthusiastic applause of at least one, Viscountess Farthingale herself.

Once more, the duchess stood. "Thank you, ladies," she said, "that was lovely. Now ladies and gentlemen, next to entertain is Miss Isobel Munroe, who is to play the piano. Her first piece will be Mozart's *Sonata in C major*. This she will follow with *Spring* from Vivaldi's *Four Seasons*."

For some reason, Peter felt himself sit up a little straighter in his chair as he watched David stand to walk over to the piano. Even if he had been aware of the circumstances, Peter's heart would have gone out to him, for his whole body was visibly trembling, and even in the candlelight he could see how pale he had gone.

What courage, he thought to himself.

In the peninsular wars, he had faced unspeakable horrors. He had watched the bravest of men turn and run and he had seen the most frightened become true warriors. But in his heart, he knew that what David was about to do equalled anything he had observed on the battlefield. For there he was, in the guise of a woman, about to sit under the scrutiny of some of the most influential members of the ton to play Mozart and Vivaldi.

The room hushed once more. Nervously, Peter watched David sit at the keyboard and adjust the stool so that he could reach the pedal beneath with his slippered foot. It was then that Peter allowed himself a wry smile as he noticed something quite extraordinary. Although Peter knew him to be a man, David's profile was everything that a young woman would want it to be. His red hair, whilst held in some kind of chignon at the back, had soft curls falling around his cheeks.

His lips were plump and his nose was small, and there was no sign of an Adam's apple that might have revealed his true gender. The dress he wore was modest but beautifully crafted, fitting so well that, in profile, Peter could even see the soft swell of breasts beneath.

Intriguingly, David had placed no sheet music in front of him. Instead, he sat and closed his eyes, his visibly trembling hands coming up to the keys in a posture that suggested he was about to start. Then he paused, and for the briefest of moments, Peter thought that stage fright might get the better of him.

Instead, David began to play, and the most sublime music filled the room. The first piece was lively and fun, and Peter observed the joy of playing wash over David's face, his head moving expressively in time to the music as all nerves seemed to have been forgotten. The second piece was far more technically difficult, yet David played the piece with passion and heart, his fingers flying over the keys, never missing a note despite the lack of sheet music.

"By God," whispered Tremain, who had somehow managed to sit next to him. "She is magnificent, is she not?"

As the final note drifted away into silence, David simply sat and stared forward at the piano, his hands folded neatly into his lap. It was then that the audience erupted into enthusiastic applause, forcing him to turn and stand, his face now glowing like the embers of a fire as he curtsied before them. And as David lifted his eyes once more, his piercing gaze locked onto Peter, somehow stealing his breath from him, and all he could do was return it with the broadest of smiles as he too applauded.

Strangely, as David started to move to the side to make way for Madame, the duchess stopped him, whispering something into her ear, only to have him nod in agreement before sitting once more before the piano. A footman appeared and placed some sheet music in front of him as the duchess once more held up her hand to ask for quiet.

"Ladies and Gentlemen. For our final performance tonight, it is my great privilege to present Madame Helena Hargreaves. Tonight, she will sing for your pleasure *Geme la Tortorella* from *La Finta Giardiniera,* followed by *Alleluia,* both of course by Herr Mozart. Unfortunately, Mr Mosley, her pianist, has taken fall from his horse this evening on the way here this evening."

"The fool was drunk again," said Madame Hargraves.

"Quite," the duchess said with a laugh. "Anyway, it appears he has broken his wrist and cannot play tonight. However, rather than disappoint, Madame Hargraves has requested that the lovely and, might I say, extremely talented Miss Munroe stand in for him, and I am pleased to announce that she has agreed to do so. So, without further ado, I would like to present Madame Helena Hargreaves, accompanied on the pianoforte by Miss Isobel Munroe."

Chapter Twelve

In the shadows of the trees opposite the duke's town house, a man stood and watched guests began to depart, as the rain, which had been threatening all day, started to fall.

"Fuck this," he said to himself.

William Drummond stared up into the sky and cursed loudly, every miserable fibre of him wanting to be anywhere but there. He turned up the collar of the heavy wool cloak that he wore, his mind wandering to the warmth of the inn at which he was staying and the buxom daughter of the innkeeper. But then another group exited the building opposite him, rapidly clambering into the coach that waited for them, forcing him once more to look through the spy glass he had brought with him.

What choice did he have but to do so? His uncle, the Earl of Falkirk, his Clan chieftain, had demanded that he go to London to find his cousin, David. Although rumours about the Earl and his son were rife, William had no real knowledge of what David might have done to incur his uncle's wrath. However, one thing was for certain. William knew the Earl to have a ready temper, but never before had he seen the Earl so angry as he had been on the day William had been dispatched to London

"Fuck David fucking Drummond," he whispered. "I'll give it three more fucking minutes." He groaned.

It wasn't as if he even knew the lad by sight. It had been nearly three years since they had last met, David having been a virtual recluse within his father's castle. All he really had to go on was his memory of the boy, a badly painted miniature portrait which now resided in his coat pocket, and a name, Lady Olivia Hamilton, Dowager Countess of Weybridge.

Just locating the countess had proved difficult. London was so different to Edinburgh, the locals treating anyone different with suspicion and mistrust. The kilt that he wore and his broad Scottish accent did little to help, either. However, from his throwing around a few coins that he could ill afford, a costermonger had eventually revealed the location of the Countess's residence, and Drummond had been watching it ever since, in the hope of spotting his quarry.

But to no avail.

Unseen for three days, Drummond had watched the countess's house, looking for anyone remotely close to the description of David. In truth, he had little idea of what David actually looked like. In vain, he had studied the miniature portrait of the lad, but David had been but fourteen when it had been painted, so it had proved next to useless. At times, the countess and her companion would come and go, always accompanied by at least one maid and one footman. He had even followed her coach that evening hoping that, just maybe, David would put in an appearance. However, the only men of a similar age to his quarry had turned out to be four young Sassenachs, none of whom even remotely resembled the miniature portrait.

Not known for his patience, the man groused to himself as the countess exited the duke's residence. With growing frustration, he watched on as the woman said her goodbyes to her hosts, and within moments she and her young companion had alighted their coach once more.

"Fuck this," he whispered to himself. "If only," he moaned.

His father, Baron Drummond, Laird of Kinross, had been born exactly three minutes after the Earl of Falkirk, his uncle. Three minutes had been all it had taken to demote *him* to the ranks, to make *him* the son of a nobody. On the other hand, David Drummond, his milksop of a cousin, stood to inherit everything — the title, the estates, and a twenty thousand fucking pound trust.

Turning, the man walked away into the darkness, pulling his cloak around himself against the cold of the night, knowing exactly what he was going to do when he finally caught up with David fucking Drummond.

Chapter Thirteen

Even though Isobel was mentally exhausted and physically drained, that night she hardly slept as every moment of the musicale replayed in her mind, over and over again.

With one notable exception, the entire evening had been a resounding success.

Once the musical part of the evening had concluded, Isobel had been *mobbed* by guests who had wanted to congratulate her on her playing. Madame Hargraves had even kissed her on both cheeks and pronounced her to be a prodigious talent. In fact, the only guests who had not spoken to her had been the *fantastic foursome,* who had studiously ignored her. Not that she minded that, especially when Viscount Stephens, Viscount Tremain, and Mr Quentin had all approached Olivia in her role as Isobel's guardian and had requested that they be allowed to call upon her! After all, whilst Olivia and Isobel both had absolutely no intention of allowing them to do so, their good opinion of her had served to bolster Isobel's self-confidence to heights unimagined.

Best of all had been the reaction of Lady Olivia, Dowager Countess of Hamilton. Seemingly, she had deliberately distanced herself from Isobel so that she could observe the reaction of others to her presence. Then, on the coach ride home, she had been like the proudest of mothers. Each moment had been dissected, critiqued and praised, the countess finding little to fault in Isobel's performance as a *lady*. In fact, she quite categorically stated that not a single person in the room appeared to suspect even a hint of subterfuge.

No, there had only been one sour moment in the whole evening and that had been Lord bloody Fairfax. With the exception of escorting her into dinner, something Isobel recalled with real excitement, he had hardly spoken a word to her. He had not congratulated her on her playing, nor had he indicated his intention to call. In fact, throughout the majority of the evening he had shown absolutely no interest at all. It was only in the coach, on the journey home, that Olivia had informed her of Peter's intention to call on the following afternoon. Seemingly, he had spoken to Olivia, without Isobel's knowledge, to seek permission to do so.

"Gor, it's like a three-ring circus downstairs this morning," said Mary. "I've never seen so much coming or going since the countess's daughter got married a couple of years back."

As Mary pulled back the curtains to allow the midday sun to stream into the room, Isobel stretched and sat up in her bed, her long red hair failing loose over her shoulders.

"What time is it?" she asked.

"A little before noon. Lady Olivia would like you downstairs in an hour for nuncheon. Then, I believe you have callers at two in the afternoon."

Isobel groaned at that thought and flopped back onto her pillow so she could pull the covers over her face. Despite the success of the evening, the last thing she needed was to be thrust even more into the limelight, especially if that limelight be before Viscount Stephens, Viscount Tremain, and Mr Quentin.

"Oh God! Tell me Mary, have I awoken the sleeping dragon? Have I made a monumental mistake in playing at the musicale last night?"

"Not from what Lady Olivia has told me. By all accounts you were a great success and were able to fool all and sundry. Not that I am surprised," said Mary. She came and perched on the side of the bed.

"What do you mean by that?" asked Isobel.

"Come and stand in front of the mirror and I will show you what I mean."

Throwing the bed clothes to one side, Isobel clambered out of her bed and walked over to the mirror dressed only in her night-rail.

"Go on . . . take a good look," said Mary. "Tell me what you see?"

"I'm not sure what you mean. I see me!" said Isobel.

"Well, what I think is this. Your hair is all mussed from your bed and you wear no cosmetics. Despite that, what I see is a very pretty and natural looking young woman . . . who incidentally used to be a boy. Were you to dress in boys clothing right this moment, I even believe that you would probably be taken for a girl, should you walk out of the house."

"Oh, I see what you mean!"

"It came as no surprise, therefore, that once you had put on your finery, you would have little problem fooling other members of the *ton*, Miss Isobel." Mary grinned as she pulled out a pretty day dress from Isobel's wardrobe.

"The countess also informed me that throughout the whole evening, she did not spot a single mistake in your deportment. She was most pleased with me, I can tell you, for teaching you what you needed to know. Now shall we get you dressed, Miss Isobel?"

Fifty minutes found Isobel skipping down the stairs. Moments later she entered the drawing room, only to stop dead in her tracks. The whole room seemed to be festooned with hothouse flowers, the heady scent of roses, bougainvillea and lilies almost too powerful to endure.

"Good heavens, what on earth?" said Isobel. With mild shock, she plonked herself down upon a chair.

"From all your admirers, Isobel," said Olivia. She had a

rather pleased expression upon her face that suggested to Isobel a cat that had just been given the cream. That she was pleased with the flowers sent to her protégé was more than a little evident. "That bunch is from Viscount Stephens, the other by it from Mr Quentin. The roses are from Madame Hargreaves as a thank you for stepping in last night . . . well done for that, by the way . . . .and the largest arrangement is from Charlotte."

Isobel grimaced. "The ones from Lady Charlotte and from Madame I don't mind, but those from Mr Stephens and Mr Quentin! Oh dear, what am I going to do about them?"

"Ah yes. I have a little confession about that," said Olivia. "Last night, the Duchess of Abingdon cornered me and quizzed me about you. I think she wanted to know if Peter were to take an interest in Miss Isobel Munroe, that she wouldn't turn out to be some sort of gold digger. I *might* have let slip that you have a dowry of five thousand pounds and a trust fund that would provide an income of at least a thousand a year."

"But I don't have a dowry of five thousand!" shrieked Isobel.

"Oh, I know that, but she doesn't. Besides, if needs be, Charlotte has already told me that she would advance you the five thousand against your trust fund. Anyway, I think Mr Francis might have overheard our conversation. Knowing him for the tattle he is, I am certain he would have reported the intelligence back to Stephens and Quentin, both of whom, I am reliably informed, are in sore need of a favourable match."

"God," moaned Isobel.

"No need to worry, though. If they become a nuisance, I will have the duchess have a word with the duke, who in turn will have a word with them. Besides, once it becomes known that you and Lord Peter Fairfax are courting, he should hopefully try his hand elsewhere."

"You mean *if* it becomes known, rather than when. He hardly endeared himself to me last night. I also notice that he has not sent flowers."

"No, I had noticed that too. Perhaps he still harbours some doubt as to the sanity of this plan we have. I am sure we will find out more when he calls this afternoon. Oh, and don't worry. I have sent notes to your other *potential suitors* to inform them that you will not be receiving visitors today."

"Thank God for that," groaned Isobel.

"Now, young lady, let us go over the ground rules for when David Fairfax comes a-calling, as he most surely will."

Theatrically, Isobel groaned yet again.

"Oh Isobel, you know perfectly well that young ladies of the ton have to do everything in their power to protect their reputations."

They both laughed at the irony contained within that simple statement.

"Anyway, it is of the utmost importance that you do nothing to attract further attention, and putting yourself in a compromising position would undoubtedly do that. Consequently, there are to be no unescorted trips with Lord Fairfax. You will take either myself or Mary to act as chaperone, and if needs be, one of the footmen to act as escort. When attending evening functions, you are to remain in the public spaces. No unplanned sojourns into the gardens or quiet room. I expect your *reputation* to remain squeaky clean."

"Yes, aunt," said Isobel, trying very hard not to roll her eyes.

It was then that there was a knock on the door and Cartwright let himself in with a curt bow.

"Lord Fairfax has arrived, Milady," he said.

"Good. Would you show him in please, and then ask cook to send up tea?"

"Yes, milady."

Peter had slept quite badly, his mind consumed with thoughts of one David Drummond, his confusion keeping him awake until the small hours of the morning. There was no doubt that, for the entire evening, David had presented himself effortlessly as the young lady he had fashioned himself to be. Even his mother had waxed lyrical about Isobel throughout the carriage ride home, praising her playing as well as her looks and deportment.

Yes, there had been no doubt that the whole evening had been a great success for *Isobel.*

But for Peter, the fact that David had been so successful in presenting himself as a young woman posed something of a dilemma. As the evening had progressed, it had become quite evident that David now thought of himself only as Isobel. Everything about him had become supremely feminine, from the way he dressed, to the way he walked, to the way he talked, to the way he held himself. And it was this very fact that had Peter extremely worried, for never before had he felt such attraction for a *woman.*

Astonishingly, there was also no doubt at all that Peter had experienced true attraction for the *girl.* Why, the simple act of her taking his arm to go into dinner had threatened embarrassment when his cock had stiffened within his trousers. Then, during the night, his dreams had been filled with a beautiful red headed woman, which had resulted in an erection so hard it was almost painful.

Even in the cold light of day, matters had not improved, for the moment he had walked into the countess's drawing room, his eyes had been instantly drawn to the young lady sitting next to her.

"Good afternoon," he stuttered as he bowed politely,

watching as David stood to return his courtesy.

"Good afternoon, Lord Fairfax," said Olivia. "I hope the day finds you well."

"Passably, Lady Hamilton. Anyway, I was hoping I might have a word with . . . with . . ." He suddenly stumbled over what name to use. He had wanted to say David, but it was blatantly obvious that the girl who sat before him was no David, for she was dressed in a peach-coloured day dress and looked as pretty as a picture.

"Isobel, my lord," said Isobel, answering for him. "My name is Isobel, and I would appreciate it if you call me by that and no other," she added, her tone of voice suggesting no argument.

"Yes, of course Miss Isobel. Anyway, I would request that I might have a little time for us to talk, Lady Hamilton, alone that is. I fear we have much to discuss."

Peter watched as the countess looked first at Isobel and then at him, almost as if she were trying to make her mind up as to whether she could trust them both together. Then she sighed theatrically and smiled a knowing smile.

"Well, I suppose that would be acceptable, given the circumstances. I will give you ten minutes. Isobel, I will be in the music room if you need me."

The room went strangely silent once the countess had exited, leaving Isobel sitting primly upon a chaise and Peter standing next to the fireplace, neither of them wanting to speak first. Unexpectedly for Peter, it was Isobel who eventually took the initiative.

"Be truthful, Peter. What did you think of last night?" she asked.

Boyishly, Peter grinned, thankful for an opportunity to be honest.

"I thought you to be incredible Da . . . er, Isobel. Your playing was simply sublime. As for the other guests accepting you as a lady, why, even my mother was extolling your virtues by the end of the evening. You definitely proved the point that you can function as Isobel in society."

"Oh!" Isobel grinned, heat suffusing her cheeks once more as she did so.

"So," said Peter.

"So," said Isobel. "So where does that leave things between us?"

"In truth, I am not quite sure," said Peter. "It is a dilemma I have struggled with all night. There is no denying that I find myself enamoured with you ... but I ... I erm ... I ... I shouldn't be."

Peter's voice cracked, his face red with embarrassment as Isobel turned her gaze upon him. But then he watched as sudden realisation flickered across her beautiful green eyes, an incredulous smile forming upon her lips.

"Oh, my goodness," muttered Isobel to herself before turning a piercing gaze back upon Peter. "You are attracted to me — the girl me, that is — and you feel as if you should not be. Is that it, Peter?"

"Yes," he mumbled, "and I know not what to think about it."

Isobel sighed, making Peter look even harder at her.

"Tell me, Peter," she asked. "What type of man do you prefer to take to your bed? Be honest, please, for your answer is of great importance."

"Someone like David," he instantly replied, not having even to think about his answer for one second. "Someone who is soft and gentle and compliant; someone who enjoys the fact that I like to take the masculine role."

"Well, nothing has changed there, for that is exactly the man I was and the *woman* I have now become."

That statement surprised Peter, for one thing was certain, and that was the person standing before him bore little resemblance to the young man he spent the night with all those weeks before. So how had nothing changed?

"What? I am not sure I understand what you mean."

"For the whole of my life, Peter, even from my earliest memories, I have truly believed that I have been cursed with the wrong gender, that I should have been born a woman and not a man. Had I been, I would have had no hesitation in finding a kind, loving man to marry, with whom I could raise a family. All my fantasies about the marriage bed involve giving myself to a man as a woman might, for in my mind and heart that is what I am.

"Now, thanks to Lady Olivia, I truly believe that I could live successfully as a woman without fear of discovery or ridicule. But the truth remains that beneath the finery, I am still a boy, the boy you so masterfully bedded that night as the Moonlight Club, and who will always be soft and gentle and compliant when with a man."

Her blatant honesty gave Peter pause for thought even if it did add to his confusion. There was no doubt in his mind that the night he had shared with David had been the most memorable of his life. But *he* was now a *she,* and the thought of that worried him intensely. Yet what she appeared to offer would solve so many of his problems, the first of which being he would not have to marry Lady Priscilla Weston or some such woman.

"So," said Peter thoughtfully, "perhaps it would appear that we are made for each other, after all. Outwardly, you are the sort of woman my family and society expect me to marry, whilst inwardly, you would be the lover I find myself wanting with a passion. Tell me. Does that mean you think we should somehow contrive to do so?"

"No, Peter, it does not," said Isobel emphatically.

Peter blanched at that, for it was definitely not the answer he was expecting. After all, was that not the very reason for them having this discussion in the first place, and wasn't he risking all to even contemplate a *marriage*? Surely the chit was not going to turn him down when he offered her . . . him . . . her the security of his name.

"What!"

Peter stared at the young woman before him.

Isobel appeared composed and confident, obviously secure in the fact that what she was about to say was nothing but the truth of the matter.

He held his breath.

"In truth Peter, I do not *need* to *marry* you, for on my one and twentieth birthday I will inherit enough money to make me financially independent for the rest of my life. Of course, I would love to have someone to share that life with, but honestly, I could never contemplate doing so on the basis of sex alone. So, for us to *marry*, there needs to be more than the physical attraction we have for each other."

"Love, you mean?" said Peter

"Yes, love," said Isobel. "That, and so much more. There has to be compatibility, companionship, a genuine friendship, too."

"And you think that two men can love each other; that we could grow to love each other and have all those other things between us."

"Yes, perhaps, but who knows?"

Strangely, the truth of what David had just said hit Peter harder that he had expected. He had never before contemplated love. How could he, when the partners he chose were men like himself? Yet he suddenly found himself yearning for what his sister had, for what his mother and father had, a loving partner with whom he could share his life. Unfortunately, there was still the ultimatum his father had given him.

"So, what do you suggest we do? You know I am required by my family to marry by the end of the season."

"What I suggest is that you officially court me. That, on so many levels, would achieve much. First and foremost, it would allow us to spend time together, to get to know each other properly and see if the prospect of *marriage* would suit. But it would also get off my back the likes of Mr Stephens and Mr Quentin, both of whom fancy their chances with one Miss Isobel Munroe, judging by the flowers they have sent."

Inwardly Peter grimaced, especially at the thought that other gentlemen might already have taken an interest in David. Not that he found it surprising, for David made a remarkable and very talented young lady, one who would shortly be in possession of a sizeable fortune. But then, he smiled and nodded his agreement. He also saw the wisdom in David's suggestion. He would court the woman David had become, get to know her, find out whether it would be possible for them to have a relationship without fear of scandal. Admittedly, it would be awkward should the story come out, but he could easily pass this off as her having completely fooled every other member of the ton as well.

"Yes. I will court you, David," he said.

"*No!* Not David. If this is to work, you must *only* think of me with a feminine gender, as Miss Isobel Munroe. On that I am final!"

"Very well, Miss Munroe," said Peter. He grinned again as he took a step closer to where she now stood. "But I have a request in return. Before we make our courtship public knowledge, I would like you to meet my sister, Alice, Marchioness of Cranleigh."

"Your sister? I did not know you had a sister."

For a moment, Peter thought back to the day on which his father had issued the ultimatum. As he had always done, he had turned to his sister, Alice, for support and guidance, and it had been her advice that had led him to David. Now, without any doubt in his mind, he knew that if he was to carry on

The Making of a Lady

with this courtship, it would have to be with her blessing.

"Yes, and an older brother too. However, of the two, Alice is most dear to me. Not only is she my best friend, she is my twin, and as a consequence we are closer than two peas in a pod. She is the only other person that knows of my preferences, if you know what I mean. It was she that suggested I see Lady Hamilton for her to arrange me a match of convenience. I would like to know that she is on our side in this matter, before we proceed."

"Would you want to tell her about me?"

"Perhaps. But take comfort in the knowledge that she has never once condemned me for the choices I have made in the past. I am certain she would keep our confidence if we have occasion to tell her."

"Very well then, we are agreed," said Isobel softly. "You will court me, officially, that is, and I will meet your sister openly."

"Good," said Peter.

"Then shall we seal our deal?" asked Isobel, her gaze now firmly locked upon Peter.

"I think we should."

Peter looked into Isobel's eyes, searching for any sign to suggest she had changed her mind about this, yet all he saw was the same need, the same want, that he felt in his heart. So, leaning forward, Peter gently kissed the woman who stood before him, adoring the touch of her soft lips upon his. He stepped closer and put his hands upon her hips as he deepened the kiss, feeling her snuggle into him, her arms snaking around his neck, her fingers threading into the back of his short hair. For the briefest of moments, their tongues danced together. And as they kissed, tiny moan slipped from her throat, the sound of which went straight to his manhood, and suddenly Peter realised that his heart now beating wildly in time with the woman he held in his arms.

It was then that a very loud cough came from the doorway, making them both jump as they snatched themselves apart with the sheepish look of school children caught with their hands in the biscuit jar.

"I see you have reconciled your differences," said Olivia, fighting to keep a smile from her face.

"Yes," replied Isobel, her hands covering the mortification that showed upon her cheeks. "Peter has agreed to formally court me."

"He has, has he? Well, perhaps next time you should bring flowers, young man," Olivia replied.

Chapter Fourteen

"Mary," shouted Isobel, "where is my reticule?"

"On the dressing table, Miss Isobel, along with your gloves and parasol," Mary called back. "Don't worry, you have plenty of time."

"I know, I know . . . but this is important," shouted Isobel, a note of panic in her words. "What about you? Are you ready?"

"Yes, Miss Isobel," said Mary.

As Mary rolled her eyes and emitted a theatrical sigh so huge that it could only have been designed to mock, Isobel stomped her foot like a petulant child. After all, today was the day that she was to meet Peter's twin sister, Lady Alice, Marchioness of Cranleigh, and the last thing Isobel needed was the bare faced cheek of her abigail. As it was, Isobel was nervous, so nervous that she had once more been sick after taking her medicine that morning. But then Mary grinned, a wide smile splitting her face, and it was all that Isobel could do to stop herself from grinning back.

As the day was set to be fine, the plan was to have a picnic in Hyde Park, where it had been arranged for Isobel to meet Alice and her children within an informal setting. She and Peter had discussed this at length, and they had agreed it to be the perfect opportunity for Peter, through Alice, to let the rest of his family know that he was formally courting Miss Isobel Munroe. At one in the afternoon, Peter would arrive to escort Isobel to the picnic, with Mary as her chaperone. Just that fact alone was enough to give Isobel palpitations. After all, even she knew the consequences of a single lady being escorted by an eligible gentleman, even if all the niceties were being observed. Should anyone see them together, as they surely would, it would be bound to set the gossip mongers a-gossiping.

"Oh God, oh God, oh God," mumbled Isobel. In a blind panic, she dashed around the room, only to be brought to a halt when Mary stood before her.

"Just stop for a moment," said Mary. Firmly, she put her hands upon Isobel's shoulders. "Take a deep breath."

Isobel did as she was told and instantly felt a little easier as she gulped in some air. Then she grinned as she glanced sheepishly at Mary. "Is my appearance satisfactory?" she asked.

Isobel had dressed in another of Lady Charlotte's gifts, a light summer dress that, yet again, appeared never to have been worn before. It was a pretty cream walking dress adorned with tiny blue primroses that had been embroidered by hand into the fabric. Mary had insisted on leaving her hair down so that long golden red curls hung artfully around her face and shoulders. A pair of short lace gloves, a pretty bonnet, her reticule and a parasol (as the sun threatened to be quite fierce) completed her outfit.

"Of course you do, Miss Isobel. Each day that goes by sees you becoming more and more feminine. I have absolutely no doubt that Lord Fairfax's sister will see you as such."

It was at that very moment came a soft knock upon her door. Mary answered it, revealing Cartwright standing there. In hushed tones, she spoke to him and then closed the door behind.

"Lord Fairfax is downstairs," she said, as she turned once more to Isobel.

"God, he's early," moaned Isobel.

"Then keep him waiting," grinned Mary. "I will go and

inform his lordship that you will be down shortly. Give me five minutes, and then come down."

Isobel stood, her hands clasped nervously together as Mary slipped from the room. Counting the seconds in her head, she once more moved in front of her looking glass, just as she had done so many times since arriving in Olivia's home. Still counting, she turned this way and that to view herself in the mirror. The dress she had chosen was perfect for a picnic, the skirts a little wider that usual to allow for ease of walking. The bodice itself was tight enough to show the swellings of her *breasts* too. For a second, Isobel fiddled with a loose curl of hair. But then she grinned as she decided how much she liked the look of having her hair loose, especially with the way it draped artfully over her shoulders and down to her breasts.

"Six hundred," she whispered to herself. Turning, Isobel gathered her things and then slipped out of her room.

When Isobel approached the top of the stairs, she paused for a moment to collect herself, for her heart was now pounding with excitement and apprehension. Mary had made her practice endlessly, for walking gracefully down a flight of stairs was not an easy thing to do in a long dress. As she had been taught, Isobel placed one hand upon the banister, her other hand holding her skirt a fraction so that her toes poked out from underneath the hem. Isobel knew she was not allowed to look down at her feet so, as she began her descent, she pushed her shoulders back and held her head high, gracefully and slowly taking one step at a time. Only then did she allow herself to look down at Peter with her eyes, her heart threatening to burst as she saw him waiting for her. He looked gorgeous. He was finely dressed in tailcoat, waistcoat, and breeches, his hessians polished to a gleam, and in one hand he held a large bouquet of flowers, what seemed to be a mixture of camellias in pink, red, and white. But best of all, he was standing at the base of stairs, a look of awe upon his face as he gazed up at her.

"Isobel . . . erm . . .oh wow! These, these are for you," he stammered as Isobel reached the bottom of the stairs. "You, er, look wonderful, Miss Munroe."

Not knowing who was blushing the most, Isobel took the proffered bouquet. The giving of flowers was a simple gesture, but for Isobel, it suddenly made her feel so incredible feminine. So she put the flowers to her nose and inhaled delicately, savouring the gentle scent, the blooms covering the pure happiness upon her face. Then she looked deep into Peter's eyes. A broad smile emerged on her face as she did so, and she watched as his mouth dropped open wide, his own eyes showing a combination of admiration and lust that set her heart pounding once more.

"Thank you, my lord, they are beautiful. I am glad to see you remembered," she said. Turing upon her heels, she handed the bouquet to Brenda, the downstairs maid who had been hovering in the entrance way.

"How could I not, after the way the countess remonstrated with me? Now, are you ready?" he asked casually as he held out his arm to her.

Isobel took his arm, and side by side, Peter led her from the house with Mary following discreetly behind. The sun was bright and at first dazzled her as they left the building, so much so that she did not see the coach that Peter had arrived in. In her mind, Isobel had expected a hackney to take them to the park. How wrong she had been. Once her eyes had adjusted to the light, the truth of it made her gasp out loud.

"I borrowed it from my father," said Peter. "That man up there, in the driver's seat, is Jenkins."

Parked by the side of the road was a magnificent barouche, a four-wheeled carriage, both heavy and luxurious, with two equally magnificent coal-black horses harnessed to it. It had a soft collapsible half-hood that had been raised as protection from the sun, and to the side of the gleaming black carriage was a short door on which was painted the ducal coat of arms. It was to there that Peter led Isobel.

"I'm afraid your maid will have to sit up there with Jenkins," he said, nodding his head towards the driver's seat. "Even though this is a four-seater, there is only room for two in the back."

Isobel looked at Mary, who grinned back at her, indicating her approval. That was, until she herself gave a little shriek. Despite an obvious limp, Jenkins had stepped down from the high driving platform, and before anything else could be said, he had effortlessly lifted Mary up into the air and onto the seat next to his. Isobel could only splutter with laughter as she watched her maid blush furiously, a silly grin plastered across her face.

"And who are those for?" Isobel asked. Peter had offered his hand, and as she clambered up into the carriage, she noted the parcels and a large picnic hamper upon the backward-facing seat.

"The picnic is for us, the parcels for my niece and nephew. They would never forgive me if I did not turn up with a gift or two," said Peter. The springs of the coach dipped a little as Peter climbed in to join her. He settled into the seat next to Isobel, making sure he kept a respectable distance from her as he did so.

Hyde Park was still relatively quiet when they entered. For that, Isobel was grateful, as during the journey, Peter had pushed back the canopy so that they could be seen together. Had Peter been sat opposite her, perhaps she would not have felt so vulnerable. But even she knew that to have him sit next to her in the barouche would certainly have tongues wagging, should anyone see them. So she sat still and tried to look pretty as she placed her parasol over her shoulder to shade herself from the sun, knowing that Peter had pulled down the canopy for this very reason.

Soon they were coming to a stop on the road that wound its way through the park, and for a few moments, Isobel sat to compose herself, her gaze darting everywhere as she looked for any possible threat of exposure. It was a beautiful spot for a picnic, with green lawns next to the Serpentine surrounded by lush green trees. A little distance away, under the canopy of a large oak tree, a beautiful woman sat upon a cashmere rug. In her arms was a babe, wrapped up in a fine knitted blanket, whilst behind her two children played a game of blind man's bluff with a young woman who was obviously their nursemaid.

Alice sat on the rug that had been spread out on the grass and sighed. Richard and Caroline were happily playing with Stephens, the nurse, and in her arms was the bundle of joy that had arrived but three months previously, Jamie. The sun was shining, and it was beautifully warm as they prepared for the picnic by the banks of the Serpentine.

Yet Alice still bore a considerable amount of trepidation.

Peter had visited her on the previous afternoon with the news that he had found the girl to whom he intended to be married. His call had left her more than a little perplexed. She had expected him to be morose, almost depressed at the prospect. However, much to Alice's surprise, Peter had been apprehensively excited by the prospect, especially when he explained that the lady was the very same Miss Isobel Munroe her mother had talked about incessantly since attending the musicale at the Duchess of Camberly's home. In fact, Peter had been so keen to introduce the girl to her that she had actually agreed to attend a picnic, reasoning it to be a good suggestion for getting the children into the fresh air.

As the ducal carriage pulled up, Alice felt her heart

suddenly ratchet up a few beats. Jenkins, her brother's man, was seated in the driver's seat next to a young lady, and both were smiling broadly. She watched as he jumped down, mindful of his wooden leg, but before he could reach the carriage door, Peter had also stepped down. Strangely, he had a warm and affectionate expression upon his face.

Like the gentleman he was, he turned and then extended his hand to help a beautifully dressed young woman alight from the coach. Instantly, her maid came to her, accompanied by Jenkins, and for a moment the girl fussed over her mistress, making sure her long red hair lay perfectly around her shoulders. As for Peter, he leant back inside the carriage to reappear with two large, wrapped presents and a picnic hamper, all of which he handed to Jenkins.

With a curious and thoughtful eye, Alice stared at the young woman. Even though she could not be called a diamond of the first water, she was most definitely pretty. She was young, perhaps one and twenty years of age, and was tall and willowy in stature, her gorgeous long red hair having been carefully styled around her face and secured beneath a pretty bonnet. The girl was expensively attired, too. She was attired in a fine muslin walking dress that Anne recognised as one of Madame LeClerc's creations, and over her shoulder, as protection from the sun, she carried a delicate parasol. There was an elegance about her also; just the way she took Peter's proffered arm to walk gracefully by his side suggesting she had been raised as a lady.

It was at that very moment when two balls of energy came hurtling towards them, screaming with excitement. Richard arrived first, as he was older and had longer legs although little Caroline was not far behind, both of them flinging themselves at their uncle, only to be swept up into his arms to be swung around.

"Uncle Peter, Uncle Peter. Have you brought us a

present?"

"Richard!" said Alice. "Mind your manners!"

Her son turned to look at her, his face now a little sombre from her chastisement. But then he grinned once more as Peter ruffled his hair and leant down to whisper something in both the children's ears, sending them scurrying over to Jenkins. Then he approached, once more with the lady's arm tucked under his own, and Alice found it hard not to miss the nervous smiles that played across both their faces.

"Alice, may I present Miss Isobel Munroe. Miss Munroe, this is my twin sister, Lady Alice Forbes, Marchioness of Cranleigh."

Alice smiled as the young woman curtsied, but she did not stand herself.

"Do excuse me from not getting up Miss Munroe, but I have just got Jamie off to sleep and do not wish to disturb him. Please sit," she said as she indicated the rug.

Alice could hardly take her eyes from the girl. There was a moment of awkwardness as she took herself down onto the rug, almost as if she were uncertain as to what to do with her skirts. But eventually she settled, tucking her legs beneath her, the skirt of her dress neatly covering her legs and feet. It was then that Alice noticed the girl's hands trembling, a true indication of how apprehensive she must feel, and she reacted instinctively as she saw the girl's eyes flicker towards her baby.

"Would you like to hold him, Miss Munroe?" Alice asked, nodding towards her sleeping son.

For a second Alice saw the fear and panic that flickered over the girl's face. But then she seemed to school her expression and simply nodded her assent. Very gently, Alice passed over her child, noting the girl's awkwardness until she found a natural position to cradle the baby. For a second Jamie fussed, and Alice thought him about to cry. Then he settled, his eyes firmly closed as his tiny cupid's bow of a mouth moved up and down, almost as if he was suckling at his mother's breast.

"Oh my," said Isobel, her eyes completely focused upon the baby. "He is so beautiful."

"I think so," said Alice, "but I am allowed to do so, as I am his mother and am totally biased. Now come, Miss Munroe, you must tell me all about yourself. Are you really Herr Mozart's successor, as my mother claims you to be?" she said. Alice kept her voice light, a note of humour in her voice to gently tease the girl.

"She plays beautifully, "said Peter, a little more forcefully than was necessary.

Intriguingly, Alice noted how Peter had instantly come to her defence. What was more fascinating was that he had *actually* placed himself right next to her upon the rug, their bodies almost touching, despite the impropriety of doing so.

"I play passably well, Lady Forbes," said Isobel

"No. Not Lady Forbes. My name is Alice, and I shall call you Isobel."

"Thank you, Alice. Anyway, I was fortunate that as a child my mother was able to teach me. She was a prodigious talent herself, although she only played for her own amusement. However, I have had no formal instruction, so do the best I can."

"A best that surpasses every other young lady I have heard play," said Peter.

Alice felt her mouth open in shock until a fraction of a second later she got control of herself and shut it again. For this was not at all how she had expected Peter to behave with the girl. Knowing what she knew about her brother and his intentions towards his *bride*, she had believed that he would be distant and aloof with her. However, the way he had now twice felt the need to offer his support suggested more than a casual relationship between the two, and this merely served to compound Alice's confusion.

"Now let me introduce you to my other two reprobates." said Alice. "Richard, Caroline, come over here," she called.

The two children obediently did as they were told, the little boy clutching the makings of a magnificent kite, the little girl grasping a beautiful wooden doll that had surely cost a small fortune. Both children came over to sit on the rug, Richard by his uncle's side and Caroline upon her mother's lap.

"You spoil them, Peter," said Alice.

"An uncle's prerogative, and yes, before you ask, they have said their thank-yous."

"Children, this is Miss Munroe. Miss Munroe, my children, Richard and Caroline."

"It is wonderful to meet you both," said Isobel kindly. Her eyes at last came away from the babe she still held in her arms, and she looked up and smiled at the children. However, she had to hold back a giggle, for as she glanced at them it was to see that their attention was most definitely not upon her.

"Will you help me make my kite, Uncle Peter?" said Richard.

"I'm hungry, Mama," said Caroline at exactly the same time.

"Perhaps, then, it is a good time to have luncheon," said Peter. "Then, of course I will help you make your kite, Richard, and if the wind is strong enough, we might even fly it."

Almost as if by magic, things began to happen once those words had been spoken. Jenkins and the footman who had accompanied Lady Alice delivered the large basket. Miss Munroe's maid, aided by the nursemaid, quickly and efficiently laid out plates of sandwiches and pies and cold cuts of meat, along with newly baked strawberry cream cakes and bottles of freshly made sweetened lemon juice. It was a veritable feast that had the children's eyes opening with delight.

The Making of a Lady

Once luncheon had been laid out, the nursemaid came over to relieve Isobel of her burden. Interestingly, as Nurse took little Jamie from her, Alice observed an unmistakeable expression of disappointment flicker across the girl's eyes. A second rug was thrown a few yards away, where another smaller basket was produced and where the servants now sat in amiable company to eat their own meal.

The conversation, as they ate, was light and relaxed, the children dominating the conversation with their chatter about the school room and all the wonderful adventures they got up to with their mama and their papa. As Alice made sure that the children ate their sandwiches before the cream cake, she took the opportunity to surreptitiously observe the couple that sat before her, noting quite clearly how their behaviour most definitely did not match what she had expected.

Every moment or two, Isobel would glance at Peter with a nervous smile upon her lips, obviously seeking his approbation. At first, she had been quiet, almost bashful in demeanour; that was until Caroline unexpectedly moved to sit upon Isobel's lap, probably so that she was closer to the strawberries, which were a particular favourite of hers. Isobel seemed to come alive at this point, giggling and whispering in her ear as she pretended to steal a strawberry or two, much to Caroline's delight.

But what surprised Alice the most was Peter's behaviour towards the girl. Just like she looked at him, Peter would glance occasionally at Isobel. But instead of the detachment that Alice had expected, there had been nothing but admiration in his eyes. She had thought that he would be angry and frustrated at being forced to choose a bride. Instead, despite the touch of nerves he seemed to display, he seemed perfectly happy and relaxed and more than a little enamoured with the girl.

No, this is definitely not what I expected.

Once lunch was over, a drowsy Caroline was taken by her nursemaid and placed next to the baby under the shade of a large parasol, where she promptly fell asleep, cuddling her new doll. Peter went off with Richard to make the kite, but not before looking back at his sister to tell her he was deliberately leaving Isobel alone with Alice. Alice almost laughed out loud, for there was more in his expression too, a narrowing of the eyes that told her to treat the girl kindly. Alice was having none of that.

"So, Isobel, tell me," she said, going straight for the throat. "Did Lady Hamilton explain to you the conditions placed upon marriage by my brother?"

She heard Isobel gasp, and watched as the girl fought to hide her embarrassment.

"Yes. She has told me that it would be a union of convenience only," said Isobel.

"So, pray tell me. Just what the hell is going on between you two?

For a second, Alice thought the girl was going to flee. The look of fright in her eyes certainly suggested it. But again, there was that flash of steel that suggested there was much more to this girl than met the eye, a strength of character that she would surely need if she were to enter into matrimony with Peter. Yet Alice desperately needed to know what was going on between them, especially as she knew unequivocally that Peter could never fall in love with such a girl.

"Peter and I . . . we have a certain regard for each other, Lady Alice. Even though I understand the terms of the proposed marriage contract, I would hope that, in time, we could get on quite amiably should we marry," said Isobel.

"Be clear, Miss Munroe, that my brother and I keep no secrets from each other. In fact, it was I that suggested he engage the services of Lady Hamilton to find him a wife who would be content in a marriage of convenience. But I have to ask,

Isobel. Why? Why settle for my brother, who might never give you the family I am certain you desire, judging by the way you behave towards my children. My mother tells me you are in possession of a handsome dowry. So why not hold out for a better match?"

Again, Alice watched the girl. This time her answer was immediate and clearly instinctive, her cheeks blushing furiously as she spoke.

"Whilst I am, Lady Alice, in possession of a sizeable dowry, I am no member of the ton. Someone in my position, the orphan child of a mere gentleman, could hope for no better match than your brother. Peter has offered me a title, a home, and the chance to be mistress there. Besides, I truly lov... er... care for him, Lady Alice," she blurted. "He is the only one for me, whatever that brings me."

"Yet I would still counsel you to think carefully about this match, Isobel. Are you prepared to love him and not have that love returned; to forgo the possibility of having children of your own?"

"I am," she replied simply.

"Very well," said Alice, somewhat tersely. "But know this, Miss Munroe. I am very protective of my brother and want nothing more than to see to his happiness. But I have to voice my concern. You are obviously an accomplished and intelligent young lady who could do so much better than a marriage of convenience. In truth, I feel sorry for you. Whilst I know it is the way of the ton, I am angry that you feel the need to sacrifice your own happiness for the sake of a home and security."

Later that evening, Peter found himself once more with his sister, this time alone in the library of her own town house. He had thought to leave this meeting for a few days, but impatience had gotten the better of him and he was desperate to know what Alice thought of Miss Isobel Munro.

Alice, he soon discovered, was not happy.

"I don't know how you can do this to that poor girl," she snapped.

"What?" asked Peter? He tried to suppress a grin, for this was most definitely not what he had expected his sister to say. "Was it not you who suggested that I find such a lady to marry?"

"Yes, but not to someone such as Miss Munroe! She is no vacuous, simpering socialite, with not enough brains to understand the situation you place her in. She is obviously intelligent, accomplished, and more than pretty enough to snare a proper catch, especially with the dowry she has. On top of that, the way you behave towards her has clearly made her fall in love with you."

That caught Peter totally off guard.

"You think that she loves me?"

"The girl is unquestionably besotted," said Alice vehemently. "But no, Peter! No! I will not allow it. I will not allow you to marry this girl, for to do so would surely break her heart. I insist, Peter! I insist you break off this courtship before it goes too far. Find someone else instead."

"But what if I love her?" said Peter softly.

"Now who is being ridiculous? We both know that is impossible for you."

Inwardly, Peter smiled. Throughout the afternoon, his admiration for Isobel had grown out of all proportion. The children had loved her, especially after she agreed to take part in their games after lunch. His sister had clearly been impressed, too, and showed absolutely no indication that she thought Isobel to be anything but an eligible young woman. Now, after what Alice had said, he was absolutely certain that she did not suspect.

Time to 'fess up, Peter, time to 'fess up

The Making of a Lady

After the picnic, once they had said their goodbyes to Alice and her family, he had taken Isobel for a walk around the Serpentine. As they walked, with Mary and Jenkins a respectful distance behind, he had explained to her how, when he had been but a young man, Alice had divined the truth about his true nature. He spoke of the tears and the anguish they had shared and of the love and support that his sister had offered. But most of all he had convinced Isobel of the trust that he had in his sister.

And it was at this point that Isobel had agreed, nay insisted, that he tell his sister the truth.

"Why would this be impossible Alice?" he asked softly.

"Because *she* is a *she*, you idiot," roared Alice.

Peter grinned.

"But what if she is not a *she* after all?" he replied simply. "What if *she* is, in fact, a *he*?"

Chapter Fifteen

"Charlotte," said Olivia. "Oh, darling. How wonderful!" she added, as she pulled the duchess into a deep hug. It was no ordinary hug either for, as they found themselves alone together, they both felt free to embrace each other lovingly.

"I thought I would pop by to see how things progress with Isobel," said Charlotte. She perched herself upon the settee placed before the fireplace and then proceeded to divest herself of her gloves.

"Things progress better that I could possibly have hoped for," grinned Isobel, "with perhaps the exception of Lord Fairfax's twin sister, Lady Alice. It seems that Lady Alice and Lord Peter are very close, and that she knows all about his sexual proclivities. So, when his parents demanded he marry, it was she who suggested he use my professional services to find him a potential wife, one who would be content in a marriage of convenience."

"I see," said Charlotte, a mischievous smile upon her lips.

"Only Lady Alice was not quite expecting the person I chose for him," said Olivia. "Seemingly, she was furious with Peter that he had chosen a lady with much potential. You know, she actually demanded that he break the courtship so that Isobel would be allowed to find a true love match with some other gentleman. So, in the end, with Isobel's agreement, Peter chose to share the truth with her. She was not best pleased, to say the least."

"I can understand that. Perhaps if I had a word with her,"

suggested Charlotte.

"No need, I think. She came to see me, you know. She is very protective of her brother and demanded I put a stop to all of this. Somehow, I managed to persuade her that she should allow the courtship to follow its natural course, for at least a few days more. I used the argument that as Isobel had fooled the entire ton, Peter's reputation would remain intact should anyone discover the truth about Isobel. Then, two nights ago, Peter accompanied Isobel to the opera and shared a box with his sister and her husband. By all account, Isobel's performance as a lady was so exemplary that Lady Alice definitely showed signs of relenting in her opinion."

"Yes. Isobel is quite remarkable, is she not? Oh, and talking about Isobel, Phoebe has sent another batch of her medicine. My footman has it."

"How is Phoebe?" asked Olivia.

"Very pregnant. Samson demanded that she go home for her confinement, so she has returned to Thorpe Hall. As for Samson, he is like a bear with a sore head waiting for the arrival of his second child. Now," said Charlotte, "where is Isobel? I have something I wish to discuss with you both."

"She is where she can usually be found at this time: practicing on the pianoforte. Come, I will show you."

Isobel was so obviously lost in the piece she was playing that when Olivia and Charlotte entered the room, it hardly registered. Instead of interrupting, they stood listening until the final notes drifted away into nothingness. Only then did Isobel turn, jumping to her feet so she could curtsey to the duchess.

"Oh, no need for that, darling, when we are alone," said Charlotte. "How many times have I told you that?"

"Lady Charlotte," Isobel said with a grin. "How lovely to see you."

"Isobel, would you come into the sitting room? Charlotte

has something she wishes to discuss with us."

Moments later, all three were seated, a tray of tea and scones delivered by Mary. At first they sat politely, until Charlotte dipped into her reticule to pull out two gold embossed invitations.

"It is to be the fifth anniversary of my marriage to the duke in a sennight's time," she began. "In celebration, we are to hold a summer ball. I would love it if you could both attend. Be it known, I have also extended an invitation to the Duke of Abingdon and his entire family, Lord Peter included."

"That is wonderful, Charlotte. I had forgotten your anniversary. We would both be delighted to accept, wouldn't we, Isobel?"

"Yes, thank you Lady Charlotte, I think!" said Isobel.

"Secondly, as is customary before the season gets into full swing, I like to spend a week or two at Thorpe Hall. Thorpe Hall is my country estate, Isobel. It is my intention to do so after the ball, and I would also like to invite you both to accompany me. It will be something akin to a house party. With a little luck, my stepson Richard will be there with his family, although my stepdaughter, Anne, may not attend, for she too is about to enter her confinement. Oh, and I thought of inviting Lord Fairfax as well."

Isobel's mouth dropped open wide with that. The thought of having an opportunity to be out of the London limelight for a while was immensely appealing, but to do so with Peter!

"But," spluttered Isobel. "Do you not mind that he and I are beginning to form an attachment? After all, he is . . . and I am . . ."

Isobel looked away with abject embarrassment. This had been a question that had been burning through her mind for some time. It was one thing for Charlotte to support her transition from man to woman, but to accept that she might also form a relationship with another man was a whole other matter. Still, she had to know, had to ask.

Charlotte returned her gaze with equal seriousness.

"As far as I can see, Miss Munroe, you are a lady, and he is a gentleman. What is more natural than for the two of you to form a *tendre* for each other? Besides, I am firm in my opinion that everyone deserves happiness in life, however that is brought about. So no, I do not mind in the least, Isobel."

It was all that Isobel could do to stop herself bursting into happy tears. Instead, she beamed at Charlotte, a smile so bright it could have illuminated even the most misty of evenings.

"Now, last but not least," continued Charlotte, "I have arranged for both of you to visit my modiste, Madam LeClerc, for ball gowns to wear to my little shindig. I will truck no argument on this either, for I cannot have my best friend and the lovely young *lady* I am sponsoring to be shabbily dressed."

Chapter Sixteen

William Drummond sat alone in his meagre lodgings, knowing the night ahead would probably be his last chance at finding his cousin. Every avenue he had so far tried seemed to have come to naught. He had tried to bribe officials in London harbour to see if the boy might have taken passage to some foreign clime. He had trawled through London, visiting every gentleman's club he could think of. Yet, despite having spent an inordinate amount of blunt buying yet more drinks, no one seemed to have even heard of Lord David Drummond, let alone seen him.

Now the only lead that remained was the Dowager Countess Hamilton herself.

He had considered approaching the countess directly, but even with the little he knew about her, he doubted she would be forthcoming with any information. Then two nights before, his luck had finally turned for the better. Having no better idea, he had followed one of the countess's footmen to a tavern and had bought him several drinks. At first, the man had been seriously tight-lipped. However, as the evening progressed and as the ale started to loosen the man's tongue, he had let slip that the countess would be attending a ball and that her servants would probably be loaned to the Duchess of Camberly for the very event.

His plan was simple. He would wait until the countess and her companion left for the ball. Then he would break entry to her house whilst all was quiet. He would search her office, make it look like a robbery perhaps, maybe even steal some blunt to supplement the meagre amount of coin left in his purse. Of course, his real goal would be to find the evidence he needed, the information that would lead to the whereabouts of David Drummond.

His instructions had been clear. Find the brat and then return him to his father. But now, he had absolutely no intention of doing so. Instead, once he *had* found his cousin, the lad would be made to disappear for good, buried in some shallow grave deep in some forgotten woods with a pistol ball through his brains. Only then would the way be clear for *him* to become the man he was destined to be—his uncle's only remaining relative, and eventually, the Earl of Falkirk.

Chapter Seventeen

"Your bath is ready, Miss Isobel," called Mary from around the dressing room door.

Isobel was stood in the one place that Mary usually found her: in front of the mirror. As was her habit, Isobel seemed to spend an inordinate amount of time before the looking glass, not through vanity, Mary supposed, but in an effort to convince herself of her ability to maintain a feminine guise. It was almost as if she could not believe who she had become and needed to look at herself regularly in order to do so. That thought always made Mary smile.

"Coming," called Isobel.

Mary watched as Isobel entered the dressing room, where the copper bath of steaming hot water was waiting for her. Without any embarrassment, she lifted her arms and stripped out of her chemise to then unwind the muslin bandages wrapped around her middle. For a moment she paused to test the heat of the water with a hand, giving Mary a clear view of the tiny swellings on her chest that were a hint of what was to come. Even thought there was yet no size, she was definitely fleshier there, her areola having darkened, and her nipples having grown somewhat. Without further ado, Isobel then stepped into the tub and eased her body down into the scented water.

"Oh, that is good," she sighed. She dipped her head beneath the surface to completely wet her hair, spluttering a little from the water that covered her face.

"Would you like me to wash your hair for you, Miss

Isobel?" called Mary

"Please. I love it when you do that."

Mary grinned and reached for the bottle that contained Miss Phoebe's magic soaps, noting that the bottle was almost empty and making a mental note to ask her for more. Then, coming to stand behind her mistress she poured a generous amount of scented soap into her hand and began to massage it into Isobel's hair. The girl practically purred with pleasure.

"Do you know, Miss Isobel," she said, "even your hair seems longer and glossier than it did before you started taking Miss Phoebe's medicine."

"I know. And is it not remarkable that hair seems to have stopped growing everywhere other than on my head?"

"That might also have something to do with the salve we put on your skin each evening too," said Mary. Isobel leaned her head back as Mary poured a jug of clean water over Isobel's head to cleanse it of the soap. "There, you will do. You dry yourself, Miss Isobel, and I will ready your room."

Mary was busying herself around the bedroom when Isobel re-joined her, a robe covering her body, a towel wrapped around her head. Mary had, by then, laid out everything she would need upon the bed, and Isobel's dress hung on the back of the wardrobe door.

Mary began by drying Isobel's hair in front of the fire. Together they had spent some considerable time experimenting with styles of hair, eventually deciding upon an elegant chignon into which tiny little peach-coloured roses made from silk would be placed. The roses gave an air of sophistication, and their colour matched perfectly the hue of the sash to be worn with Isobel's dress. For her makeup, Isobel had insisted on something a little more dramatic, even though Mary had been reluctant to do so. After all, Mary had no intention of allowing the gossipmongers to suggest her mistress was some painted strumpet. However, once Mary had finished applying the cosmetics, even she had to admit that Isobel had been right to insist. For, as if by magic, Isobel's appearance had been transformed from merely pretty to something that could only be described as truly beautiful.

When the time came to dress, first came Isobel's bandages. Once those were in place, Mary helped Isobel into a new pair of sheer white stockings secured at the thigh with ribbons, and Mary could not help but smile to herself when she imagined how Lord Fairfax might react should he see her dressed in such a fashion. Being careful not to disturb Isobel's hair, Mary then helped her into her chemise. It was not the garment that Isobel had been expecting. Instead, it was a chemise that was cut much lower in the bodice than she was used to and which caused Isobel to raise an eyebrow when she viewed it in the mirror. From the bed, Mary retrieved the next item of clothing to be worn, an unusual looking set of stays, and she had nearly laughed out loud when she observed Isobel's reaction at seeing them.

"It is called a *corset*, Isobel, and is very new and very French," explained Mary. "Like with your stays, I have added padding, although I am hoping for even more than the normal effect," she said.

"What do you mean?" asked Isobel as she swivelled to look at her.

"You'll see," said Mary. Grinning in a conspiratorial fashion, she tapped the side of her nose with a long, elegant finger.

The corset was made out of much stiffer material than a set of stays, with long laces at the back. In preparation, Mary had loosened the laces as much as she could so Isobel could step into the unusual garment as if they were a pair to trousers. Then, once her mistress was standing in the middle, Mary pulled, tugging the corset up over her slim hips to settle it snugly around her torso. Only then did she start to pull firmly upon the laces.

"Oh my God, Mary," groaned Isobel. "Does it have to be so tight?"

"Just wait and see, Isobel," said Mary. "Wait and see. I am sure the discomfort will be worth the finished effect."

When Mary was certain that Isobel was about to cry *pax*, she tied off the laces, not wanting to take things so far that she might faint during the evening. Then she moved around to the front of her mistress, and without a by your leave, pushed her hand down between Isobel's chest and the corset material. By means of a little indelicate pulling and pushing, she arranged what flesh she could grasp on top of the sewn-in padding. This she repeated on the other side until, once satisfied, she pulled Isobel in front of the mirror once more.

Her gob so obviously well and truly smacked, Isobel stood and stared. The tight laces had nipped in her waist and made it as if she had quite womanly hips. But best of all were the small globes of flesh that peeked out from the top, globes of flesh that could only be seen as belonging to the breasts of a woman.

"Dress," she demanded. "I need my dress. I need to see."

Mary retrieved the gown that Madame LeClerc had made for Isobel, looking at it longingly. In cream satin and lace with lovely little sleeves, it was modestly cut in the empire style with a lovely peach-coloured satin sash that fastened beneath the bust. She first undid the buttons at the back before very carefully lifting it over Isobel's head. For a few moments, Mary then fussed, tying the satin ribbon a little more tightly, umming and ahhing as she did so.

"There," she said. The girl was grinning broadly at what she could see, obviously more than a little pleased with the outcome of her efforts. "A perfect fit, Miss Isobel. I had a seamstress at Madam LeClerc's adjust it slightly with the corset in mind. What do you think?"

Once more Isobel stood before the mirror, her hand over

her mouth in abject shock. When choosing her dress from a pattern book, Isobel had lusted after the sort of gown many young women currently liked to wear, one which left little to the imagination when it came to their breasts. But of course, she had no such things, so had settled for something far more modest, or so she thought. But now, thanks to the padded corset and some slight modification in the décolletage of her dress, for all intents and purposes Isobel appeared to have perfectly modest and very feminine breasts. Better still, the opal necklace which Isobel had previously donned nestled perfectly within the crease of flesh, serving only to draw the eye towards them.

"Bugger," whispered Isobel, unable to stop herself from using a most un-ladylike word.

"Yes, quite, Miss Isobel. No one looking at you now could possibly believe you to be a boy."

"Bugger," she said again. "I'm not sure about this, Mary." Isobel turned this way and that to view her outline. "I feel almost naked. Everyone will stare at me, and I do not want them to."

"Don't be such a ninny," replied Mary. "Ladies are supposed to show a little flesh, and your doing so will only serve to convince others of your feminine status. Besides, your dress is positively modest compared to the way many will be dressed, I can promise you that. Now wait there and I will see if Lady Olivia is ready. Let's see what see thinks, shall we?"

Moments later Mary followed Olivia back into Isobel's room to find her still standing in front of the looking glass. Mary had obviously taken a few moments to explain to the countess what the issue was, and the look on her face was serious and sombre.

"Come on, let me have a look at you then," said Olivia.

Coyly, Isobel moved to the centre of the room, her hands clasped nervously before her, the effect of which was to make her *breasts* look even larger.

"My, my, my," said Olivia as she circled around Isobel.

"Effective, was it not, milady?" asked Mary.

"I'll say. Not a single person would now ever suspect that beneath the surface is a . . . well, you know. Yes, truly, Isobel, you look more and more feminine with every passing day."

"That's what I said," added Mary.

Isobel grinned at both of them but said nothing. Not that she had to, for her smile spoke the volumes for her.

"Downstairs in ten minutes then," called the countess as she walked imperiously out of the room.

"Oh, Lady Hamilton, don't forget you have given me the rest of the evening off," called Mary.

Isobel rounded on her.

"And what is this?" she demanded. "You did not tell me about that."

"*Well*," said Mary, drawing out the word for emphasis, and failing to look at all innocent. "If you must know, as you will be at the ball until the small hours of the morning, I have arranged an evening out for myself."

"What, where, who?" demanded Isobel. "Come, 'fess up."

"Mr. Jenkins, Lord Fairfax's man, has asked me to accompany him to Vauxhall Gardens, and, oh, Isobel, I am so very excited."

When a nervous Peter entered the ballroom, he was not at all surprised by the crush that he discovered. The room was packed with just about every member of the ton who presently resided in London, all of them dressed in their finest. As for Peter, he had travelled to the event alone, thus allowing him to slip inside practically unnoticed. As was his habit, he always did this when attending a ball. It gave him the chance to get his bearings, to observe the *battleground* before *play* commenced, to plan his strategy for avoiding the mothers with daughters upon the marriage mart. Stealthily, he kept to the shadows as best he could, only pausing when he found himself in a position where he could observe without himself being observed.

Across the room, he first located his mother and father. Of course, his mother was royally decked out, with the Abingdon rubies around her neck and feathers in her hair to rival a peacock. Stood next to them were his sister and her husband, Richard, Marquis of Cranleigh, as well as several others, all of whom seemed to curry the duke's favour.

But then, across the room, he caught sight of Isobel, and his breath caught in his throat as he did so. She was standing by Lady Hamilton, and even with her back to him, Peter had instantly recognised her. Whist he could not make out every detail, it appeared that she was attired in the most stunning of gowns, her glorious red hair dressed in the most fashionable of styles. Unobserved for the time being, Peter took the opportunity to study her.

He had thought, nay expected, that like him, she might have felt nervous. Instead, what he saw had him shaking his head in wonder. Even from across the room, he could see that there was most definitely something different about her, something that had been missing at the musicale and on the day that she had met his sister. For a few moments, he pondered on this revelation, wondering what might have changed for her. Then he realised what it was. Even with her back to him, he could see that Isobel had an air of confidence about her that had previously been absent. Yes, that was it. Just the way she carried herself, the set of her shoulders and the angle of her head, suggested her to be a lady of culture, a lady who looked eminently comfortable in these lavish surroundings. Instead of looking at the floor, she held her head high with self-assurance, and she was obviously making eye contact with those around her as she conversed confidently with them.

It was then that she turned, her eyes searching across the room, and in that moment Peter understood why.

Holy Mother of God!

As she turned, his eyes were magnetically drawn towards her décolletage. The dress she wore was elegant and quite modest by modern standards. Yet there was no denying what he could see. Isobel had breasts, or what appeared to be so. And between the soft swelling of flesh, an opal pendant sat, drawing the eye towards the two small but significant globes.

"Fuck me," he said once more, but this time aloud.

But Isobel was also much more than just her breasts. Her beautiful red hair had been artfully dressed to show off her graceful neck and stunningly pretty face. The gown she wore draped beautifully over her lithe body, her arms encased in long white gloves so that they appeared slim and feminine. Like every other young lady, in one hand she confidently held her dance card, a card that was presently being vied over by several of the young men who clamoured around her.

Something quite extraordinary then occurred.

As he realised what was happening, as he saw these fops fawning over her, a sudden inexplicable and uncontrollable surge of jealousy hit Peter like sledgehammer beating against a wall. To make matters worse, principle amongst Isobel's suitors was none other than Viscount bloody Stephens, a man who was practically drooling upon her skirts.

"God," he mumbled to himself, "does she know what danger she places herself in?"

He could imagine what might happen. Stephens would take her onto the dance floor, would flatter her, woo her. Then he would take what he supposed to be a naive Scottish lass outside for fresh air where he would try and compromise her in an effort to coerce her into marriage. After all, he had heard that the man had serious gambling debts and was in need of the fortune that Miss Munroe was rumoured to have. What better way to get his hands on her money than to ruin her reputation, forcing her to *marry* him. Instantly, his mouth went dry and his heart began to beat as he fought to control the urge to march across the room and plant the man a facer.

But then he laughed, a deep guffaw spluttering from his lips. With intense pleasure, Peter watched the object of Stephen's desire shake her head to politely decline his offer, before turning her back upon the man. It wasn't quite the *cut direct*, but judging by the look upon Stephens' face, he had seen it as such.

As a lady, Peter knew that Isobel would usually be expected to dance with different partners. However, Lady Olivia had suggested he be Isobel's only partner that evening, and she had two very valid reasons for doing so. First and foremost, it would keep Isobel away from the potential danger of dancing with any other man, thus protecting her anonymity. More importantly, it would also subtly announce their intentions towards each other, especially as Isobel had his name on no less than three dances. They would first share a cotillion, which would be followed a little later by a quadrille. That was to be the dinner dance, which would then allow him to escort Lady Olivia and Isobel into the supper room. After dining they would share one more dance, the third being no less than a waltz.

Three dances, one of them a waltz! That was sure to set tongues a-wagging and discourage the likes of Lord bloody Stephens. For sharing three dances, one of them a waltz, would most definitely announce his intentions towards Isobel, almost as clearly as would a headline in the St James's Chronicle.

"Oh God!" he groaned as he moved deeper into the ballroom.

Whilst he wanted nothing more than to rush to Isobel's

side, propriety and manners dictated that he say hello to his parents first, even though he had yet to greet the hosts. So, he wandered in their direction ... only to find himself face to face with none other than Viscountess Salisbury and her daughter Lady Felicia Farthingale.

"Lord Fairfax, what a pleasant surprise," said the viscountess. She dipped a perfunctory curtsey before him. "You remember my daughter, Lady Felicia, do you not?"

Inwardly Peter grimaced, for this was exactly why he normally gave himself time to view the room. However, he had allowed himself to become distracted, and now he had been waylaid by the very type of woman he sought to avoid. He bowed politely to give himself time to school his face into his well-practiced impassive expression and then look back at both ladies.

"Indeed, my lady, and don't you both look beautiful this evening," he replied.

In truth, Lady Felicia did look quite pretty, if perhaps a little overdressed for someone of her age. Her golden blonde hair had been nicely arranged, and she wore an expensive-looking gown that left little to the imagination, especially in the area of her breasts. Like all the other young ladies, she held her dance card in one hand, pencil poised at the ready, and Peter was suddenly under no illusion as to why her mother had placed the girl before him.

He was having none of that. He politely bowed once more so as to not appear impolite.

"If you will excuse me, my ladies, I was on my way to say hello to my mother and father. I wish you joy of the evening."

With that, he took a step to the side and smartly marched away, desperate for the sanctuary that his parents would offer. Fortunately, Alice was the first to see him and she instantly gathered him into their group. A good thing too, for as he had glanced back at Viscountess Salisbury and her daughter, both had the look of lemons on their lips,

"Peter!" she exclaimed. "At last!" she added as she kissed him lightly upon the cheek in greeting.

Peter smiled, for this was an Alice he had not expected. Instead of the open hostility he had experienced of late, the sister he loved and admired, the sister who had always given him unconditional support, seemed to be back. Turning, he kissed his mother on the offered cheek and then shook his father's hand.

"Darling," said his mother with a touch of sarcasm in her voice. "So good of you to join us."

"Mother, you look wonderful as always. Where are Thomas and Sara?" he asked.

"There is good news and bad there," smiled the duchess. "It seems Sara is with child once more, so I am to be a grandmother again."

Peter almost winced at those words. After all, they were said in a way that left no doubt that his mother was continually disappointed in the fact that he had yet to marry and produce even more grandchildren for her to dote upon.

"That is the good news," continued his mother. "The bad news is that Sara suffers dreadfully from morning sickness so has been confined to bed. Your brother has decided to stay with her, as a husband should. Anyway, what chance is there of you finding such a lady for whom you might do the same sometime in the future?"

"Mother," said Alice. "Leave poor Peter alone. After all, has he not agreed to choose a bride by the end of a season? A season that has not yet even started!" With that she turned to her husband and smiled sweetly at him. "Now darling, will you please excuse me for a moment, for I need to have a few words with my baby brother alone. Then, when I return, you can whisk me onto the dance floor as much as you like."

Grateful to his sister, Peter offered his arm, and together

they started to circle the room, only stopping when they found a quiet spot beside a giant fern of some kind. Alice then turned to him, the sparkle in her eye suggesting to Peter that all was going to be well. Surprisingly, she turned to look to where Isobel stood.

"I would like to apologise, Peter," she said softly, clearly not wanting to be overheard.

"Whatever for?"

"Over the past few days, I have given this matter a great deal of thought, as you might imagine I would. When I met the *lady* in question you know she had me . . . yes, me . . . completely fooled into thinking she was exactly the sort of girl I suggested that you find for a wife. But then, when you explained the situation, I have to admit that all I could see was the potential for scandal and not the opportunity for you to find happiness. But God, look at her. I do not know how it is possible that she does this, but even I must admit that she is beautiful and every inch the *lady*. Whilst I will always worry, I would even go so far as saying that she will make you the perfect *wife*."

Peter hissed, not even knowing that he had been holding his breath. There it was, in those few brief words. Alice was saying that she understood, that she accepted the choices that were about to be made, and he could not help but smile as he pulled his sister in for a brief hug, relief washing through him as he did so.

"Thank you, Alice. You know not what that means for me to hear," he whispered in return.

His sister gripped him by the arm. "Just promise me that you will be careful," she said.

"Always, sister, always." he replied softly as he kissed her upon the cheek.

As his sister walked away to return to her husband, Peter heard himself take in a deep breath. He turned once more to stare at Isobel, only to discover that she had seen him, that she had locked her gaze upon his as the broadest of smiles suffused her beautiful face.

And in that very moment, as sometimes happened on the battlefield, Peter had a flash of absolute clarity: an all-consuming thought that staggered him almost as if a lance had speared him through the heart.

There was no denying it.

He loved her. He loved Miss Isobel Munroe.

"Oh fuck," he whispered to himself.

Almost from the moment that she and Lady Olivia had entered the ball room, the one thing that Isobel had feared would happen, actually happened. They had been surrounded, practically mobbed, and Isobel had found herself inundated with requests to dance. One young man in particular, none other than Viscount Stephens, seemed quite insistent, almost desperate in pursuing his cause. But with her newfound confidence, Isobel was having none of that. She was polite. She was courteous. She was ladylike. Yet she still declined the man's request, turning from him to speak to Olivia upon some trivial matter instead.

"Stick to the plan Isobel, stick to the plan," she whispered to herself. Carefully, yet quite deliberately, she tucked her dance card into her reticule, a public announcement that her card was as she wanted it to be.

The plan was simple, really. Tonight was the night when Peter would publicly announce his interest in Miss Isobel Munroe by dancing no less than three dances with her, one being a waltz towards the end of the evening. Tonight was the night when Isobel would also publicly announce her interest in Lord Peter Fairfax by dancing with none other. So, after placing her dance card inside, she firmly closed the drawstring on her reticule. Then she glanced around her, even though she knew she should not do so, instinctively searching for any indication that someone might have seen something amiss with her actions.

It was at that moment, across the room, that she saw Peter for the first time that evening. And what she saw took her breath away.

He was immaculately dressed and groomed, his suit being modest in style and colour, unlike some of the other fops in attendance. In fact, to her eyes, his short hair and unassuming waistcoat made him look even more handsome than any other gentleman there. Fascinated, she watched him intently as he moved farther into the room, his eyes searching the crowd. To one side was a gaggle of women, Viscountess Farthingale and Lady Felicia Farthingale amongst them, and Isobel gasped inwardly as the viscountess had the temerity to place herself before him. The move had been so blatant, so obvious. Lord Peter Fairfax was a very eligible bachelor, being a son of a duke, no less, and Lady Felicia was in need of a husband, was she not? So perchance, the viscountess hoped he would ask her daughter to dance and perhaps form a *tendre* for her. But much to her relief, Peter merely bowed and sidestepped, his parting words leaving more than a little pout upon the lady's face from his curt departure.

She thought perhaps he would come to her next. Instead, from the corner of her eye, she followed him as he crossed the room to stop before his mother and father, whom he greeted warmly. It was then that Isobel saw exactly who they were standing with, her heart leaping into her mouths as she did so.

With the duke and duchess stood Peter's sister, Alice, and a man whom she knew to be Alice's husband, and Isobel shuddered from the apprehension she felt at seeing her once more. Alice and Peter had argued quite vociferously when he had told her the secret which they both kept, and their parting had been conducted in anger. Isobel hated that thought, for she knew how close the two of them were and detested the fact that she might come between them. Nervously, she looked away, but then, unable to stop herself from doing so, she looked back. Peter and Alice had moved to a quiet spot to the side of the room and were deep in conversation.

Then she saw them embrace, a huge grin appearing upon Peter's face as they did so, and once more, Isobel found the wherewithal to breathe.

As Peter walked away from his sister, Isobel willed him to look in her direction. She did not have long to wait, for moments later, his eyes captured her own from across the room. For Isobel, the effect of this was quite remarkable and left her almost breathless. It was so utterly bizarre. As she returned his gaze, she felt herself smile, and as she did so, every other person in the room seemed to fade away into nothingness. A mist descended, and for the most magical of moments, it appeared to her that, despite the crush around them, they were both completely alone in a sea of insignificant humanity. And oh, how she wished it were so.

Then he returned her smile, and in that very instant, Isobel become supremely conscious of a very important fact.

She loved him. She, Isobel Munroe, a man dressed in women's garb, loved Lord Peter Fairfax, and loved him with every fibre of her heart.

It was then that a touch on her arm dragged her back into reality, a touch that was so startling that it almost made her shriek.

"I say Miss Munroe, are you certain that I cannot have the next dance?" said Viscount Stephens. "A cotillion has been announced, and it appears you have no partner. I would deem it an honour."

Inwardly Isobel grimaced, every fibre of her being

shuddering from the nasal quality of the man's voice, a voice that did little but set her teeth on edge. Cringing, she turned to Olivia to beg for salvation, not expecting the deliverance that came.

"Sorry old boy," said a strong voice, just as it had done before dinner at the musicale. "Miss Munroe has already promised me this dance. Miss Munroe."

Peter was holding out a gloved hand, having somehow materialised by her side, despite the crush that had tried to prevent him from getting to her. In return, Isobel beamed at him, her eyes never leaving his for a moment. At first his expression was severe, and for a second, Isobel actually thought she had done something to annoy him. Perhaps he even thought she had encouraged Viscount Stephens. But then he snorted and shook his head, letting out a sharp bark of a laugh as some sudden notion occurred to him.

"So, you find Lord Stephens attentions to me amusing, do you?" hissed Isobel from the corner of her mouth.

He laughed again. "No, not at all. Judging by his expression, you were quite successful at putting that popinjay in his place."

"Then what is it that has you so amused, my lord?" asked Isobel, hissing the words through her clenched teeth.

Peter, not caring about propriety, leant into her ear to whisper. "What has me smiling, *Miss Munroe*, is that I have just realised that this is the very first time I have ever stood up to dance with a lady and have actually looked forward to doing so."

Her cheeks burning so furiously that she was certain that everyone would be looking at her, Isobel somehow found herself standing next to Peter in a square of eight, with her hand held firmly in his. Despite her training and practice with Mary, Isobel was now nervous. The reel was one in which each gentleman would dance with each lady until the reel was complete, and this was not something Isobel had been looking forward to. The dance was complicated and would require absolute concentration if she were not to step on someone's foot. In addition, she had absolutely no desire to get *so* close to another man that she risked exposure.

But then music started, and the complex reel began to unfold. Isobel plastered a smile onto her face and began to count as Peter turned her in the reel before handing her to the next gentleman. As he did so, something occurred which very nearly caused her to stumble. For as she looked at her new partner, an older man in the scarlet uniform of the army, she discovered that his eyes were clearly focused not on hers, but on her décolletage instead. The man was actually glancing at her breasts! Fortunately, the dance moved on swiftly, and Isobel was soon handed off to another gentleman . . . who then promptly did exactly the same thing.

As the dance ended and the music stopped, Isobel once more found herself hand in hand with Peter. His grip was a little firmer than it should have been, and in that Isobel found comfort as she curtsied to first him and then to the circle. Only then did he lean towards Isobel to whisper in her ear.

"And where, Miss Munroe, did you get those?" he asked as his eyes flickered towards her chest.

Isobel grinned broadly as she whispered in return.

"That is for me to know and for you to find out. After all, even a lady such as I must have her secrets, Lord Fairfax," she replied.

"Seriously, Miss Munroe, you continue to astonish me," said Peter.

"A good thing, I hope," she said softly.

"Most definitely," he whispered, as they arrived next to Lady Charlotte.

On completion of the quadrille, tongues really did start to wag, for whilst the evening was still young, they had already shared a second dance. To compound this, as the music ended, Peter had extended his arm to Isobel so as to escort her back to a smiling Lady Olivia, walking straight past the Farthingales as he did so.

"Oh Isobel," she gushed. "Well done. Did you see the look upon Felicia Farthingale's face? She was not at all happy that you have both shared a second dance."

"That harpy had been trying to get her claws into me for months," groaned Peter. "At least Lady Weston is not here."

"Who?" asked Isobel.

"Lady Priscilla Weston. Laugh like a braying donkey, and the first lady my father suggested I might consider for a wife."

It was at that moment that the dinner gong was sounded, and tongues began to wag once more when Peter extended his arm to Isobel.

A sumptuous feast had been laid out with a veritable army of footmen and maids to serve at table. As propriety dictated, when they sat, it was with the countess between them. Nervously Isobel found herself glancing around the room as she ate, everything for some reason tasting bland, even though she knew every morsel to be delicious. The problem was that in her mind everyone seemed to be staring at them, including the Duchess of Camberly and Peter's mother, who both seemed deep in conversation with each other.

"Oh God," she whispered.

For not only were Lady Charlotte and Lady Mary looking at them, they were now walking over towards them. Peter stood.

"Mother. Your Grace," he said as he bowed politely. "Mother, you remember the Dowager Countess of Weybridge, Lady Hamilton, and her ward Miss Munroe."

Both Lady Olivia and Isobel had now stood, both of them curtsying briefly.

"Of course, darling. I was only now remarking to Charlotte

as to how beautifully you play the piano, Miss Munroe."

Isobel coughed, a gesture that Peter had come to know as Isobel preparing to speak in her feminine voice.

"Thank you, your Grace," she said.

"And might I say how lovely you look this evening, Miss Munroe. That dress is so becoming on you."

"I'll say it does, Katherine," added Charlotte. "I had Madame LeClerc commission her gown especially for this evening, and I will say she did a marvellous job, did she not Lord Fairfax?"

"Erm, yes," he replied as he glanced at the duchess. "You do look exceptionally lovely tonight, Miss Munroe."

"Peter," his mother then said. "I have been meaning to ask you. When was the last time you visited Winsworth Manor? I am told the estate is doing exceedingly well."

Almost as if in agony, Peter groaned.

"Not for some time, Mother," he said. He felt a shiver run down his spine, causing him to squirm a little as he gave his terse reply, knowing the game that his mother was playing.

"Winsworth Manor?" asked Lady Olivia, obviously deciding to play as well.

"Mm, Winsworth Manor was my childhood home. It is the estate that will become Peter's on his marriage, Lady Hamilton. It has a lovely house set in three thousand acres of the most beautiful countryside."

It was another hour before dinner was over, an hour that to Peter seemed like a day, a month, a year. Subtle had not been the word for his mother, but he was thrilled to think that in her own rather unique way, she was giving her blessing to Isobel. That in itself was quite remarkable, for had Isobel been a genuine member of the fairer sex, had her father really been a mere sea captain, her *lack of title or family connections* might easily have prejudiced his mother against her. So too did the Duchess of Camberly, in her own way, signal her approval for the match. For that, Peter was truly grateful, as someone as influential and powerful as the duchess could only add credibility to Isobel's claim to be a woman.

Once dinner was complete, the dancing started again. By this time the guests had consumed their fair share of wines and champagne, so there was a much lighter and more jovial atmosphere in the room. It was as the first set ended that a voice cried out, a voice that instantly commanded attention.

"My lord, ladies and gentlemen, if I could have a moment of your time,"

Peter turned to see a young man and a young woman standing beneath a picture that hung upon the wall, a picture that was as yet covered with a pristine white sheet. He recognised the man instantly as Lord Richard Beaufort, son and heir to the Duke of Camberly. Stood next to him was an exceptionally beautiful woman. With golden blonde hair, Peter recognised her as Richard's sister, Anne, the Marchioness of Blandford.

"Mother, Father, would you come and join us," said Lady Anne.

Peter watched as the duke took hold of his wife's hand, and even from a distance, Peter could see the love that they shared from the way Charlotte looked at her husband with adoring eyes. They joined the duke's children. At first, they kept their backs to the crowd, but Richard was having none of that, so taking them by the shoulders, he gently turned them around to face the company.

"Ladies and Gentlemen," continued Lady Anne, "as many of you know, a little over five years ago, in this very room, a most remarkable lady marched up to my father and asked *him* to dance a waltz with her."

"And to say that my father was a little shocked that this

lady had the audacity to do so is, without doubt, a mild understatement," said Richard. "However, I am pleased to say that he had the eminent good sense to do as she asked."

"As if I had any choice," said the duke, a huge grin upon his face.

"And that was the start of it. For you see, ladies and gentlemen, exactly five years ago today, my father had the singular honour of marrying that very same lady," said Richard.

"So here we are," said Anne, "to celebrate the fifth wedding anniversary of James and Charlotte, the Duke and Duchess of Camberly. But I ask, ladies and gentlemen, what does one get as a gift for the couple who already has everything a heart could desire?"

"Mother, Father, it was all Anne's idea, honestly," joked Richard. "I thought it would be enough to have Mr. Samson and Mistress Phoebe to attend the ball. If you would look over there, Mama." He grinned.

Everyone's eyes swivelled in the direction that Richard was pointing. There stood Mistress Phoebe, her enormous belly suggesting that she might have the babe she carried at any moment. Stood next to her was the biggest man, black or white, that Peter had ever seen. Of obvious African descent, the man was simply huge, both in height and in the build of his athletic body. Charlotte shrieked with pleasure and practically ran across the room to greet them both with a sound kiss upon their cheeks.

"However," said Anne, "my brother and I both agreed that we should also do something special celebrate that moment all those years ago. So without further ado, Mother, Father, if you would do the honours!"

Enthralled, Peter watched as Richard took Charlotte's hand and as Anne took her father's, each leading them to either side of the picture upon the wall. For an instant, Charlotte looked at the duke and he looked at her. Then together the two of them pulled the covering away.

There was a collective gasp from the audience.

The picture was simply stunning. A life-sized likeness of a tall handsome man, so obviously the duke, held a beautiful woman in his arms as they danced what could only be a waltz. The lady, Charlotte, was looking at him, her eyes locked upon his, the love that they shared in that moment perfectly captured on canvass for all eternity.

Charlotte promptly burst into tears. At the same time the whole room erupted into applause, and Peter watched as the duke suddenly swept his bride into his arms to kiss her, the tears of joy and love pouring down her face as she returned his embrace.

"And with that, ladies and gentlemen, would you please gather your partners and join Mother and Father for the first waltz of the evening."

It took more than several minutes for everyone to compose themselves. Charlotte needed a moment to dry her eyes, as did the duke. There were hugs and kisses to be given and hands to be shaken and partners to be found. Eventually, all those who were to waltz found themselves standing respectfully around the edge of the dance floor, whilst the duke and duchess stepped off to the music.

Peter watched in awe, for they danced in perfect harmony, giving a master class to those who watched. But then Anne joined in with her husband and Richard with his wife, and soon several other couples were enjoying the delights of the waltz. Formally, Peter bowed to Isobel, and she curtsied in return before taking his hand. For a moment they stood together, their bodies so close that they almost touched. Then Peter nodded his head in time to the music and stepped off, Isobel following his every move.

Even in the height of battle, Peter had never felt so alive. As they danced, he could feel the heat of her body, the slight tremble in her hand, the frantic beating of her heart, and never before had he felt so intoxicated. It was as if she were made for him. Whilst he was tall, so was she, their bodies seeming to fit like the pieces of a jigsaw as they stepped in perfect unison to the music. In fact, there was only one thing that worried Peter. Every now and then he would feel the soft round swelling of a breast as it pressed against his chest, breasts that were where breasts had no right to be. As he glanced down at Isobel, he could see that she also felt the emotion of the moment. Her chest was heaving as if she had run a mile, and her soft and dreamy eyes were shining as she looked back at him.

Eventually the music stopped, as did the dancers. Reluctantly, Peter stepped back and bowed politely whilst Isobel curtsied once more in return. She took his arm, and he was about to escort her back to Lady Olivia when Peter felt a tap on his shoulder. Turning, he found a serious looking footman behind.

"Excuse me my lord, but there is a Mister Jenkins here demanding to see you. Says he's your valet and that it is extremely important."

As quickly as was polite, Peter returned Isobel to Lady Olivia. Then he followed the footman out into the entrance way to find Jenkins standing there with yet another footman, knowing that he would never have interrupted unless it was a matter of great importance.

"What is it, Jenkins?" he demanded.

"Lady Hamilton's town house, my lord. It's been broken into. Someone forced their way in past Cartwright, the footman, and bludgeoned him something good. He was the only one in the house, as all the others had the night off. The blackguard left him for dead before ransacking the countess's office."

"My God! How do you know all this?"

"I was returning Mary, Miss Munroe's girl, to the house.

She and I had been to Vauxhall Gardens. We found Cartwright unconscious just inside the servant's entrance."

"You did not leave her alone, I take it?" Peter demanded.

"Nay, sir. I called for the watch and for a surgeon, and only when they was at the house did I set off for here."

"Good man, Jenkins, good man."

Olivia had worked up a considerable rage by the time she walked imperiously into the house with Peter, Jenkins, Isobel, and none other than Lady Charlotte's man, Samson, as her escorts.

"Where is Mr Cartwright? Is he well?" demanded Olivia the moment she walked through her front door.

Mary was waiting for her, a uniformed man that Olivia took for a member of the watch standing next to her. She appeared resolute although visibly shaken, her face ashen from the shock of what had transpired.

"He's in the parlour my lady," said Mary. "Dr. Davis is with him. Has a lump the size of a duck egg on the back of his head, but the doctor says he is going to be all right."

"My name is Jones, of Bow Street, my lady," said the constable. "Appears to have been one man. Hit your man with a sand-filled cosh, I would guess. Your man is conscious again, I am glad to say, but he could not give much of a description. Big man, by all accounts, wearing a cloak and hood, his face covered with some sort of scarf. Got four other runners out combing the district looking for him, but he is likely long gone."

"What happened?"

"Your man was in the kitchen when someone came uninvited through the servant's entrance. The next thing he remembers is waking up a few minutes ago in the parlour. The man worked him over good and well, he did."

"Thank you, Constable," said Olivia, her anger barely under control.

"My lady," the constable continued. "Would you be so kind as to check to see if anything is missing from your office? That seems to be the only room to have been touched. A list of anything val'able would be a might useful in tracking the man down."

The room was a complete mess. Her desk had been broken into, the drawers emptied out onto the floor. Books had been stripped from the bookcases in such a manner that suggested a great rage, and a small cash box, which had been forced open, lay empty upon the floor.

"Was there much in there?" asked Peter. He had followed Olivia into the room and was bending down to retrieve the box.

"A little under thirty pounds, I would guess. All my real valuables and confidential documents are in a hidden steel strong box that would take four Mr. Samsons to lift, let alone open."

"And this has not been touched?" asked Peter.

For a second, Olivia's eye flickered to the panel in the wall behind which the strong box was hidden, but 'twas clear that the intruder had not even suspected it was there.

"I am certain, Lord Fairfax," replied Olivia. "Other than the missing cash and the mess, I cannot see anything amiss... except perhaps..."

"What is it?" asked Peter.

"My appointment book," she said. "It is the only book left upon my desk!"

It was at that moment that Samson entered the room, followed by the constable, who was viewing the man with awe. Samson's expression was grim, yet some of the tension that had been in the man's shoulders seemed to fade away as he made his report

"I have searched the house from top to bottom, Lady Olivia. Like the constable said, there is no sign of anyone having been in the rest of the house."

"I would guess, milady," said the constable, "that the intruder was an opportunist burglar, taking advantage of the fact that you was out this evening. Thirty pounds is a huge sum of money to the likes, so it's doubtful that he will be back. Chances are he is in some tavern celebrating his good fortune, but to be on the safe side, I will leave a man here overnight, if you wish."

"I can stay," said Peter. "Or I could leave Jenkins."

"That, Lord Fairfax, would not be appropriate," rumbled Samson. "I will stay."

"Neither of you will stay," said Olivia adamantly. "Samson is right, Lord Fairfax. It would be highly inappropriate for you to be in the house overnight. And you, Samson, need to get back to Phoebe, who might be delivering your child as we speak. We will be safe enough with a constable outside."

Chapter Eighteen

It had been seven days since he had broken into the countess's home. Now, from his hiding place deep in the woods, William Drummond watched the country mansion as several carriages began to arrive. Yes, breaking into the house had been risky, especially as he had nearly been caught by that blasted footman who had no rights to be there in the first place. But it had offered a lead that he could not resist. Whilst he had found no direct evidence of David, the stupid mare had written down the dates of a visit to somewhere called Thorpe Hall in her appointment book. This turned out to be the Duchess of Camberly's country home, and it had occurred to Drummond that this would be the perfect place for his cousin to hide out.

It had taken a couple of days for him to discover the location of Thorpe Hall. Even so, he had still managed to arrive ahead of the party. With the thirty guineas he had stolen from the countess, he had rented a half decent horse and had ridden hard, taking lodgings at an inn located in the nearby town of Kings Langley. He had also bought himself a hunting rifle, although he did not carry it at present for fear of being mistaken for a poacher.

Reaching into a pocket, Drummond extracted a small spy-glass which he opened and rested upon a branch of a tree. With it he observed the comings and goings of the party that had arrived, looking for any indication of his cousin, David. He recognised the countess and the duchess immediately, for the servants clearly deferred to them. There was the huge black man, too, along with a very pregnant black woman, both of whom were dressed as genteels. There were maids and footmen and grooms, and even a gentleman on horseback whom he did not recognise.

And then there was the countess's companion!

The girl was attired in a travelling dress and cloak. As she alighted from the coach a breeze had caught her, wrapping her skirt around shapely legs and pulling the fabric around small but pert breasts. Her golden red hair was loose around her shoulders, and that too caught the wind, blowing around a beautiful face that was smiling broadly at the man who had dismounted from his horse.

"She's a beauty, there's no doubt," he said softly to himself. "Wouldn'a mind tupping that!"

He focused his glass more tightly upon the young redhead and watched her as she walked towards the house, her arm linked with no less than the duchess herself. Then, dragging himself away, he scanned the rest of the building, hoping that he might catch a glimpse of his quarry.

But of David Drummond, or for that matter, anyone remotely like him, there was no sign.

Patience, Will, patience!

Chapter Nineteen

It was still early when Isobel awoke on the next morn. Everyone had been tired after the journey from London, so after a simple meal, the entire party had retired for the evening. Mary, she knew, would probably have been awake until much later, sorting out not only her wardrobe, but the countess's, too. So as Isobel lay there in the warmth of a very comfortable bed, she decided to allow her abigail to sleep in.

Isobel clambered from the bed, pulling back the sheets and blankets that kept in the warmth. Quietly, she padded over to her window, and drawing back the curtains a little she peeped out through the glass. Her bedroom had the most magnificent view. In the distance, she could see a lake sparkling in the early morning sun, the trees surrounding it rustling gently in a light breeze. Opening the window slightly, she breathed in a deep lungful of crisp fresh air and smiled, for judging by the lack of cloud in the sky, the day promised to be fine and warm.

As a young man, David had grown fond of the outdoors. Whenever he could, he would take a horse and ride out alone onto the lands that surround his ancestral home. For him it was a time of peace — away from his responsibilities as the future Earl, away from his domineering father, away from the thoughts of womanhood that haunted his dreams. And now that she was Isobel, she strangely found herself missing the boy that she had once been and the freedoms that he had enjoyed.

"Come on my girl," she said, smiling ironically to herself.

"I'm sure that no one would object if you take a stroll around the gardens before breakfast, even if you are now a *lady*."

It took Isobel a half an hour to dress herself. She chose a light day dress with buttons she could reach, and her new walking shoes that Olivia had purchased for her in London. She brushed out her hair and tied it with a pretty ribbon before applying a little of the makeup she had grown so fond of. Mary had been teaching her how to use the various powders and paints, so she even made quite a good job of it. Then, after grabbing a bonnet, she slipped quietly out of her room and walked down the stairs.

Whilst the house was large, it was laid out like many others. It therefore took Isobel a matter of moments to find her way down to the kitchens, a room that was already full of bustle as the staff worked to prepare breakfast. A portly woman smiled at her as she entered the room.

"Good morning, Miss. I'm Mrs. White, the cook. Can I help you with something?"

Isobel smiled in return. "Good morning Mrs. White, I am Miss Munroe, Lady Olivia's ward. I was hoping someone might show me how to get into the gardens. After yesterday's journey, I feel the need to stretch my legs a little before breakfast."

"Oooo, a Scottish lassie," said Mrs White. Her smile was broad and genuine, and Isobel found herself taking an instant liking to the woman. "My Arthur, God bless his soul, was from Scotland. If you would like to follow me, Miss."

From a large teapot that sat in the middle of a huge pine table, Mrs. White poured a mug of tea, adding a little milk from the jug beside it. Then she smiled once more and gestured for Isobel to follow her out of the door and into a large kitchen garden. There, tending to the plants, was a wizened old man of at least seventy years, his severely wrinkled face almost the colour of Samson's.

"Here, George," said Mrs. White. She handed the man the mug of tea. "This is Miss Munroe. She is the ward of Lady O'. Miss Munroe, this 'ere is George Harris. Used to be the head groom, but the mistress retired him a couple of years back. Now, to keep him out of mischief, he tends the garden for me instead."

"My grandson, Billy, is 'ead groom now, although I could still do the job," said George begrudgingly.

"Of course you could," said Mrs. White, "what with your rheumatics and your gammy knee. Anyways, Miss Isobel would like a once round the garden, if you can spare the time, that is."

Isobel could not help but smile at the banter between the two of them, for it would be obvious to anyone that they shared a great deal of affection and respect for each other.

"Always happy to escort a pretty lass," said George.

Together they walked through the gardens, part of her still amazed that she was able to do such a thing without any fear of discovery. George, for his part, had simply accepted her for whom she was, and for that she was incredibly grateful. George was also so easy to talk to, and he prattled away as he showed Isobel around the extensive gardens. The gardens were beautiful. They first visited the kitchen garden, which displayed a variety of produce. Next came the formal garden, and even Isobel recognised the promise of the roses which were yet to bloom. It was as they walked through a small orchard that George paused to pull a weed from in front of a marker stone.

"Never seen the like of it, Miss Isobel," he said. "Old Hermes is buried here. That old pony was a particular favourite of her Grace. Wept buckets, she did, when we put him in the ground."

Slowly, for he truly could not walk very fast, George then led Isobel back through the gardens and into the purpose-built stable block, where a quadrangle of stables held a variety of horses, all with their noses poked out into the morning air. A red-headed young man waved as he led one of the horses out, leading the saddled mare towards a paddock for exercise. George waved back, a self-satisfied smile upon his face.

"Do you ride, Miss Munroe?" George asked.

"Yes. I love to ride, but it has been some time since I have been able to do so."

"Well, that rapscallion over there is my grandson, Billy. Thanks to 'er ladyship, 'e is 'ead groom here, in my stead. 'E's only one and twenty but is as good with the 'orses as I ever was. If you want a ride, ask him, and he will find you something suitable. Mind you, you will need a groom to accompany you, as Mr Samson would have 'is 'ide if he were to let you ride out on your own."

"Why?" asked Isobel.

"Mr Samson is a big black bloke," he replied, obviously assuming that Isobel had not yet met him. "As fine a fellow as you can imaging too. He is 'er Grace's estate manager now, and 'e takes the safety of all those in his care extremely serious like."

"You like the duchess, don't you?" Isobel asked.

"As fine a lady as can be found in the whole of England. Treats her staff like royalty, she does. Do you know, since her Grace bought the estate, only two members of staff have left, and one of those was Gracie, who was even older than me."

"She has been very kind to me too," said Isobel.

"Just make sure you keep on her right side though," said George with a mischievous grin. "Come, let me show you why, Miss Isobel."

To one side of the quad was a large barn, and as they approached, Isobel could hear some very strange sounds coming from within. Without calling out to announce their presence, George motioned for her to go inside so that she could see what the fuss was about.

The barn was like nothing Isobel had ever seen, with perhaps the exception of the studio of David's old fencing master. The floor was laid with polished oak boards, and the walls were covered in painted plasterwork on which mirrors had been mounted. In one corner hung a large well-worn leather bag, similar to the one that Isobel imaged Gentleman Jack might use to practice his boxing skills. In racks around the room there were also weapons of all shapes and sizes, swords of every type, spears and wooden staves, and even a pair of brass tipped quarterstaffs.

And in the middle of the room, Lady Charlotte danced a violent dance with Samson himself.

The duchess was dressed almost as a man. Her hair was plaited into a thick rope to keep it out of the way, and she was attired in shirt and trousers that did little to hide her feminine shape. On her feet she wore soft leather shoes, and in her hands she held two staves of hickory, each the length of her forearm. Samson also held two similar staves, only he was naked from the waist up, sweat dripping from his incredibly muscular body as he danced effortlessly around his mistress.

As a boy, David had been forced to practice with the sword, and whilst he had not enjoyed doing so, had become proficient with foil and sabre. But what Isobel saw was skill way beyond anything that David had achieved. In awe, she observed the two protagonists strike at each other with incredible speed and deadly accuracy. Yet each blow seemed to be parried, the sound of wood on wood echoing through the barn. Faster and faster they went, Charlotte's feet jumping and dancing in a deadly pattern as she fought desperately to find an opening, her aggressiveness forcing Samson onto his back foot to parry each and every blow.

Suddenly Charlotte gave a yell of triumph. One of her sticks slipped inside of Samson's defence, and with remarkable control, she tapped him lightly upon the arm.

Samson stepped back with a grin on his face. "Bravo, Missy Charlotte, bravo." he said. "You are almost too good for poor old Samson."

"Pah! Old, you, never. And I could never best you in Dambe," said Charlotte. She turned to wipe the sweat from her brow with a cloth, catching sight of Isobel as she did so. "Oh, hello, Isobel."

"That was incredible, Lady Charlotte. I have never seen the like."

"These are the fighting sticks of Samson's tribe. He makes me practice with them whenever I am home. Even though I bested him this morning, it is a rare occurrence that I do so, for he is a master with the sticks."

"What is Dambe?" Isobel asked.

"It is a form of fighting with fist and feet, Missy Munroe, and is especially effective for close quarters," said Samson.

Suddenly, Samson turned with incredible speed. His arm shot out with the accuracy of an arrow from a bow to strike at the leather bag with only the palm of his hand. The blow was so violent that the bag nearly touched the beams that supported the roof above.

"He makes me practice that, too," grumbled Charlotte.

"For it has saved your life on more than one occasion," retorted Samson.

"Good morning," called another voice. In unison their heads swivelled to find that Peter had also joined them, an easy smile upon his face as he glanced about. For once, he was not fully dressed, his shirt open at the neck to reveal a hint of manly chest beneath, the effect of which was not lost upon Isobel. "Good gracious, this is quite the facility you have here your Grace," he said as his fingers caressed the hilt of a sword.

"Welcome to my training room, Peter," said Charlotte. "I had it built after I bought the estate. Samson insists that all the members of the family are taught to protect themselves. He has even made little Henry his own set of fighting sticks, and he is only three and one half. We also have pistol and archery ranges outside."

"You are welcome to train with me, my lord, should you wish to," said Samson. "Were you not once in His Majesty's army?"

"Yes, but I am not at all familiar with your type of hand-to-hand combat. My expertise lies with the sabre and pistol, although I am passable with a foil."

"Shame, for I have no real fondness for any of those," said Samson.

Isobel felt the heat in her cheeks once more as a seriously wicked idea came into her head. Before she could even attempt to stop herself, the words came tumbling from her mouth.

"I have always wanted to learn the foil, Lord Fairfax. Would now be appropriate for a lesson?" she asked.

She watched as Peter grinned.

"A short one, perhaps," he replied.

Samson insisted that the two of them don the extensive protective clothing that he had within the training room. For Isobel, he had Charlotte's padded leather fencing jacket, which he buckled firmly around her from behind. Peter put on a similar garment, and then each was given a mask to protect face and eye and leather gauntlets to protect the hand.

Throughout, Isobel had a very hard time keeping a straight face as Peter patiently began to teach her the basics of fencing. It soon became quite obvious that Peter had not considered, even for a moment, that *David* would have been trained in the use of small arms. So, as he demonstrated the correct stance and grip on the sword, she feigned ignorance, even though, judging by the smirk on Charlotte's face, she had not fooled the duchess for one moment.

Then came the time when they faced each other off.

"I will go slowly at first, Isobel," said Peter, "a simple thrust and parry to start with. I will thrust, you parry and then we will swap places."

Behind her mask, Isobel grinned as she took stance, trying hard to make it look as if she did not know what she was doing. Slowly Peter advanced, his hand pushing forward his foil in a gentle thrust. Like lightning, Isobel parried and followed up with a thrust of her own, the blunt end of the blade striking him on the heart as the blade bent almost double from the force.

"Oh, my lord," she said innocently. "Is that how you do it?"

They sparred for about thirty minutes before Samson called a halt.

"Bravo Missy Munroe," he said as he grinned broadly. "I see there is nothing Lord Fairfax can teach you with regards to the foil."

"I'll say," groaned Peter with mock indignation. "You could have told me you knew how to fence."

"And what would have been the fun in that?" she replied.

Whilst Isobel divested herself of her protective jacket, she could not help but smile back at him, for in truth she had held her own with Peter. And judging by the look of appreciation upon his face, he had found the experience just as invigorating as she.

"Now, Lord Fairfax, I believe you to be a cavalry man," said Samson.

"Why yes," replied Peter. "Why do you ask?"

Again, Samson grinned. "I usually do rounds of the stables first thing in the morning, and I was wondering if you might like to accompany me before you break your fast. I thought you might like to check on your stallion, Ajax. Her Grace has also recently purchased a beautiful two-year-old gelding which I am schooling to be her mount. I believe Billy will be exercising him in the paddock.

"Come on," said Charlotte, as she linked her arm into Isobel's, "you are going to want to see this.

Together the four of them walked over to the fence surrounding the paddock, where the young red headed man Isobel had seen earlier was indeed attempting to school a gorgeous chestnut horse of about sixteen hands, with white socks and a flash of white upon his nose. Even Isobel could appreciate the graceful lines and rippling muscles possessed by the gelding. Billy had a lead rope upon him, but the spirited horse was fighting him.

"Oh, he is stunning," said Peter. "What is his name?"

"I have called him Blaze," said Charlotte. "He is still untutored as of yet, but I hope to ride him to the hunt next season."

It was at that moment that, despite Billy's calm demeanour, the horse shied, dancing up onto his hind legs for a moment. Cautiously, Billy took a step back, and as he did so, Isobel saw Samson move to climb over the fence, only to have Peter beat him to the punch. Her heart in her mouth, she watched him walk slowly but confidently towards the horse, his firm hand coming up to grasp the bridle that the horse wore. Isobel could see his lips moving even if she could not hear the words Peter was saying.

Instantly the horse calmed, and she watched as Peter stroked the horse's cheek before turning to slowly lead the horse in a gentle circuit around the paddock. Soon he had the horse walking in a circle around him on the lead rope and only then did he hand the rope back to Billy.

Isobel suddenly became aware that her heart was hammering in her chest. She knew that the duchess had expected Samson to take charge of the situation, but it had been Peter who had so expertly steadied the horse and Isobel could not have been more proud. As Peter walked back to the fence, he had a huge grin on his face, and Isobel could do nothing but return his gaze as his sparkling eyes captured her own.

And in that very moment, Isobel realised that her heart was, and would always be his, irrespective of what might befall them in the future.

"Miss Munroe, I was wondering if you might like to go for a walk this afternoon," said Peter. "If that is permissible, Lady Olivia?"

They had sat down to luncheon at midday and had enjoyed a very relaxed meal. Now Peter itched to spend time with Isobel, and a walk seemed just the thing. If only they could get away without a chaperone, that was, for the countess was sure to insist upon one if Isobel's *reputation* was to be spared. For her part, he watched Isobel look first at the countess and then at the duchess, an eager smile upon her lips.

"What a wonderful idea, Olivia," said the duchess. "There is a splendid walk around the lake that takes about an hour. No need for a chaperone either, I would say," she added, "for you will be in plain view from the house for most of it."

"Well," said Olivia, "be off with you then. Oh, and Isobel, make sure you take your parasol. The sun looks like it will be something fierce this afternoon."

Peter could hardly believe his luck and fully intended to take advantage of the situation. It took but a few minutes for them to find the path that led down towards the lake. Isobel had taken his arm with hers and had put up her parasol to shade herself from the sun. She wore a pretty walking dress and had left her hair down, and had Peter not known different he would have taken her for any other beautiful young miss out for a stroll in the countryside.

Once they were alone and away from prying ears, Peter had a question for Isobel, one which had consumed a deal of his time.

"Tell me, Isobel, does the duchess know your secret, and by association, mine?" he asked softly.

His companion kept walking, although he felt her hand tense upon his arm.

"Yes," she replied simply. "How did you guess?"

"I have had my suspicions all along. Lady Olivia and Lady Charlotte are so close that I cannot fathom the reason why they would not share such a thing."

"I know," said Isobel. "Have you noticed how alike in appearance they are? Why, they could be mistaken for sisters."

"Perhaps not sisters, but instead, mother and daughter. Putting that aside, there is the question as to why someone such as the Duchess of Camberly would risk so much to help someone such as yourself."

"I know," sighed Isobel. "The thought of it has kept me awake on many a night. She once told me that there had been someone there for her in her darkest hour and that she wanted to pass forward the kindness she received. All I can say with truth is that I believe her conviction and that I trust her implicitly."

"As do I," replied Peter. "Whilst I don't like the fact that she knows about us, I cannot help but offer thanks to her for providing the opportunity of us spending time together like this, especially when you take into consideration the circumstances of our relationship."

Isobel laughed. "Yes, in fact I think she is doing what she can to encourage us. Remarkable, is she not."

"I wonder why."

"I asked that very question. She told me that as I am a lady and you are a gentleman, it was perfectly natural for us to be together."

Soon, they reached the lake and paused, each of them staring out over the crystal-clear water. The atmosphere between them was tense so they stood in silence for a few moments, both seemingly lost in their own thoughts. That was until Isobel spoke her mind.

"Peter," she said, "do you think me insane for wanting this?"

Peter laughed. "I did, at first. When you told me about yourself, that day at Lady Olivia's, I thought you to be completely out of your mind. After all, it is simply not natural for a man to want the things you want. But now? No, I do not think you insane."

"But . . . but . . ." stammered Isobel.

"Is the world not full of buts and what if's, Isobel? Someone once told me that God did not make mistakes, but what if *He* did when *He* made you? For weeks now, I have watched you blossom, I have watched you become the person you were meant to be. But in truth, my opinion matters little. It is what you think that truly counts."

Now he turned Isobel, so that they were facing each other. He took her hands in his and looked down upon her, her own eyes cast down to the ground.

"There are times," she said as she lifted her eyes to his, "that I think I should end all of this before I bring scandal down upon the shoulders of those I care for. Perhaps I should go back to being David before anyone else discovers what I am."

"And would that make you happy?" asked Peter.

"No," she said adamantly, shaking her head for emphasis. "It would likely be the end of me, in all reality. For I think I would not care to live if I could not be the person I am now. As I said before, it is so hard to put into words why I need do this. It is a compulsion, an addiction, a need so entrenched within me that I could not deny it even if I tried. But I still worry endlessly that I would bring shame to Lady Olivia, to the Duchess, to you."

"Well let me tell you something, *Miss Isobel Munroe*," said Peter. "Before the duchess's musicale, I had all but made up my mind to put a halt to this. But Isobel turned up and from the very first moment began to prove that she, not David, was the person you were meant to be. I had never before seen the courage that you displayed by sitting on the piano stool. Then at the ball the other evening, it was so obvious that not a single person in the room would ever suspect that you are not who you seem to be, a beautiful red-headed Scottish lass who I am rapidly falling in love with."

Peter watched as Isobel's eyes widened, her mouth dropping open as he said those words.

"You . . . you . . . you love me?"

"Yes, Miss Isobel Munroe, I think I love you," he grinned.

Without warning, Isobel threw her arms around his neck, and Peter felt her reach up to him, her lips searching for his. He dipped his head and met her, pouring every ounce of passion that he felt for her into that one embrace. Part of him had worried that he would feel revulsion when kissing a woman, even if that woman was in reality a man. But this was so different, oh so different, for he could not imagine anything more perfect than the moment they shared. They kissed and kissed and kissed, Isobel running her hands through his hair in the most delightful way, pulling him deeper with every passing moment. It was if he had no control. His hands roamed over her body to feel the soft contours of her bottom, to linger upon what felt like a soft pert breast, his cock now hard and expectant, pressing against her thigh as if it had a will of its own.

Isobel giggled and pulled away.

"They are only padding, my lord," she said. She nodded down towards her chest to indicate her breasts. Then to Peter's astonishment, she allowed a hand to drop between them so that she could lightly caress his member through the fabric of his breeches. "But I think this is not."

Peter stepped back. "God Isobel, you realise that we are in full view of the house."

Isobel grinned and once more Peter felt his heart stop.

"I care not," she said, "for I love you too, Peter."

From a window in the house, Olivia watched, a smile drifting across her face as the young couple came together and embraced. She sighed, for part of her remembered the passion and love she had shared with her first husband and the kisses they had stolen when standing in the very same place. Suddenly a tear dripped from her eye, a tear born of pain and a tear born of joy: pain for the loss of a love that that she still felt deeply; joy for the couple only just starting out in a difficult life.

From behind, she felt a pair of hands snake around her middle, and looking up, she found Charlotte standing behind her, her chin now resting upon her mother's shoulder as their cheeks pressed together. Tenderly, she lifted her hand and stroked her firstborn's face.

"Look," she said as she nodded to the couple that stood by the lake.

"Oh, how wonderful," sighed Charlotte.

It was then that something else caught Olivia's eye. From deep within the woodland by the side of the lake, there came a single flash of reflected sunlight.

Chapter Twenty

The evening meal was a quiet affair, with Peter, Isobel, Olivia, and Charlotte sitting down to eat together. It had been a marvellously serene day, a day spent without worrying about the approbation of others. Wandering the grounds with Peter had been wonderful and it had soon turned into a day of talking and kissing and of falling even more hopelessly in love.

And now, at the dinner table, Isobel remembered, in intimate detail, each time they had stopped, each time they had kissed. Just the thought of Peter pressing his body against hers set a fire within her and had it not been for the bandages wrapped tightly around her, she knew she would have surely embarrassed herself. The passion they had shared that night at the Moonlight Club, also consumed her thoughts. Even now she could *feel* Peter's hands upon David's body, part of her reliving every searing caress, every lingering touch, and she knew that the heat upon her cheeks would surely give her away as her thoughts turned to repeating that night.

After dinner, the evening had dragged interminably for Isobel. They had sat in the parlour, and she had half-heartedly played the piano for a while. She and Peter had *enjoyed* a game of chess whilst Charlotte and Olivia sat before the fire with embroidery in hand. The four of them had even entered into a game of whist, although Isobel's mind being on other things meant that she had played quite atrociously. Much to her relief, at a little before eleven by the clock on the mantle, the party had retired for the evening, each returning to their own bedrooms upon the first floor of the house. Thus came step one in Isobel's plan, as she took careful note through which bedroom door that Peter went.

When she entered her own room, it was to find herself alone, just as she had expected to be. Before dinner she had instructed Mary to prepare her room, after which she would be free to join the other servants for dinner. Mary had readily agreed, for Isobel knew that she was looking forward to spending more time with Jenkins. The fire had been banked and her bed turned down, the long handle of a bed pan peeking out from beneath. As she had arranged, on the bed also lay a nightgown. However, it was not a gown she had ever seen before, but one which literally took her breath away.

"Oh my goodness," she whispered to herself as she picked it up.

The nightgown was made of the finest pure white silk, silk that seemed to have a life of its own as the material slithered between her fingers. Delicate Honiton lace fringed the hem and bodice, and if Isobel had not known better, it looked almost as if it had been made especially for her. Isobel giggled as she considered where the night gown might have come, heat flaring in her cheeks as she did so. The answer was obvious.

"Oh, my," she said. As if her legs could no longer carry her weight, Isobel sat heavily on the bed, holding the nightgown before her to view it once more.

This was a nightgown that had been made for one purpose in mind—the seduction of a man, and its mere presence in her room could mean but one thing. It was obvious. Those wonderful scheming ladies, Charlotte and Olivia, had not only guessed what she had in mind, but they actually approved of her doing so!

Swiftly she stripped out of her gown and undergarments until she stood before the fire, now dressed only in the silk stockings she had worn for dinner and the bandages that secured her phallus. Smiling, she pulled her stockings a little tighter to remove any wrinkles and re-secured the blue ribbons that held them firmly upon her thigh. Then she unwrapped herself before rubbing gratefully at her little cock to bring back the blood to her flesh, groaning with the pleasure of it as she did so.

So dressed, she sat before her dressing mirror to take the pins from her hair, allowing it to fall around her shoulders in loose curls which shone like burnished copper in the light of the fire. Mary, she was pleased to see, had laid out all of her cosmetics and brushes upon the table. Isobel set to work on her face, adding a little more kohl to her eyes and a little more colour to her cheeks. She even added a touch more of the ruby-coloured stain to her lips, for she adored the way it made her look.

When satisfied with her handwork, Isobel picked up the nightgown and carefully pulled it on overhead, groaning with pleasure as she felt the silk slither its way down her body. As she suspected it would be, it was a perfect fit. Slim little straps held the lace edged bodice upon her shoulders, and it moulded to her chest so snugly that her puffy and expectant nipples seemed to stand proud through the material. The skirt of the nightgown draped itself over her hips in the most delightful way, but then flared out a little in the shape of a bell to provide a modicum of modesty for her sex.

Isobel was enthralled by what she saw in the looking glass, for her image was everything she had ever dreamed it could be. Even with her own demanding eye, Isobel could find little to criticise. Yes, she was a little taller than she would have liked. Yes, her hands were a little larger than some and her breasts were non-existent. But in every other respect Isobel was the lady she wanted to be. Her beautiful red hair hung in masses of curls around her shoulders and face, giving her a soft and dreamy look. Miss Phoebe's medicine had definitely softened her facial features a little, so that with the applications of cosmetics not even the slighted hint of the boy she had once been remained.

Suddenly, Isobel hissed, letting out a breath that she had held for some time, knowing that her heart was beginning to pound with the audacity of what she planned. Yes, she was nervous, yet very fibre of her being wanted, nay, needed what she was planning to do.

For a few moments, she pressed her ear against the oak door of her chamber and listened for any sign of movement. On hearing nothing, she opened the door a crack and peered into the darkened corridor that was illuminated by a single candle mounted in a glass covered lantern. The landing was deserted, so Isobel slipped from her room, closing the door behind her as she walked into the darkness.

Peter was in bed, book in hand as he tried to settle his mind, knowing that if he did not do so, he would find it immensely difficult to sleep. Yet even though the candles by his bed provided enough light, he was finding it impossible to focus, having just discovered that he had read the same passage for the third time without registering a single word.

"Damn and blast it," he said as he threw down the book.

Reaching over to one side of his bed, he blew out one of the candles and was about to do the same to the other when there came a gentle knock upon his door. Before he could react, the door opened, and he watched in awe as Isobel slipped into the room. At first she stood there, her back against the door as she reached for the key in the lock. As soon as there was a satisfying click, Isobel smiled, and Peter once more felt his heart begin to beat.

She looked simply spectacular. Her glorious red hair was

loose around her shoulders, just as he liked it to be, a riot of curls surrounding a face that could have graced a goddess. She was dressed in a stunning pure white nightgown that draped over her body in the most seductive of ways, and Peter fancied he could even see the tell-tale signs of a small bulge between her legs.

Without saying a single word, he pulled back the covers of his bed, revealing to her that he was already naked, his cock lying thick and heavy against his leg. Isobel needed no more invitation. Gracefully she walked across the room and slipped herself into the bed next to him, lying on her back with her head on the pillow, her glorious hair fanning out beneath.

Peter turned onto his side and slipped an arm under her head, the other coming to rest upon the flat expanse of her stomach. His heart lurched as she looked up at him, her beautiful eyes beseeching him as her hands cupped his cheeks. Very slowly, she brought his face down to meet hers and in the most tender of ways she kissed him, slowly, softly, her lips teasing at him, her tongue dancing with his own.

Oh so gradually their kiss deepened, and as it did, Peter caressed the woman beneath him through the silky fabric of her night-rail, knowing that the sensuousness of his touch through the silk would bring exquisite pleasure. His hand lingered on her flat chest, feeling the hardness of her nipple, hearing her moan as he did so. He explored, moving his hand down, a finger now tracing the outline of her cock through the silk of her gown, moving further down until he found the hem around her ankles. Without breaking his kiss, he slipped his hand beneath the silk, purring a little in his mind as he found the stocking-clad legs that led the way to his prize.

He felt Isobel reach for him then, the elegant fingers of one hand wrapping around the base of his cock. God, he was so hard, his cock throbbing in time to his heart, and as she slowly moved her hand up and down, he very nearly spilled his essence like an inexperienced schoolboy. Instead, he stopped her, pulling her hand away, feeling her pout against his lips as he did so.

"No, Isobel" said Peter firmly. "Let me. Let me do everything. Do as I ask, please!" he demanded.

Isobel nodded and snuggled back into the bed, her eyes acknowledging that she understood his need to be in control. Slowly Peter allowed his hands to move once more as his fingers began to explore her again through the fabric of her nightdress. He lingered appreciatively on the bow of the ribbon which held her stocking before his hand moved slowly to trace the outline of her taut nipple, pinching it hard through the silk. Then his fingers moved up even further, to her face and neck, and she closed her eyes again as he delicately traced the outline of her nose, her lips, her eyes, with his fingers.

Little by little, Peter pulled upon the hem of Isobel's nightdress, tugging it up over her thighs as she wriggled her bottom. Impatiently, Isobel sat up, and Peter grinned as he watched her deftly remove the gown. Naked now except for the stockings, she lay back on the pillow, and Peter once more came to her and kissed her deeply.

"My God, Isobel," he whispered. "You are so beautiful, so perfect for me."

He kept his touch soft and gentle and was rewarded by the rise of goose pimples and an expectant shiver. Then he suddenly moved and took her nipple into his mouth and sucked hard.

Clearly not expecting this, Isobel arched her back in pleasure, pushing her into him even more deeply.

"Oh God, Peter!" she moaned.

He moved to the other breast, not wanting it to feel left out, and Isobel let out a hiss of pleasure through her clenched teeth

Lifting his head from her, Peter pushed her silk-encased legs apart. Then he knelt between them and reached delicately for her penis. Very gently, he took her into his hands and pulled back the skin to reveal the crown of her cock. She was oozing with excitement, the first few drops of slippery fluid escaping from her cock, making her skin glisten in the candlelight. Peter licked his lips as if he were about to taste the finest caviar and then slipped her into his mouth.

Once more her back arched, her moan so loud that anyone passing his door would surely have heard. Not caring, Peter licked her and caressed her, in one moment taking her cock into his mouth a fraction and then, in the next, forcing her cock into the depths of his throat. Within moments, she was panting and keening and moaning as he sucked her faster and harder, all the time her orgasm threatening to explode in his mouth. But Peter sensed this, too, and every time she was on the verge of erupting, he would stop, back off, slow down, mischievously prolonging her agony until she could stand it no longer.

"Peter, please. Oh, please, my sweet," she begged, her voice hardly a whisper.

He came to her then, pushing her into the bed as he covered her body with his muscular frame, his cock rubbing deliciously alongside her own. Once again he kissed her, this time his embrace hard and passionate, both of them sensing that the moment was near. With sudden thought, he then jumped up and dashed over to his dressing table, searching for a small bottle that he knew would be located within his housewife. Finding what he wanted, he once more came to her, pulling the little cork stopper from the crystal bottle with his teeth as he did so.

"A little body oil, love," he said softly.

He poured some of the oil onto his fingers and then reached for her, coating her flesh with the slippery liquid. From experience, he knew that his size could be painful, so he carefully smothered her opening, allowing an oily finger to enter her. Then another few drops of the oil coated his own flesh before he once more came to her.

Isobel wrapped her long stocking-clad legs around his hips, positioning herself, her body speaking the words he needed to hear. She was ready for him, and he wasn't going to disappoint her. With a hand, he placed his cock at her entrance, its huge head pushing in an effort to overcome the resistance it felt. Harder and harder he pressed, and he heard her hiss out loud from the pain of it. But Peter was not to be denied. Urgently he forced himself on and with a huge moan from him and an equally loud groan from Isobel, he felt himself slip inside.

They lay like that for some time, Peter's body tense as he fought to prevent his own premature orgasm, Isobel's gasps of air telling him of the discomfort she must be feeling. But soon, he felt her relax, her hips pushing up a little, informing him that the pain was gone and she was ready for what was yet to come. Little by little, he began to move, gently at first to allow Isobel to become used to his size. But his strokes soon became long and urgent and oh so exciting, her own cock rubbing delightfully between their bodies. They kissed, they caressed, they made love. As he thrust into her, Isobel wrapped her legs around his hips, her heels digging delightfully into the small of his back. Her arms snaked around Peter's back, too, her nails digging into his flesh as she clung to him, almost as if she were trying to climb into his very soul.

But then he paused, and he heard her hiss with disappointment as he pulled himself from her. He could quite easily have brought them both to fulfilment that way, but Peter had a different idea. He tugged at her body, making it clear he wanted her to turn over, and he was soon knelt behind her as he raised her up onto all fours.

This time, as his cock slipped effortlessly into her pert little bottom, he could tell there was no pain, only pleasure. Peter felt his lover push back into him, urging him on. So as soon as he was fully seated, he began to fuck her, really fuck her, his hips almost a blur as he thrust in and out. Faster and faster he went, and he watched as her arms buckled so that her face was pushed into the pillow beneath. The inevitable began to build, and even though her head was pressed into the mattress beneath, he heard her keening and moaning, urging her lover on.

"Oh God, Peter, oh dear God," she moaned. "Don't stop darling, don't stop, please don't stop, fuck me, darling, fuck me harder."

Isobel didn't even have to touch herself, for the act of being taken from behind proved to be more than enough. Within moments her back was arching as wave after wave of intense pleasure swept through her and as spurt after spurt of her scalding cum shot onto the sheets beneath. Faster and faster, harder and harder he fucked her, the very tip of his cock seeming to prolong her orgasm until, moments later, he too came, equally hard, his cock twitching madly as he orgasmed deep inside her body.

Slowly Peter relaxed behind Isobel, pushing the weight of his body down onto her back as he fell forward. As he did so, Isobel twisted slightly and turned with him so he was spooning her from behind, one arm under her neck as the other pulled her tightly against him. They lay that way for some time, Peter's cock still buried within her, until it started to soften and left her with an almost audible pop.

As Peter's manhood left her body, Isobel felt a moment of loss. Her whole body ached deliciously, a wonderful languid and lethargic feeling washing over her. She felt Peter snuggle behind her, his cock nestling in the cleft of her buttocks, and she could easily have fallen asleep that way. Instead, she turned so that they were almost nose to nose, her eyes focused upon his own. Reaching for him, Isobel kissed him once more, a slow soft tender kiss that spoke more than all the words of love ever written, and it was a kiss that Peter returned in equal measure.

"So," she whispered, "that was rather ... er ..."

"Mm, it was, wasn't it," Peter said, a rather satisfied and smug look upon his face.

"Better than the first time?"

"Much. I am told it always is when you love the person you are with," said Peter.

"Oh, I like the sound of that," said Isobel. "For I love you, too, Peter. In truth, I think I have loved you since the very first day we met at The Moonlight Club."

"So now beggars the question. What are we going to do about Lady Hamilton's plan that we *marry*? You know that if I am to inherit Winsworth Manor, I must do so."

For a moment Isobel lay silent, her eyes flickering over his, a serious and thoughtful expression upon her face.

"Will you tell me about the estate, Peter?" said Isobel.

Peter turned to lay on his back, pulling Isobel with him so that her head lay upon his shoulder, one of her hands coming to rest upon his chest. Lazily she began to play with the light down of hair that she found there, her fingers occasionally fondling his tiny nipples.

"Mm," said Peter. "Winsworth Manor was my mother's childhood home. As she was an only child and as the estate was un-entailed, she inherited the property on the occasion of her father's passing."

"What of the house?" asked Isobel.

"The house is a few miles outside Stow on the Wold, and it is, in style, very much like this one. There are twelve bedrooms, including the master and mistress suites. At present the house is managed by, I think, eleven staff. Mr. Figg is the butler, and his wife, Mrs. Figg, is cook cum housekeeper. They have been at the estate forever, and whilst they are strict beyond measure, the other servants seem to love them. Then there is Mr. Yates, who is my mother's estate manager, and who oversees the estate farm and the eighteen or so tenanted farms that make up the three thousand acres. I love it there. The family would often spend the summer there, and I have fond memories of my sister and I learning to ride and swim when we were children. The stables and paddocks of the estate farm are so magnificent that I even have a fancy to breed horses."

"In what way?" asked Isobel.

"Well, if there is one thing I know, it is horses."

"Yes, you do," said Isobel, thinking back with pride on how Peter had handled Blaze that very morning.

"Well, I have often thought about starting a stud farm. I still have many contacts in the army, and they are always looking for superior mounts. Only last week, at Tattershall's, I saw a Colonel bid four hundred guineas for a gorgeous Arabian, only to be outbid by his own commanding General. Anyway, Winsworth would be the perfect place."

For a moment, Isobel allowed herself to speculate, to imagine what life might be like if she were to *marry* and become *mistress* of Winsworth Manor. In her mind's eye she could see an idyllic yet quiet life in the country. Days would be spent managing the estate, something she would enjoy being involved with. There would be picnics in the countryside, an occasional dinner with friends, children . . . Shaking her head, she fought back the tears that threatened when she thought of children. Perhaps the horses could be her children. Starting a stud farm would require considerable investment, yet soon, on David's twenty-first birthday, she would have a considerable amount to invest, would she not?

But on the other side of the coin, Isobel knew she would find some things more than a little daunting. There would be a house to manage. Whilst David had knowledge of how to run an estate, he had not a clue as to how to manage a house. As Isobel, she would have to be like a commanding general to her troops, troops who in an instant could turn around and accuse her of being someone she did not appear to be.

"I hope you realise that the thought of Winsworth Manor makes me quite apprehensive," said Isobel. "Whomsoever you marry will be mistress of the house. For my part, I am not sure I could do that. In truth, I have not an inkling of how to do such a thing. Even the notion of it sends shivers of fear up and down my spine, especially of what the staff might think of me . . . because of . . . well you know."

"Well, don't be. If a lady can find the nerve to sit in front of dukes and duchesses to entertain them so splendidly on a pianoforte, then I am certain that the very same lady can find the wherewithal to run a small family home."

"I like it when you call me that," said Olivia as her hand slowly moved down to his cock.

"Mmm, call you what?"

"A lady," she said. As she spoke, she took him in her fist, relishing the way his flesh began to swell at her touch.

"Well, is that not what you are? My very own and very *special* lady . . . God, Isobel, if you keep that up, I will not be answerable for what happens next."

"No, you will not, for *I* will be. After all, is it not my turn to pleasure you, my lord?" she said.

Giggling to herself, she jumped from the bed to fetch a dampened washcloth from the nightstand. With it she cleansed herself before bringing the cloth to Peter. Climbing back onto the bed, she straddled his thighs. Peter lay motionless as she began to gently stroke the cloth over his muscular body, knowing he was enjoying the attention from his smile. She wiped his face, ridding his brow of the perspiration that was there. She wiped his neck and chest, lingering upon the hard pebbles of his nipples. She stroked the cloth over the muscles of his stomach and hips, then took his cock into her hands. He was so much bigger than she, and she could not help but lick her lips with the anticipation of what she had in mind.

At first, she merely grazed the single eye with the tip of a polished fingernail. But as he moaned his appreciation, Isobel washed him with such tenderness that his cock once more became hard and engorged with blood, every vein throbbing to her touch.

And when all was as it should be, she nonchalantly threw the cloth over her shoulder before placing her hands upon his chest. Grinning wildly, Isobel leant forward, her hair pooling down over her face as she kissed the man who lay beneath. She took her time, worshipping his mouth, exploring it with her tongue. She nibbled on his ear, then kissed the side of his neck. She licked his neck underneath his chin and caressed his nipples, teasing them between her teeth. She planted tiny little kisses on each of the ridges of muscle on his stomach, slowly making her way down to her prize.

Moving so that she knelt between his outstretched legs, Isobel first let her hands tease the hair upon his thighs, her gentle fingers tracing the ugly scar that she found there, Moon-shaped, and the length of her outstretched fingers. Isobel could only guess at the suffering it must have caused him. Yet somehow, he had survived the horror of it; had been returned so that he could find his way to her. And the thought of it had her sending up a brief yet silent prayer of thanks.

Peter was massively hard when she finally took him in hand once more. Isobel paused and smiled at her man, and then, without further ado, she opened her lips and took him into her mouth. Peter's hips bucked upwards, and Isobel smiled around his flesh with the pride of a woman who was bringing pleasure to her man.

"Bloody hell," he whispered.

Slowly she began to rock her head, her tongue swirling around his crown each time the head of his cock threatened to pop from her mouth. At times she was slow and gentle and teasing, at others she took him deep into her throat, her mind recalling the first time she had done this to him as she did so. When she had first met Peter at the Moonlight Club, she had been in the guise of a boy. But that night, when they had made love, in her mind it had been Isobel whom Peter had taken to bed, not David. To her, the act of pleasuring a man was the act of a woman, and the thought of doing so once more thrilled her to the core. Just as she had before, she began to lick him, her tongue lapping at his flesh as one hand gripped his length, whilst the other gently cupped his magnificent balls. After a few moments, Isobel felt Peter move a little, and as she glanced up, she could see that he had propped a pillow behind his head. It was as his hand smoothed her hair behind her ears that Isobel realised why.

He wanted to watch

Obligingly, she again took him into her mouth, and this time it was his turn to groan. As her lips stretched to accommodate the contours of his flesh, she once more began to move her head up and down. At first she moved but a fraction, relying on her tongue swirling around the crown of his cock to bring him pleasure. But as she grew in confidence, each time she pushed forward, she took a little more of his length into her throat, until every last part of him was buried in her mouth, his balls resting against her chin. She held him there for as long as she could, the gag reflex in her throat flexing and stimulating him until with a gasp, she released him. Again and again, she took him deep, her lips surrounding his flesh as he watched on in awe, his breath coming in shorter gasps now as he occasionally threw back his head in delight.

Suddenly he pushed her away from him.

"Turn around Isobel," he demanded as he pulled at her body, making it quite clear what he wanted her to do. She was more than happy to comply, and within moments her knees straddled his head. Isobel felt his hands upon her hips, pulling her down towards his head and she felt herself respond as she shuffled backwards, gasping as she felt the warmth of his mouth upon her own rock-hard flesh. God, he knew how to suck cock too, and she had hardly taken him back into her own mouth before she felt him swallow her whole, causing a huge spasm of pleasure to shudder through her body. For her part, she made love to his massive cock with her mouth whilst all the time the sensations, those incredible feelings he was generating in her, made her pant even more with desire.

Now Isobel wanted more, wanted to try something she had always imagined doing.

She pulled herself from his mouth and sat up, moving to kneel between his legs. It took but a few seconds for her to locate the oil bottle, and soon his cock and her depths were liberally coated once more. Then facing him, she straddled his hips yet again. Slowly she raised herself up and over his body, swiftly positioning him at her entrance, her own expectant cock still erect and hard in front of her. Little by little she pushed herself down to impale herself upon him, every inch of his cock that penetrated her body making her hiss with a combination of pain and pleasure. She took him all, and when he was buried deep inside, she paused and reached to kiss him awkwardly on the lips, allowing herself a moment time to get used to his size once more.

Then she began to ride him like the prize stallion he was. She began with a gentle rocking motion of her hips. As she became sure of her balance, she increased her speed, her thighs pushing up and down as his cock slid effortlessly in and out of her. Faster and faster she went, her breath now coming in short gasps from the effort, her own sex flapping wildly in front of her.

To Isobel's delight, Peter was starting to moan and groan as his body began to respond beneath her, his hips beginning to buck upwards to match her rhythm. Something wonderful then happened. With neither rhyme nor reason, they found themselves in perfect unison, their bodies in perfect harmony as they matched each other thrust for thrust.

As Isobel imagined he would when in a cavalry charge, Peter won the race. His head went back and his teeth clenched, his body visibly pulsing and throbbing as his back arched, pushing his hips high into the air, causing his cock to grind even deeper into her body.

On and on Isobel went, not wanting to stop, milking every last ounce of cum from him until moments later she too came, Peter's hand upon her cock as her own cum launched into the air, landing in little globules on his chest and stomach.

When Isobel awoke, she found herself in her own bed, even though she could not remember how she got there. Once more, her body was covered by the beautiful nightdress, a body that ached with the deliciousness that could only come from a night filled with passion.

And on the ring finger of her left hand sat the most stunning sapphire and diamond promissory ring.

Chapter Twenty-One

According to the carriage clock in her room, it was a little after eight in the morning when Mary came bustling in to help Isobel dress for the day. Of course, the first thing that Mary noticed had to be the ring that Isobel now wore upon her left hand, and the shriek of delight that Mary let out was probably heard in London.

"So he has asked you?"

"Yes, last night, and I have accepted."

Isobel, unable to keep the worry from her voice, had captured her bottom lip between her teeth before swinging her legs from the covers to sit the edge of her bed.

"And why do I think that this does not excite you, Miss Isobel?" asked Mary as she sat next to her. "Any who knows you can see in your eyes that you love him, despite the peculiarity of your situation!"

"Oh, I don't know why," replied Isobel sarcastically. "Perhaps it is that I worry endlessly that this, like a barrel of gunpowder on a bonfire, is going to blow up in our faces when someone exposes me for what I am. Besides, how can I marry him? No matter how much I love him, I can hardly stand in church, before God, as if I were a true born woman!"

"No, perhaps not, but there is always the anvil priest in Gretna Green," grinned Mary. "'Tis a legal marriage, but one where they ask no questions, provided enough money changes hands. You could *marry* Lord Peter there and no one would be the wiser."

"Yes, the thought had crossed my mind. But there are other

considerations," whispered Isobel. "There is the fact that Peter's family will be disappointed not to see him marry. There is the fact that I cannot bear him children. There is the fact that I will become mistress of his home. Then there is you, Mary."

"Me?"

"Yes you, Mary. You are like a sister to me, one in whom I have absolute confidence. I couldn't bear the thought of leaving you behind. Who else could I trust with my secret?"

Isobel stared in surprise as Mary grinned happily back at her.

"Have you ever thought of asking me direct to come with you?" she replied, her voice soft and gentle.

"Why? It is clear that you would never leave the employ of Lady Olivia."

"Well, about that," said Mary sheepishly. For some reason, she then placed her hands over her own flaming cheeks.

"What? Come on! 'Fess up, missy," demanded Isobel.

"'Tis Will, William Jenkins that is, his lordships valet. He and I . . ." she mumbled.

"My God, you little strumpet. Did you spend last night in his bed, *young lady*?" demanded Isobel, unable to keep the broadest grin from her face.

"I might have done!" said Mary. "Oh Isobel, he says he loves me and wants to marry me," she gushed. "Yes, I know he lost a leg in the war, but he is so kind and strong and handsome. Would it not be wonderful if he and I . . . well."

"Oh, this is simply perfect. Provided Peter agreed, it would mean that you and I could stay together. But what about Lady Olivia?" she said with sudden thought.

"I have already taken the liberty of speaking to her and she has given her whole-hearted blessing should this be the way things work out."

Mary and Olivia were still hugging when a knock came upon the bedroom door. Mary hopped down from the bed and practically danced over to the door to find Phoebe standing there with a straw-filled wooden box in her hands. Her hugely pregnant belly preceded her, and she was puffing a little from shortness of breath, her cheeks red with the effort of having to climb the stairs. Yet still she had a smile upon her face.

"Good morning ladies," she said as she waddled into the room.

"Oh my goodness," said Mary as she relieved Phoebe of the box. "You should have sent for me and I would have come to collect these. You should not be climbing the stairs carrying such things, not in your condition. What would Mr Samson think?"

"What Samson does not know will not hurt him. Besides, many such as I continue working in the fields until the very day they drop a child, some even birthing them there." Phoebe grinned ruefully as, with her hand upon her back and with Mary's support, she sat upon a chair.

"And you know what I think of that," said Mary. She wrinkled her nose up in disgust.

"What is it you bring, Phoebe?" asked Isobel.

"It is a new supply of your medicine, Miss Isobel. Mary informed me that you are running low, so I made you a new batch. I would also like to take the opportunity of examining you, with your permission Miss Isobel. This is a powerful medicine, and I would like to check that it is doing you no harm."

"Of course. What would you have me do?"

"If you would take off that rather lovely night-rail and then sit upon the edge of the bed for me, Miss Isobel."

As Mary took the crate of bottles into Isobel's dressing room, Isobel did as she was asked, even though she was naked beneath the nightgown. With a supreme effort, once Isobel was sat, Phoebe heaved herself from her chair and waddled over to the bed.

"So, Miss Isobel, tell me. Did you suffer any sickness?" she asked.

"Only at first, but some of that I also put down to stress of the situation."

"And have you suffered from any other symptom, dizziness, megrims, aches and pains in the body?"

"No, not really," replied Isobel.

"If you would please stand, Miss Isobel."

Isobel did as she was asked and stood before her. Phoebe then conducted a thorough examination. She pressed her ear against Isobel's chest and listened to the pounding of her heart. She checked her eyes and smelled her breath. She poked and prodded, feeling the muscles within Isobel's arms and thighs, and then, much to Isobel's embarrassment, inspected her phallus.

"Have you seen any impairment in function?" she asked.

Isobel blushed furiously as she thought of the previous night and how Peter had brought her to fulfilment no less than four times.

"No, none at all," she replied.

"And are you regular with your toilet, Miss Isobel?"

"Yes."

"Good, good, you may put on your robe Miss Isobel," said Phoebe. With a groan she lowered herself down onto the chair once more.

Isobel slipped on her robe and tied it around her middle before sitting upon the bed, waiting for Phoebe's verdict. She did not have to wait long.

"Well, Miss Isobel, you seem to be making excellent progress. From what I can tell, your skin has softened beautifully, and I can already see that your body hair growth has been significantly reduced. You appear to have lost some muscle in your arms and legs, and I already see some enlargement of your hips and seat. Best of all, I see some growth in the area of your breasts, Miss Isobel. The rings of colour have definitely darkened, and your nipples are much enlarged."

"Yes, I had noticed, and they are much more sensitive too," whispered Isobel. "When do you think my real breasts will begin to grow?" she asked.

"I have three strengths of my medicine, Miss Isobel. Currently I am giving you the middle one, to allow your body to become used to it. The weakest preparation will merely maintain your current body state. The middle one, should you continue to take it, will effect gradual change, perhaps over a number of years. The strongest is the one to take should you desire rapid breast growth. In your case, however, I would not recommend it, especially with the current situation with Lord Fairfax, for it would, without doubt, seriously affect the function of your phallus."

"Ah . . . oh . . . yes," replied Isobel. "Perhaps it is wise to stay with what I have then."

"Indeed," said Phoebe as she once more heaved herself to her feet. "Now, if you would excuse me, I have a lot to do before the arrival of our guests."

Isobel looked on as Phoebe waddled slowly over to the door, her massive belly preceding all else. It was there that she paused and turned to look at Isobel.

"Oh, and by the way, congratulations on your betrothal, Miss Is . . ."

It was at that very moment that it appeared as if someone had upturned a pail of water beneath Phoebe's skirts. With a splatter, a pool of fluid splashed upon the oaken floor as Phoebe groaned and clutched her at her belly. She hissed in pain as she leant her hands against the wall to brace herself, her cheeks puffing and panting as she did so.

"Oh dear," she whispered. "I think my waters have broken, and on today of all days."

It took but six hours. In Isobel's very bed, a beautiful little baby girl was born, followed, a mere eight minutes later, by her equally beautiful sister.

Chapter Twenty-two

"I'm sorry to have dragged you away from your family Samson, but pray tell, what have you discovered?" asked Charlotte, as they walked through the garden together.

"Well Missy Charlotte," said Samson. His voice was low, as if to guard from being overheard, even though there was no on there. "The man's name is William Drummond, and he is cousin to Viscount David Drummond. Their respective fathers are twins. David's father was the elder, so he became Earl. Drummond is staying at the Cock and Bull in Kings Langley and is currently in the trees over there, watching us through a glass."

"I thought he might be."

"I had Michaels spend the night in the bar of the Cock and Bull last night, my lady, so do please forgive him if he sports a headache today. According to the landlord, William Drummond took rooms two days before your party arrived, so I suspect he was the one who broke into Lady Hamilton's home and read the entry in her appointment book."

"My thought exactly," said Charlotte. "And in your expert opinion, what do you think his intentions are?"

"In my *humble* opinion, he can only be here to do David Drummond harm. He followed Master David's trail to London and to Lady Hamilton, then followed you all here, thinking that we might be hiding him in Thorpe House."

"Yes," mused Charlotte. "It occurs to me that there are two possibilities. First Drummond may be under orders to locate David before reporting back to his father. More sinister would be a plan to kill David, for that would probably leave open the door for him to become Earl in his stead. Either way, we must stop him before he discovers David's whereabouts."

"Would you like me to kill him, my lady?" said Samson. He spoke as if the deed would be of little consequence, as if Drummond was a merely an annoying tick that needed removing. There was no malice or hatred in his voice, only matter of fact.

For a second, Charlotte paused and considered the offer, for it would not be the first time she had ordered Samson to do such a thing. In fact, in Jamaica she had once watched Samson crush a man's head between his hands, and had relished the occasion. But to kill Drummond would certainly raise suspicion with his family and would likely bring more looking for David.

"No," she said. "You now have three children, and I will not risk the hangman's noose for you. I think I have a better idea. Would you be so kind as to find Billy for me and ask him to come see me?"

Isobel sat, her face ashen as she listened to Lady Charlotte, an overwhelming desire to be sick almost consuming her. This was her worst nightmare, the powder keg that she had feared, and it was about to explode in her face.

"So that is my plan," said Charlotte softly. "I do not think that Drummond has recognised you, Isobel, but we must act before he does."

"Can I not kill the man?" said Peter, the darkness in his eyes telling everyone of his murderous intent. "I could bury him deep and no one would be the wiser."

"N . . . no . . . Peter. I cannot allow you to do that for me," stammered Isobel.

"Besides, what if he has already sent letters to David's

father? We cannot take that risk," said Olivia. "Lady Charlotte's plan seems to be the only way."

"I still do not like it." said Peter angrily. "It puts everyone at risk. What if the man is armed with pistols?"

"Have no worry. Samson will not allow harm to come to anyone," said Charlotte. "You have my word on that." She then turned to Peter and set her piercing gaze upon his. "But I will need your co-operation, Peter, if this plan is to work."

"I still do not like it!" Peter roared.

"I am sure you do not," said Charlotte, "but it is the only way."

William was at the end of his tether. He was hungry and he was bored and all he wanted to do was to get back to the inn and that comely bar maid he hoped to get into his bed. For days he had watched the house, and in all of that time there had not been a single sign of David Drummond.

However, being on his own had given him time to plan his next step, should Drummond fail to appear.

The key to David's whereabouts remained Lady Hamilton, and if she was not hiding David in the house, she would surely know more of his current location. On more than one occasion, he had seen the countess and her companion taking a walk together. What he would do would be to snatch one or both of them at gunpoint, take them deep into the wood, have his fun with them and then make them talk. The girl was certainly comely and would be worth his attention. But in saying that, the countess was also definitely worth a roll, even though she was much older.

"One more day," he whispered to himself.

The day wore on. He made a meagre lunch of the pie he had bought and drank a bottle of beer, knowing that the thirty pounds he had stolen would not last much longer. Once in a

The Making of a Lady

while he would scan the house, the small telescope trained upon the bedroom windows in the vain hope of spotting someone resembling David.

It was then that he observed the party riding out.

Instantly his mind was alert as he reached once more for his telescope. There were six people in the party. The first was the huge black man. He was riding an equally big black horse, but thankfully, after saying something to the party, he rode away at speed. This left five. The duchess was astride a beautiful grey, whilst the countess rode side-saddle upon a pretty mare. Behind them was the man that Drummond had seen squiring the pretty redhead, a man who rode alongside the pretty redhead herself. Finally came a fifth rider, and instantly Drummond felt his heart begin to beat with excitement.

The fifth rider was on a handsome black stallion, a mount that could only belong to someone of importance. He was dressed as a gentleman in coat and breeches, and on top of his head sat a mop of bright red hair. Drummond stared and stared, hardly daring to believe. It had to be David! He was the right age, the right size, and the man even rode in the style of a Scottish gentleman.

"Fuck," he whispered to himself. "I was right."

Frantically he grabbed for the blanket which lay upon the ground, and from under it he pulled out the hunting rifle he had secreted there. It was already loaded, so he placed it across the bough of a tree and trained it onto the party of riders, assessing their distance to be still well over a mile.

Patience, Will, patience. Let them get closer.

He watched and waited, only to groan once more under his breath when the party stopped in a pretty clearing by the side of the lake, some six hundred yards from where he was concealed. Both men instantly dismounted, and, like gentlemen, started to help the ladies of the party dismount. Then from saddle bags appeared blankets and flasks and packages of food, all of which were laid out upon the ground.

"They are having a fucking picnic!" he whispered to himself as he left his rifle and once more picked up his spy glass.

He again trained the glass upon the party. The man he did not know was sat next to the pretty redhead, whilst the other, the man he suspected to be David, sat between the countess and the Duchess. William stared at the man intently through the lenses of his glass, the image now large enough for careful scrutiny.

"It has to be him," said Will to himself.

The young man was no older than one and twenty and was stylishly dressed. Although William was expecting his hair to be long, instead it had been cut short, presumably in an effort to disguise his identity. However, there was no denying it to be the shade of red that all of his family sported. Even the man's face looked familiar: the same shaped nose; the same roundness of jaw. Searching in his pocket, he pulled out the miniature portrait and stared at intently. Then he looked back at the lad, then back at the painting, his mind convinced. Yes, it had to be him.

William once more picked up the rifle and looked down the sights.

"Shit," he said, as he realised that one of the ladies now blocked his shot.

But William smiled to himself. After all, had he not been brought up hunting the wild stags of the Scottish Highlands? Such hunts were born of patience, and William considered himself to be an expert in the art of the *stalk*. Even his father's gillie had told him so. Little by little, so as to not disturb the leaves of the tree against which he rested, William pulled back his gun. Crouching low, he then backed away deeper into the woodland.

Very slowly, he began to make his way to the left, closing the range, looking for a more advantageous spot. He soon found it, a deep thicket of trees that had the perfect view, the perfect angle for a shot at Drummond. There was even the hint of a trail behind that would offer him an easy method of escape once the shot was taken. He paused to control his breathing, and then, taking extreme care not to step on ground that would give him away, William chose his spot and lifted his rifle once more, scanning the party to check whether anyone suspected his presence.

All seemed well as he silently extended his glass. The duchess and the countess were sat upon the rug with Drummond still between them. From this distance, his face was much clearer, and it was obvious that the brat felt uncomfortable with his situation, simply by the way his fingers fidgeted with his cravat. The other man and the countess's companion, however, were stood in the shade of a nearby tree, partly hidden from their companions. The woman had her back to Drummond, and he could see how her long red hair draped beautifully down a very shapely back. He grinned as he saw the girl glance towards the countess, presumably checking to see if they were unobserved, since moments later she was in the man's arms and was kissing him deeply, a kiss that he was returning in equal measure.

To his mind his choice of position was perfect, and even though he could see the couple embracing, Drummond doubted that they would be able to see him. Once more he lifted his rifle and placed it upon the branch of a tree. He pulled back on the hammer, wincing as it locked in place with an audible click. He checked the flint and the frisson, making sure the priming powder was dry before pulling the rifle stock hard into his shoulder. Automatically, his mind turned to the shot. He judged the distance; he considered the wind, for he knew that he would only get one chance.

He aimed, his finger resting lightly upon the trigger, waiting for the perfect moment.

It was then that all hell broke loose.

From behind him, a hand grasped the rifle barrel, forcing it into the air so that when his finger jerked upon the trigger, the shot flew harmlessly into the sky. Instinctively he turned, and there stood the biggest black man that Drummond had ever encountered. It also was the last thing he saw, for a massive fist shot out, hitting him in the face, shattering his nose as he fell unconscious to the ground.

Chapter Twenty-three

"How is she?" asked Charlotte as she strode back into the house some fifty minutes later.

"Not good, darling," replied Olivia. "She has locked herself in her room, and will not even let Mary enter, let alone Peter."

"I surmised as much" said Charlotte. "She is probably petrified that someone else, if not Drummond, is going to expose her secret to the world."

"I know," said Olivia, "but what are we to do about it?"

Charlotte stood in thought, knowing that she needed to do the one thing she had avoided so far. However, she could see no other way out of this dilemma, so she sighed and then smiled at her mother.

"I will speak to her, Mama," she said softly.

Slowly, Charlotte ascended the stairs, giving herself time to compose the things she wanted to say. When, moments later, she found herself outside Isobel's room, it was to find Peter and Mary standing there, both looking quite perplexed.

"She will not let us in," said Peter. His voice and his face were a mixture of rage and panic.

"Both of you, go downstairs," said Charlotte. Her voice was soft yet commanding, and even though Peter was about to argue, he obviously thought better of it and turned away.

Silence pervaded the corridor, and Charlotte paused for a moment to gather herself. Then she knocked upon the door.

"Isobel, it is Charlotte, and I am on my own." Again, she kept her voice gentle yet firm, hoping that Isobel might respond. "Be so kind as to open the door, Isobel, for I would so hate to have Samson break it down."

Charlotte listened, and to her surprise, she heard the key turn in the lock. She had known that Isobel would be upset, but when the door opened, even she gasped in shock with what she saw. Isobel, it seemed, had tried to eradicate all sign of herself. Her dress was torn, as if she had tried to rip it from her body, and all traces of makeup had been violently scrubbed from her face. In her trembling hands she held a pair of shears, and there was no doubt in Charlotte's mind that Isobel had been about to rid herself of the locks that hung lankly around her face.

"Oh, darling," said Charlotte. Instinctively, she stepped into the room, her arms outstretched to gather her in.

Isobel flew to her, throwing her arms around Charlotte's middle as she pressed her face into her shoulder. The tears flowed, tears which soaked into Charlotte's dress, uncontrollable tears that wracked Isobel's body, and all that Charlotte could do was to hold her and hug her as if she were her very own child.

"There, everything will be well, Isobel," she whispered. "You have my word on it."

"But how?" she moaned. "How can it be well? The whole world will know of what I am. I cannot do that. I cannot do that to Peter, to Olivia, to you. I cannot. I will not. I will be David once more. I will move away. I will get my inheritance, live simply. No one need be associated with me. I will not allow it!"

"So, you are going to live alone for the rest of your life, are you?"

"If I must, yes," said Isobel.

"Well, I for one think that you should not do anything rash. After all, Drummond is no longer a problem."

"But only if he believed Billy was David Drummond."

"And why should he not, for thanks to Mary's talents, Billy looked the twin of the portrait we found upon Drummond. And then there was the fact that whilst *David* sat with me, *Miss Isobel Munroe* was clearly seen to be kissing her betrothed behind a tree."

"But what if he wasn't fooled" said Isobel, the tears once more streaming down her face. "How can I possibly maintain this subterfuge? How can I possibly make anyone believe that I am Isobel? What if my father was to send someone else? I can't Charlotte, I can't. No one could!"

Charlotte sighed; her mind made up about the things she needed to say. Slowly she walked over to Isobel's wardrobe to extract a clean dress for her.

"Do you trust me, Isobel?" asked Charlotte.

"Yes, but . . ."

"Then do me one favour. Put on this dress, brush your hair, clean your face, and come for a walk around the lake with me. If when we return you still feel the same way, I will help you to return to being David, if you so wish it."

It took a few moments, but Charlotte had to smile as Isobel finally nodded her assent.

The day had turned out to be typical of an English summer, and cotton wool clouds floated across a sun that gave warmth to the day. Peter had tried to insist that he accompany them, but Charlotte had put him off with a stare. Now the two of them walked arm in arm with the comforting warmth of the sun on their faces as they made their way slowly towards the lake.

"Isobel," said Charlotte. "I know you worry endlessly about the choices you have made, but really, you should not. For I am certain that you can be successful in this endeavour, despite your fears."

"But how, Lady Charlotte, how can that be?"

"For that, I have a story to tell. However, before I do so, I must have your word that you will speak of this to no one, no one at all."

"Yes, of course," said Isobel. "You have my word."

"Very well, but know you, Isobel, that the consequences will be dire for everyone if you break your word."

"I understand."

"My story begins a little over five and thirty years ago when a child was conceived in that very house," said Charlotte. Turning she waved to the manor house behind them. "Nine months later, Sir Oliver Royce and his wife Olivia . . . yes, our Olivia . . . were overjoyed to be delivered of a son, whom they called Charles. Sir Oliver's lifelong friend, the Duke of Camberly, even agreed to be godfather to the child. Life here was idyllic. That was until disaster fell upon the family. When the boy was but eight years old, his father died in what appeared to be a riding accident whilst out hunting. Suffice it to say that both Lady Olivia and her son Charles were completely distraught.

"Enter the villain of the story, George Hamilton, Earl of Weybridge, a supposed friend of the family. On the day that Lady Olivia came out of mourning, he was on the doorstep, determined to take her as his wife. At the time, Lady Olivia saw him as something of a saviour, for she was not coping well with the death of her husband. She had an estate to run and a boy child whom she believed needed a father figure in his life. What she didn't know was that the earl had long coveted her and the estate and had determined to have both by facilitating the murder of her husband."

"Oh my goodness!" gasped Isobel.

"Well, Lady Olivia married the earl, and he took both her and Charles into his household. Now the only problem that remained to him was ownership of the land that should have come with them. You see, the estate was un-entailed, and as such had been willed to Charles on the occasion of his twenty-first birthday. Until that time, the estate had been left in trust with his mother, Olivia. Now the Earl was a profligate man, and he badly needed the vastly superior income that the Thorpe estate generated. So he decided that Charles must be taken out of the picture. When the boy was but fourteen years old, the earl arranged for Charles to be kidnapped when on his way to his school. He ordered that he be murdered and buried in some shallow pit, knowing that should this happen the estate would revert to Olivia and thus, through marriage, to him."

"But how do you know all of this?" said Olivia.

"I will come to that in a moment. Fortunately for Charles, the kidnapper had other ideas and saw this as an opportunity to make even more money than the Earl was offering. Instead of shooting him, as ordered, he took Charles to Liverpool, where he sold the boy to the captain of a slaver, a truly evil man. For the next seven months, Charles was locked in the captain's cabin and subjected to every perverse act that the Captain could devise.

"Oh, the bastard," whispered Isobel.

"By the time the ship arrived in Kingston, Jamaica, Charles had determined to escape. He was, of course, caught, beaten and then sold once more, this time to a Madam who ran a brothel. She needed a boy to add to her stable, one who would service any man who was so inclined. Charles was forced to become that boy. Then something strange began to happen. As the boy grew, he started to enjoy the attentions of the men that paid for him and even started to fantasise about being one of the *girls* in every respect. One day he was caught in a room, trying on a dress that belonged to one of the girls. Instead of being beaten, the madam thought this to be a brilliant idea and had the girls make him up to look like one of them. It was on that day that Charles became Charlotte."

As Charlotte uttered those words, Isobel abruptly stopped

walking, almost as if she had walked into a dry stone wall. Her mouth dropped open in shock, her eyes wide, as she turned to Charlotte and stared.

"No," she whispered. "It cannot be!"

"Oh, but it is, Isobel. I know of this story, for the boy was me," she replied simply.

"But . . . but . . ."

"No, let me finish. Now, one of my regular clients was a man called Sir David Winters who happened to be one of the wealthiest plantation owners in Jamaica. Fortunately for me, he took a fancy to the boy named Charlotte, and for an extraordinary sum of money, purchased me from the madam. I was not quite sixteen years of age at the time. He took me to his home, and it was there that I first met Phoebe. Sir David was an extraordinary man who, like Peter, wanted a *wife*. He treated me with ultimate kindness, and for the next two years, I shared his bed and was taught everything I needed to know about being a lady. I also began taking Phoebe's remarkable medicine. Then, when I was but eighteen years of age, he introduced me to Jamaican society as his wife."

Wistfully, Charlotte paused as she remembered, a tear forming in her eye as she did so. Her David had taken a frightened, confused young man out of a veritable hell and had gently introduced him into the delights of being a woman. And she had truly loved him for doing so.

"My life was wonderful, Isobel. I was accepted as the woman I appeared to be, as the woman I had always known to be buried inside of me. I had a man who loved me and whom I loved in return. I became involved in the running of the estates, especially in the welfare of the slave workers, and even persuaded David to free many of them in return for indentured service. Unlike many, we paid them a small wage, provided education for their children and basic medical care. It was at this time that Samson entered my service after I saved him from the hangman's noose, his only crime having been to prevent a sadistic overseer from beating a horse half to death."

There was pride in her voice as she related this part of her story, for having helped her workers this way had brought her a great deal of personal satisfaction. Yet her words were tinged with sadness as she continued her account.

"It was ten years later that yellow fever took my David."

"I'm sorry," said Isobel.

"For a while I was quite bereft. But to my surprise, David left me everything he owned in his will, and I became a very wealthy woman. It was then that something occurred that was to change the course of my life. I was in Hamilton when I saw the ship captain that had brought me to Jamaica. In a matter of seconds, every ugly memory came flooding back, and in that moment, I resolved to have my revenge on those that had caused me hurt."

Charlotte paused as she became lost in yet another memory, one that even she was unwilling to share. That day she had been with Samson, and together they had waited until darkness had fallen. They had followed the captain from tavern to tavern until he was almost too drunk to stand. Only then had they lured him into a dark alley where, on her orders, Samson had crushed his head between his hands.

"So I returned to London as the fabulously wealthy and extremely beautiful, even though I say so myself, Lady Charlotte Winters. I leased a townhouse and set about establishing myself as a member of the ton. One of the first things I did was to make myself known to the Duke of Camberly, my godfather, and also somehow agreed to be chaperone for Anne's come out season. It was during this time that I engineered a situation which forced the Earl of Weybridge to sell me Thorpe and its estates, even though they actually belonged to me. Having to sell did not sit well with him, for shortly afterwards, he succumbed to a seizure which took his life. I also revealed myself to my mother, Lady Olivia, as her long lost son—now daughter. Oh, and I also fell in love once more.

"For me, that proved to be the most trying of situations, as you most probably can imagine. After all, James is a duke and cousin to the royal family. In addition, James is not like Peter. He is most definitely a man's man, if you know what I mean. Accordingly, like you, I had all sorts of doubts and constantly questioned my sanity. But, as luck would have it, he fell in love with me too and here I am today, the Duchess of Camberly, a man in a woman's dress yet still one of the leading feminine figures in the ton, thanks to the influence of my husband."

"So that is why both you and Lady Olivia agreed to help me," said Isobel softly.

Charlotte stopped and took Isobel by the hands, forcing her to turn and look at her. Very gently she caressed Isobel's cheek, hoping that the girl could see the sincerity she felt.

"How could we not, Isobel? You were so much like me, other that the fact that you are far more feminine than I was at your age. You deserved a chance of finding the same happiness and peace of mind that I have as a woman."

"That still does not negate the danger of scandal that we both face daily."

"No, it does not. But look at me. Have I not done so successfully for the past five years in London and for ten years before that in Jamaica?"

"But what about my cousin, what about my father?" said Isobel, a look of real pain flitting across her face.

Charlotte's reply was immediate and firm and designed to set Isobel's mind at ease, even if in her own mind there was doubt. The truth was that Charlotte thought her arrangements to be the only way that Isobel's identity could be protected, short of having Samson stick a blade through

Drummond's heart.

"What about them? If we stick to the plan, all will be well. Your cousin will believe what he saw, that David Drummond sat next to me whilst Isobel Munroe kissed her betrothed behind a tree. To support that, David Drummond will write to his father informing him of his decision to take up a post in Jamaica. That way, David is taken halfway around the world and away from your father's influence. If need be, David can *die* from yellow fever or some such thing. In the meantime, Lord Peter Fairfax and Miss Isobel Munroe can elope to Gretna where they marry and live happily ever after. What could be more perfect?"

"And what of Peter's family? How can we explain to them the need for an elopement?"

Now Charlotte was beginning to believe she had swayed the girl into her way of thinking. Why else would she be thinking of the consequences of a marriage? This time, when she replied, she had to fight hard to keep the smile of triumph from her lips.

"Oh, that is easy. We tell them that some distant relative was trying to force you to marry him in order to get his hands upon your dowry. So in order to protect you, Peter persuaded you to elope to Gretna Green and marry him instead."

"Oh, my inheritance!" said Isobel suddenly. "If David is in Jamaica or maybe even dead, how can he collect his inheritance?"

"Oh darling, you need not worry about that. I have heard that Peter intends to start a stud farm to breed superior mounts for the army. I have been looking for an investment opportunity, say twenty thousand pounds, payable on the date of your marriage."

Chapter Twenty-Four

"Do you know who I am?" asked Charlotte. She towered over Drummond as she stared down at him, the contempt that she felt for the man written all over her face.

He was in a filthy state and still groggy from the laudanum that had kept him unconscious for the last three days. Nor had Samson been gentle with the man when trussing him to a stout iron ring in the wall of an unused root cellar. His face and eyes looked as if he had gone ten rounds with Gentleman Jack himself, and blood from his broken nose had covered his shirt. In addition, judging by the way he winced each time he moved, Samson had also broken at least one of the man's ribs.

"Fuck off, ya bitch," snarled Drummond.

A hard wooden stick lashed out, catching the man upon the shin. Drummond howled with pain, his body writhing against the bonds that held him, his breath coming in short gasps as he fought the agony of the blow.

"I will ask you again. Do you know who I am?" asked Charlotte.

"The Duchess of bloody Camberly," he groaned.

"Good, then you will also know that my husband is the Duke of Camberly and cousin to his Majesty the King. Now Mister Drummond . . ."

"That's Laird of Kinross to you."

"Oh, and we both know that is not true, for the last I heard your father was still hale and hearty, Mister Drummond. Now, I am going to ask you a simple question. You will answer truthfully, or the consequences will be dire. Have you,

Mr Drummond, sent any form of communication in reference to David Drummond to either your father or to the Earl of Falkirk?"

"Piss off," said Drummond. He hacked and then spat upon the earth floor.

"You were warned. Samson, if you please," sighed Charlotte dramatically.

Samson, who was stood behind his mistress, grinned as he pulled an evil looking ten-inch blade from the special sheath sewn into the lining of his boot. For emphasis, he ran his finger along the blade to test the sharpness before turning to his mistress once more.

"Which part of him would you like me to remove, your Grace?" he said. Samson's eyes were now fastened upon Drummond, eyes which glinted with maniacal pleasure in the lantern light. "Or shall I kill him and be done with it?"

"I think his manhood, such as it is," said Charlotte sympathetically.

"Very good, my lady," said Samson. Grinning evilly, Samson moved to place the wicked blade upon the crotch of Drummond.

Charlotte kept her expression severe as Drummond screeched in fear, his body twisting in an effort to evade the blade. The result, unfortunately for him, was the opposite for, as he turned, the razor-sharp knife sliced the material of his trousers, a thin line of blood appearing upon his inner thigh.

"No . . . please . . . please your Grace."

Drummond's face was ashen, and Charlotte almost felt sorry for him . . . almost.

"Wait, Samson," she said softly, her words so gentle that they appeared evil. "Perhaps he has a mind to answer me now."

"Yes, anything. No, no I have not sent any messages. You have my word on that as a gentl . . ."

"Do not say gentleman, *Mister* Drummond, for you are anything *but* a gentleman. I will have you know, *Mister* Drummond, that my husband is not so forgiving as I. As Lord Lieutenant of this county, he has already issued a warrant for your arrest for attempted murder and armed burglary. Each of these, should you be found guilty, would see you swing, Mr Drummond."

In truth, the duke had done no such thing, but Charlotte saw no reason to tell him of this.

"But you can't, for I am . . . ."

"You are *not* a member of the ton, *Mister* Drummond, not yet, that is. You have no title and can therefore be tried under common law. This means you will swing, *Mister* Drummond, swing by the neck until dead, *Mister* Drummond."

"Please. Please, your Grace."

"Do not interrupt," snapped Charlotte. She continued then, her voice once more soft and thoughtful. "My husband, however, has given me the honour of deciding what to do with you."

"Fucking hell," he whispered.

Sweetly, Charlotte smiled, yet her words were spoken with real intent. "If he interrupts me once more, Samson, take his tongue."

"Gladly my lady," replied Samson, his grin truly evil.

"Be it known, Drummond, that I am in a generous mood this day. David Drummond, whom I hold I high regard, is as we speak on one of my ships, bound for Jamaica. There he will be apprenticed to my Man of Business who runs the three sugar plantations I own, with the eventual aim of having him succeed my man, who desires retirement. David has written a letter, in his own hand, to his parents, explaining the circumstances of his departure. I have also written a brief note to his father, the Earl, explaining my part in these proceedings. Both of these letters have been dispatched by special courier.

"As of yet, I have made no mention of what I intend to do with you, Mr. Drummond. As you know, in my possession I hold not only the warrant for your arrest, but no less than four witness statements attesting to your attempted murder of David."

Of course Charlotte held no letter, for as yet she had no intention of involving her husband in this matter, even though she knew he would give her every support should she ask him to do so. Still, Drummond had no need to know that.

"As a consequence," Charlotte continued, "I have considered a number of options. First, I have considered having your throat slit before burying you in the woods where no one would ever find your body."

Charlotte paused to allow this to sink into the man's tiny brain, grinning wildly as she saw the look of horror that slowly suffused the man's face.

"Fortunately for you, however, Samson's wife has only just delivered twins, so I will not risk him being hung for your death. Second, I could have you arrested and tried for attempted murder, but whilst justice would most definitely be done, it would mean dragging my name and those of my friends through the courts. This I would like to avoid."

And that was the truth of things. After all, the last thing Charlotte wanted was for the courts to place Miss Isobel Munroe upon the stand so that some penny lawyer could cross examine her.

"So, perhaps against my better judgement, it would appear that my preferred option is to let you go with the understanding that you will return to Scotland and never again set foot in England. As of yet, no mention has been made of your involvement in this matter, so if you return home, you may yet be able to salvage something and perhaps make a life for yourself. But be very clear, Mr. Drummond. If I discover that you have broken my conditions or have tried to harm the good name of David Drummond in any way, I will have Samson deliver your arrest warrant personally and in the most violent of manners. Do you understand, Mr. Drummond?" said Charlotte.

Drummond sat without uttering a word, his head nodding up and down like that of a string puppet.

For a moment Charlotte could not understand why he would not speak until she suddenly had to suppress the urge to giggle. For had she not told the man to be silent just minutes before, on pain of having his tongue cut out?

"You may speak now, Mr. Drummond. What is to be, the gallows, or banishment back to Scotland?"

"I will return to Scotland. You have my word that I will never speak of what has happened, nor will I ever return to England without your permission, your Grace," he whispered.

"Very well. Samson, would you please release him and then escort him to the county line?"

Samson did not look at all happy, yet still he moved to free Drummond form his bonds." I still say option one would have been the best, my lady," he grumbled.

Epilogue

Isobel was sat in the library of her home, the housekeeper's books open before her upon a table. She could have used Peter's office, but in truth, she favoured this room, as it received the warmth of the sun for most of the day and allowed her the space to move and think. Whilst not overly large, the library was a beautiful room. The centre was dominated by a large fireplace by which had been placed two extremely comfortable chairs, one for Peter and one for her. It had rapidly become one of their favourite places in the whole house, and they could often be found arguing over a game of chess or with Isobel curled up on Peter's lap as he read to her.

It had been three months since the hammer had come down upon the anvil in the Blacksmiths Shop in Gretna Green. With Drummond still securely locked up in the root cellar at Thorpe Hall, they had made the six-day coach journey to Gretna, where not only had they married, but so had Mary and William Jenkins, both of whom had insisted on accompanying them to Scotland. Even now Isobel could not decide who had been the happiest on the day.

Since then, much had happened. Peter's parents, especially his mother, had not best received the news that they had married in Gretna. But once again, thanks to the intervention of the Duchess of Camberly, they had relented, finally rejoicing in their union by holding a ball in their honour.

Two weeks later, they had taken possession of Winsworth Manor, and for Isobel, it was like she had at last found the one place in the world where she was truly meant to be.

The house had been built on the bones of a much earlier Tudor mansion by Peter's grandparents and had served for many years as their own family home. It was a stunning red brick country house, with sumptuous gardens surrounding it, some formal and some less so, all requiring an army of gardeners to keep them in a pristine fashion. The interior was equally opulent, as most had been designed by the eminent interior designer, Richard Adams. Here there was little for Isobel to do, as much had been invested into the fabric of the building to maintain it over the years, so that it was already in a magnificent condition.

Within the house itself was an army of servants so large that, at first, Isobel had quailed at the prospect of its management. Fortunately, she soon discovered she had allies who were only too willing to help. Mrs. Figg, housekeeper and cook extraordinaire had, like a mother hen, taken Isobel under her wing, and with endless patience, had taught her what she needed to know. What helped was that not once did Isobel try to pull rank, instead preferring to discuss all issues pertaining to the house with Mrs. Figg. Matters were not harmed either by the fact that Mr. Figg, the butler, very much deferred to his wife in most matters.

Thanks to the investment made by the Duke and Duchess of Camberly, building work to expand the stables started almost immediately. It did not take long for an army of carpenters and masons to build three new blocks of twenty stables from a mixture of brick and wood, each block facing out upon its own ten-acre paddock, providing plenty of space for the brood mares that Peter had started to purchase. There had, of course, been but one man that Peter trusted to lead the day-to-day activities of the project. William Jenkins, whilst in the army, had proved himself to be an admirable horseman as well as a capable sergeant. Within weeks, he had the operation of the stables running like a well-oiled military machine.

The Making of a Lady

His promotion had also come with an estate cottage, a home he now shared with his brand-new wife, Mary.

As a complete surprise, one afternoon a groom had arrived, sent by Peter's father, along with a belated wedding present. On horseback himself, the groom held the reins of the most magnificent Arabian stallion that Isobel had ever seen. At least sixteen hands high and a glorious chestnut in colour, Zeus had been, until recently, the duke's favourite hunter. However, a tendon injury had ended Zeus's days in the hunt and his father had sent him to stud with Peter. Whilst he had been thrilled with the acquisition, it had left Peter with something of a headache. On Zeus's arrival, Peter's stallion, Ajax, had instantly become jealous and now the two were most definitely spoiling for a fight to assume dominance over the herd.

Peter could not have been happier.

Neither could Isobel, for on the following day another cart arrived, this time carrying the very same piano that Isobel had played that night at the musicale, yet another belated wedding gift.

Once more Isobel sighed with contentment, wondering for the thousandth time what she had done to deserve such happiness. As a consequence, knowing that her mind was not on the books, she closed them firmly, then stood to gaze through the window, allowing her mind to wander as she peered out over the glorious countryside.

With each day that passed, David seemed to fade more and more into history, so much so that Isobel sometimes had difficulty remembering who she had once been. For Isobel, that was a glorious thought. In truth, the only time she was reminded of David was when in the bedroom that she shared each night with her husband. Peter delighted in her, adoring her body with his mouth, his hands, and his cock and Isobel loved him all the more for doing so.

In the whole three months of married life, there had been

but one minor hiccup for Isobel. Recently, Peter had remarked about the puffiness of the flesh about her chest. Then, one morning, Peter had chanced upon her as she drank her medicine. Of course he had demanded to know what it was that she took, only for them to have a heated disagreement about the whole matter. Not really understanding what it meant to Isobel, he had demanded that she stop taking the medicine. Isobel declined to acquiesce and for a whole day, Peter had sulked, refusing to speak a single word to her in return. That was, until she took matters into her *own hands*. Fed up with his attitude, she had cornered him in a stable, and, after ordering every servant to vacate the building, had gone down on her knees before him, not to beg for his forgiveness, but to instead take his cock into her hands and into her mouth.

The memory of it made her smile as she stared out of the window, only for her mouth to drop open in surprise as she saw what now approached the house. Some distance away, on the road that led up to the house, was a carriage. Ordinarily this would not have been strange, but even at a distance, Isobel could see that this was no commonplace coach. Instead, four magnificent and perfectly matched horses pulled a huge and stately Brougham coach, one so highly polished that it gleamed in the morning sunlight.

Isobel gasped as she felt her heart begin to pound, the pessimist in her assuming the worst.

The coach was obviously owned by someone of significant status, for it was driven by a coachman with a groom by his side, a pair of liveried footmen stationed to the rear. But Isobel was not expecting anyone to call, especially anyone who might own such a coach, so her mind instantly began to assume that something dire was about to happen, that someone was about to burst the bubble of happiness that she now resided within. It was at that moment that a knock sounded upon the library door and Isobel turned to see Mary enter the room.

"Lady Isobel!" she gasped, "I think we are about to have visitors."

Nervously, Isobel smiled at her friend, grateful yet again for her presence. Since this episode in her life had begun, Mary had been the one constant, the one person, other than Peter, to whom Isobel could turn with absolute trust. When they had arrived at Winsworth Manor, Mary had insisted that she continue in her role as her lady's maid. For her part, Isobel had insisted that Mary not live in the main house but instead live in the cottage with her husband, and all were happy with the arrangement.

"Yes, Mary, I have seen the coach," she said glumly. "Will you inform cook that we will need tea for as many as six and then ask someone to go and find my husband? I think you will find him in the stables office."

Mary curtsied and scurried away.

Knowing it would be expected of her, Isobel moved to the parlor, a room where she would normally receive guests, pausing before a looking glass to check her appearance as she did so. It was a matter of moments before Mr. Figg was knocking politely on the door, a silver tray upon an upturned hand.

"Her Grace the Duchess of Camberly and the Dowager Countess Hamilton are here to see you my lady. Shall I tell them you are . . ."

Even before he could finish his words, Isobel had let out a shriek of pleasure and had dashed from the room. Within moments, she had thrown herself into the open arms of Olivia, only seconds later to have done the same to Charlotte.

"Oh what a wonderful surprise," she gasped as she jumped up and down on the balls of her feet in excitement.

"Well, look at you," grinned Charlotte. "I must say married life suits, my darling."

"It does, it does. But why did you not inform me that you

were coming?" Isobel demanded. "Will you be staying? I can ask Mrs. Figg to make up rooms for you, if you like."

It was only then that Isobel saw the third woman, a sight which stopped her almost as effectively as if she had run blindly into a brick wall. As if she had been punched, the wind left her lungs, and her heart started to beat so violently that she thought it might burst from her chest. All in black, the woman was stood behind Charlotte and Olivia, her hands clasped nervously before her and apprehension fixed to her face. Yet despite her obvious anxiety, her eyes were locked upon Isobel, eyes which shone brightly with the same sort of determination that Isobel herself had often displayed.

"So, it is true, then," the woman whispered.

"Yes," replied Isobel, her voice croaking with fear.

Isobel could do nothing but hold her breath, waiting for the outburst; the indignation and hatred that would surely come. She steeled herself, every fiber of her being prepared to defend the choices she had made.

Isobel faced her guest for a long moment, not knowing who would break ominous silence that had grown between them. Only then did the woman open her arms.

"My God," said Isobel's mother. "Oh, darling, you are so beautiful."

Relief flooding her very soul, Isobel threw herself at her mother, her arms wrapping around her in the fiercest of hugs as she was gathered into her waiting embrace. And then the tears began to flow, tears of a mother and daughter that had been long time coming, both of them shaking with the emotion of the moment. Together they sobbed, their bodies wracked with feeling, and as tears poured down her face, Isobel's only thought was of the unconditional love her mother had always given David as a child. Yes, there was weeping, but suddenly there was laughter too, and as joy flooded her heart, Isobel heard herself giggle nervously through her tears.

"What the blazes!" said Peter, as he came storming in.

Almost guiltily, Isobel pulled away from her mother. Yet she refused to let go of her hand. Instead, she turned to Peter, and despite the tears that streaked her cheeks, the biggest broadest smile of her life slashed across her face.

"Mother," she said breathlessly, "this is Lord Peter Fairfax, my husband. Peter, may I introduce Lady Elspeth Drummond, Countess of Falkirk, my mother."

"Mother?" said Peter, the anguish in his voice betraying what he thought about the whole situation.

To Isobel's complete surprise, her mother took a stride over to Peter, and before he could react, she kissed him upon the cheek. Caught completely by surprise, all that he could do was to stand opened-mouthed, his eyes wide with shock.

"Lord Fairfax, said Elspeth softly, "it is so good to finally meet my *daughter's husband.*"

Her words were simple, yet Isobel's heart threatened to burst with happiness. Her mother had called her *daughter,* and in doing so had clearly demonstrated acceptance of the woman she had become.

Only once before had Isobel felt such joy. On the day that she and Peter had stood before the anvil priest, Isobel had felt such elation that it had left her breathless. And now her mother was here to share in the bliss that resided in her very soul.

That was, until another horrendous thought shot through her mind and her happiness came crashing down like a rotten tree in a hurricane.

"God!" she said. "Father is not here, is he?"

"Fear not," said Charlotte. "He is not here, my darling."

Isobel breathed once more, the relief she felt sweeping through her.

"There is much to tell you . . . er . . . Isobel," said Elspeth, gravely, "much to discuss. Perhaps there is there somewhere private that we may talk."

It took but a few moments for the party to enter the drawing room, Charlotte sitting next to Olivia, Isobel next to her mother, Peter standing supportively next to his wife.

Such thoughts were going through Isobel's mind. Why had Charlotte and Olivia betrayed her secret to her mother? Had someone realized who she was? Had her father discovered her whereabouts? Was the scandalous tale of Lord Peter Fairfax and Viscount David Drummond about to be headline news? Isobel swallowed hard, her knuckles now firmly in her mouth.

"Isobel," continued Olivia, "first of all let me apologize for not warning you about all of this. Elspeth, your mother, arrived at my home in London but yesterday, with news of such importance that I thought it wise to tell her all that has transpired."

"And I insisted that we come to you immediately," said Charlotte.

"What is it?" said Isobel. Her other hand was now white from the way she gripped her husband's fist.

"There is no easy way of saying this, Isobel," said Elspeth. "I am sorry to report that your father has been shot and killed by Hamish Russell. Russell was also killed."

Isobel gasped. Silently, she sat as still as a church mouse, not quite knowing how to respond. Yes, she knew she should be distressed, for he had been her father, had he not? But for some reason she could not bring herself to be so. In fact, her whole body was quivering with excitement, with relief, a very large part of her glad that her father was dead. Russell too, for that matter, for he was yet another person whom Isobel had come to fear would try and find her.

Slowly, Isobel let out the breath she had been holding. She looked first at Peter and then at her mother.

"What happened?" asked Peter.

"It seems that this Russell was trying to blackmail your father, who in turn went to confront the man. There was an exchange of gunfire and both were killed. I am so sorry, Isobel," said Elspeth.

Isobel looked up and smiled tentatively at those around her. "Is it so terrible of me to say that I do not care?" she said, her voice so soft it was almost inaudible.

"No, darling," said Charlotte. "For we all know how David suffered at his hands. However, do you not realise what this means?"

"No," replied Isobel simply.

"What it means, *Lady Isobel Fairfax*," said Elspeth, "is that *you* are now the eighth Earl of Falkirk."

"Oh bugger," was all she could reply.

The End

YOU MAY ALSO ENJOY THE FOLLOWING FROM EXTASY BOOKS INC:

Lady Charlotte's Revenge
Charlotte Johnson

Excerpt

"Yes, what is it, Stevens?"

"There is a lady caller, your grace, requesting a moment of your time. I told her that you were unavailable, but she was most insistent. She asked me to give you this." The man held out his silver tray.

On the tray was a calling card that was clearly of superior quality and, after picking it up, James viewed it carefully, noting that the name was beautifully embossed in real gold leaf.

Lady Charlotte Winters.

Instantly, James's interest was aroused. Lady Charlotte Winters! He had heard that name bandied around his club over the past couple of weeks, where speculation about the woman was rife. By all accounts, she was a widow recently returned from the West Indies and was said to be as rich as Croesus himself. She would have to be, if she was to rent Conway House for the whole of the season, the townhouse only four doors away from his own in Belgrave Square.

Looking up he smiled at the butler.

"You had better show her in, I suppose. Is she chaperoned?" he asked with a sudden afterthought.

"Yes, your grace. By the biggest African man I have ever seen. But she has requested that she speak to you alone."

"Oh, very well. Show her in, Stevens."

"In here, your grace?" Stevens gave him an incredulous look, his expression leaving no doubt in James' mind that his butler thought the study was a highly inappropriate place for such a meeting.

"Yes, in here," he snapped.

"Yes, your grace." Stevens sighed and gave a cursory bow before turning back to the door, leaving James in no doubt that his butler disapproved of his choice of room.

As he waited, James could not help but speculate as to who or what this woman was all about. Just the fact that she had requested to see him alone suggested she might be a woman of advanced years, for no respectable lady would risk her reputation by being un-chaperoned.

Yes, she's probably as old as the hills and as ugly as sin, too.

A few moments later there was another knock, and James watched as Stevens opened the study door, standing to one side to respectfully permit his visitor to enter.

"Lady Winters, your grace," Stevens announced, so as to facilitate some form of formal introduction. "His grace, the Duke of Camberley."

In preparation for meeting the woman, James had schooled his expression into one of benign indifference, and he suddenly found himself offering a silent prayer of thanks to the gods for doing so. For had he not, he knew, without any shadow of doubt, he most probably would have gasped aloud when he first glimpsed his visitor.

Old she was not. Nor ugly as sin.

James had always been an admirer of the feminine form, and the lady who stood before him matched, in every way, his ideal. She appeared to be around thirty years of age and was dressed in a beautiful cream coloured day dress that must have been expensively tailored to perfectly fit her slim, graceful body. She was tall for a lady, yet still a good head shorter than he. Her arms were slender and graceful, her breasts small yet pert, her waist trim, and her lovely auburn tresses had been expertly crafted into a very pretty chignon, a style that left little tendrils of hair framing her face to perfection.

And what a face it was.

Contrary to fashion, she wore cosmetics upon her skin. Unlike some women of his acquaintance, who seemed to plaster the stuff on with a trowel, Lady Winters wore but a subtle application of makeup. She was enhanced with a light dusting of powder on her perfect skin and a little rouge on her cheeks to emphasise her high and aristocratic cheekbones. She also wore kohl on her lashes, which only served to draw his gaze to her startlingly blue eyes, and a little ruby stain on her plump and very kissable lips.

In short, Lady Charlotte Winters was undeniably beautiful.

Suddenly, James felt the heat rise in his cheeks as he remembered his earlier uncharitable thoughts. So he bowed politely to allow a moment to compose himself, shaking his head a little to clear his mind of all the improper thoughts that seemed to be lodged there.

Graciously, he indicated an armchair to one side of the room. "Please, Lady Winters, please be seated. May I offer you some refreshment? Tea perhaps?"

"No, thank you, your grace," she replied.

Lady Winters took the offered chair, smoothing her skirts beneath her so she could sit demurely, and James moved to a second chair, deliberately maintaining a neutral expression as he contemplated the woman's speaking voice. From her appearance, he had expected a soft, high pitch to her words, but she had spoken with a deeper, huskier tone that, in his mind, only added to the woman's allure.

James was intrigued.

"So, of what service may I be to you, Lady Winters?" he

asked, noting the growing nervousness in the expression on his visitor's face.

The woman sighed uneasily, her gaze, at first, cast nervously down to the floor. But then she lifted her head and looked back at him with a deep penetrating stare, her brilliant blue eyes searching his face in a way that instantly reminded him of someone he had once known. The memory of it was there, in the back of his mind, yet for some reason, he could not place it, could not recall who it was that Lady Winters reminded him of.

He stared back at her, suddenly feeling small. For there was something in her expression, an air of stubbornness perhaps, that suggested she was observing him in a manner that would allow her to judge the character of the man before her. Then she smiled, and James could not stop himself from smiling back, knowing, perhaps, that he had passed some unwritten test.

"I have something of great consequence I wish to discuss with you, your grace. But before I begin, I must ask . . . I must ask for your word as a gentleman that what we are to converse about remains between these four walls. Please, your grace, your word. It is of the greatest import to me."

James felt a surge of annoyance as he heard these words. After all, he considered himself a man of integrity, one of high office, and to have someone, especially a young woman, impugn that by actually asking for him to give her his word, irked him considerably.

But then he looked closely at the young woman once more. He noted how she had captured her bottom lip tentatively between her teeth and how her hands were clasped nervously in her lap, and something in him, perhaps an innate ability to judge someone's character, sensed there was no malice intended. Instead, it was quite apparent that the request had been made with but one thing in mind — an obvious desire to protect herself from some ill-conceived scandal, perhaps.

He did not hesitate. "Of course, madam, you have my

word as a gentleman."

Lady Winters took a deep breath, and her gaze flickered anxiously away from his. Then her eyebrows furrowed for a moment as she looked back, her expression now one of purpose and resolve, giving James the feeling that he, somehow, had yet again passed some undisclosed test.

She sighed, and her eyes narrowed with fierce determination. "Your grace, I am here with news of Charles Royce, son of the late Sir Oliver Royce and the now Countess of Weybridge . . . and . . . I believe . . . your godson."

In shock, James gasped as all the air seemed to abruptly vacate the room as he registered her words. Then his pulse began to race.

Charles Royce, son of his lifelong friend, Sir Oliver Royce, had disappeared on his way to Eton school for his first term, never to be heard of again. At the time, it was thought he had been taken by a press gang, men who roamed the countryside looking for willing volunteers to crew the ever-growing number of ships needed in the war against France. Enquiries had been made, of course, but from that moment on there had simply been no trace of him, and after seven years, he had been presumed dead.

And now this chit of a woman was sitting before him, as bold as brass, saying she had news of him.

"What!" Instantly, James moved to the edge of his seat, closing the distance between them and stared intently into the woman's eyes. "Please, Lady Winters, tell me. Is he alive?"

"Alive and well, and here in London," Lady Winters replied.

"What? Where?" James demanded. "This is incredible news. If this is so, you must take me to him immediately." He jumped to his feet and glared at the woman, hardly daring to believe what he was hearing.

Lady Winters remained motionless on her chair, yet he could plainly see that she was desperately struggling to retain her composure. Apprehension and dread swept across her eyes, and for a moment, he even feared that she was going to rise, that she was going to flee. So with a conscious effort to control himself, he took a step back and breathed deeply in an effort to still his mind.

"Please, madam," he begged. "Can you not tell me where he is? Can you not take me to him?"

"I cannot." Her voice was now almost a whisper as she pointed back to his chair, her gesture beseeching him to sit once more. "I cannot take you to him."

"And, pray tell, why not?" James struggled to contain his anger, his impatience surely evident as he refused to sit. Yet Lady Winters was not to be intimidated, and, in total amazement, James could only glare as she stared back at him, her beautiful gaze holding his own, her small breasts heaving as she once more took a deep breath.

"I cannot take you to him," she whispered, "for he is already before you. You see, your grace, I am, or should I say I once was your godson, Charles Royce."

About the Author

Charlotte Johnson is an English author with an obsession for writing romantic transgender fiction. The Making of a Lady is her second full length novel, which combines her passion for all things Jane Austin with an absolute belief that transgender people throughout the world have an unconditional right to respect and to love. Charlotte, who lives with her family near London, has also penned, to some critical acclaim, over 50 other short stories.

Made in the USA
Coppell, TX
06 February 2022